MARY JO
PUTNEY

MERLINE
LOVELACE

GAYLE WILSON

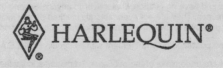

Bride
BY ARRANGEMENT

HARLEQUIN®

TORONTO • NEW YORK • LONDON
AMSTERDAM • PARIS • SYDNEY • HAMBURG
STOCKHOLM • ATHENS • TOKYO • MILAN • MADRID
PRAGUE • WARSAW • BUDAPEST • AUCKLAND

ISBN 0-373-83437-3

BRIDE BY ARRANGEMENT

Copyright © 2000 by Harlequin Books S.A.

The publisher acknowledges the copyright holders of the individual works as follows:

WEDDING OF THE CENTURY
Copyright © 1994 by Mary Jo Putney

MISMATCHED HEARTS
Copyright © 2000 by Merline Lovelace

MY DARLING ECHO
Copyright © 2000 by Mona Gay Thomas

Visit us at www.eHarlequin.com

Printed in U.S.A.

CONTENTS

To Mama Rekus, who always loved a good story.

WEDDING OF THE CENTURY
by Mary Jo Putney

Chapter One

Swindon Palace
Spring 1885

After two weeks of dizzying social activity in London, a visit to the English countryside was an enchanting change of pace. Nature had cooperated by blessing the garden party with flawless weather. Puffs of white cloud drifted through a deep blue sky, the grass and trees were impossibly green, and the famous Swindon gardens were in glorious flower.

Yet the grounds were not half so splendid as the guests, who were the cream of British society. All of the men were aristocratically handsome and all of the women graceful and exquisitely dressed. At least, that was how it seemed to Miss Sarah Katherine Vangelder, of the New York Vangelders. As she surveyed her surroundings, she gave a laugh of pure delight.

The woman beside her said, "Don't look so rapturous, Sunny. It simply isn't done."

Sunny gave her godmother a teasing glance. "Is this the Katie Schmidt of San Francisco who scandalized English society by performing Comanche riding stunts in Hyde Park?"

A smile tugged at the older woman's lips. "It most certainly is *not*," she said in a voice that no longer held any trace of American accent. "I am now Katherine Schmidt Worthington, Countess of Westron, a very proper chaperon for her exceedingly well-brought-up young American goddaughter."

"I thought that we American girls were admired for our freshness and directness." A hint of dryness entered Sunny's voice. "And our fortunes, of course."

"The very best matches require impeccable manners as well as money, my dear. If you wish to become a duchess, you must be above reproach."

Sunny sighed. "And if I don't wish to become a duchess?"

"Your mother has spent twenty years grooming you to be worthy of the highest station," Lady Westron replied. "It would be a pity to waste that."

"Yes, Aunt Katie," Sunny said meekly. "If I'm very, very impeccable, may I view the rest of the gardens later?"

"Yes, but not until you've met everyone worth meeting. Business before pleasure, my dear." Katie began guiding her charge through the crowd, stopping and making occasional introductions.

Knowing that she was being judged, Sunny smiled and talked with the utmost propriety. She even managed not to look too excited, until she was introduced to the Honorable Paul Curzon.

Tall, blond and stunningly handsome, Curzon was enough to make any woman gape. After bowing over her hand, he said, "A pleasure to meet you, Miss Vangelder. Are you newly arrived in England?" His question was accompanied by a dazzling smile.

If it hadn't been for her rigorous social training, Sunny would have gaped at him like a raw country girl. Instead, she managed to say lightly, "I've been in London for the last fortnight. Before that, we were traveling on the Continent."

"If you'd like to visit the Houses of Parliament, Miss Vangelder, I'd be delighted to escort you. I'm a member." Curzon gave a deprecatory shrug. "Only a backbencher, but I can show you what goes on behind the scenes and treat you to tea on the terrace. You might find it amusing."

"Perhaps later in the season Miss Vangelder will have time," Katie said as she deftly removed her charge.

When they were out of earshot, Sunny said with

awe, "Mr. Curzon is the handsomest man I've ever seen."

"Yes, but he's a younger son with three older brothers, so he's unlikely ever to inherit the title." Lady Westron gave a warning look. "Not at all the sort your mother wants for you."

"But as a Member of Parliament, he actually does something useful," Sunny pointed out. "My grandfather would have approved of that."

"Admiral Vangelder would *not* have wanted a penniless younger son for his favorite granddaughter," Katie said firmly. "Come, I want you to meet Lord Traymore. An Irish title, unfortunately, but an earl is an earl, and he's charming. You could do worse."

Dutifully Sunny followed her godmother to the next knot of guests, though she promised herself that she would slip off and view the famous water garden before she left. Until then, she would enjoy the color and laughter of the occasion.

She was also guiltily glad to be free of her mother's rather overpowering presence for a day. Augusta Vangelder was the most devoted and solicitous of parents, but she had very firm ideas about the way things ought to be. *Very* firm. Unfortunately, she was laid up in their suite at Claridge's with a mild case of the grippe, so Sunny had the benefit of the more liberal chaperonage of her godmother. Not only did Lady Westron know everyone, but she made racy comments about them. Sunny felt very worldly.

While a courtly old judge went to fetch them refreshments, she asked, "Where is the Duke of Thornborough? Since he ordered a special train to bring his guests from London for the day, I should at least know whom to be grateful to."

Katie scanned the crowd, then nodded toward the refreshment marquee. "That tall fair chap."

After a thorough examination, Sunny observed, "He's almost as handsome as Mr. Curzon, and has a most distinguished air. *Exactly* what one would expect of a duke."

"Yes, and he's delightfully witty, as well," Katie replied. "Very prominent in the Prince of Wales's Marlborough House set. I'll introduce you to him later."

Sunny glanced at the other woman suspiciously. "Am I to be paraded in front of him like a prize heifer?"

"No," Katie said with regret. "Thornborough won't do—his taste runs to ladies who are…rather excessively sophisticated. He's expected to offer for May Russell soon."

"The American Mrs. Russell?" Sunny asked, surprised.

"Mad May herself. She's a good choice—having had children by two husbands already, she shouldn't have any problems giving Thornborough an heir, and her fortune is immense." Katie gave a little sniff. "Heaven knows that Thornborough needs it."

"Who's the man standing by the duke?"

"Oh, that's just the Gargoyle."

"I beg your pardon?" Sunny glanced at her godmother, not sure that she'd heard correctly.

"Lord Justin Aubrey, Thornborough's younger brother, better known as the Gargoyle," Katie explained. "He manages the duke's estate, which means he's scarcely more than a farmer."

A line etched between her brows, Sunny studied the dark young man. While not handsome, his face had a certain rugged distinction. "Why was he given such an unkind nickname? He's no Mr. Curzon, but neither is he ugly."

"The Aubreys are known for being tall, blond and aristocratic, and Lord Justin is none of those things. He's always scowling and has no conversation at all." Katie smiled naughtily. "One would have to question what his dear mother had been up to, except that every now and then the Aubreys produce one like him. The youngest Aubrey daughter, Lady Alexandra, resembles him, poor girl. I imagine she's around here somewhere. She's known as the Gargoylette."

Sunny's frown deepened. "I'm sorry to think that these handsome people have such cruel tongues."

"They are no more and no less cruel than New

York society,'' Lady Westron said dryly. ''Human nature is much the same everywhere.''

Sunny's gaze lingered on Lord Justin. Though not tall, neither was he short; he appeared to be of average height, perhaps an inch or two taller than she. She guessed that he was in his late twenties, but his stern expression made him seem older. He also looked as if he thoroughly disapproved of the splendid gathering around him.

Her thoughts were interrupted by Katie exclaiming, ''Lord Hancock is over there! I had hoped that he would be here today. Come along, dear, you must meet him.''

After another wistful glance at the gardens, Sunny obediently followed her godmother.

The eighth Duke of Thornborough sampled a strawberry from one of the mounds on the refreshment table. ''Splendid flavor.'' He reached for another. ''You've been getting remarkable results from the greenhouses.''

Justin Aubrey shrugged. ''I only give the orders, Gavin. It's the gardeners who do the real work.''

''But someone must still give the right orders, and it isn't going to be me.'' The duke consumed several more strawberries, then washed them down with champagne. ''Relax, Justin. You've worked for weeks to make my fete a success, so you should try to enjoy the results. Everyone is having a cracking good time.''

"That's fortunate, considering that this little event is costing over two thousand pounds." Money which could have been much better spent.

Gavin made an airy gesture. "The Duke of Thornborough has an obligation to maintain a certain style. After I marry May, there will be ample money for those boring repairs that you keep talking about."

Justin gave his brother a shrewd glance. "You and Mrs. Russell have reached a firm understanding?"

Gavin nodded. "We'll be making an announcement soon. A late summer wedding, I think. You can plan on fixing the roof directly after, so it will be right and tight by winter." He cast an experienced eye over the crowd. "I see that Katie Westron has a lovely creature in tow. It must be the Gilded Girl. I hear she's cutting quite a swath through London society. The Prince has already invited her to visit Sandringham."

"Then her social reputation is made," Justin agreed with barely perceptible irony. "But who *is* the Gilded Girl?"

"Sarah Vangelder, the fairest flower of the Vangelder railroad fortune." The duke's tone turned speculative. "They say she's the greatest heiress ever to cross the Atlantic."

Justin followed his brother's gaze to where the heiress stood talking with three besotted males. As soon as he located her, his heart gave an odd lurch.

Sarah Vangelder was the quintessential American beauty—tall, slender and crowned with a lustrous mass of honey-colored hair. She also had an engaging air of innocent enthusiasm that made him want to walk over and introduce himself. A beautiful woman, not his. The world was full of them, he reminded himself. Aloud, he said only, "Very fetching."

"Perhaps I should reconsider marrying May," Gavin said pensively. "They say Augusta Vangelder wants to see the girl a duchess. Should I offer her the noble name of Thornborough?"

Justin's mouth tightened. Though he loved his brother, he had no illusions about the duke's character. "You'd find a young innocent a flat bore."

"Very likely you're right," Gavin agreed. His gaze lingered. "Still, she's quite lovely."

Three peeresses and two Cabinet ministers came over to pay their respects to their host. Justin seized the opportunity to escape, for the constant chatter was driving him mad. He would have preferred to be elsewhere, but he could hardly avoid a party taking place in his own backyard.

Avoiding the formal parterre where many of the guests were strolling, he made his way to the rhododendron garden, which had been carefully designed to look like wild woods. There was a risk that he would find some of Gavin's fashionable friends fornicating beneath the silver birches, but with luck, they would all be more interested in champagne and gossip than in dalliance.

Half an hour in the wilder sections of the park relaxed him to the point where he felt ready to return to the festivities. Not that anyone was likely to miss him, but he liked to keep an eye on the arrangements to ensure that everything ran smoothly.

As he walked through a grove of Scottish pines, he heard a feminine voice utter a soft but emphatic, "Drat!"

He turned toward the voice, and a few more steps brought the speaker into his view.

It was the Gilded Girl. But that was too flippant a nickname, for the sunlight that shafted through the pine needles made her honey hair and creamy gown glow as if she were Titania, the fairy queen. He halted unnoticed at the edge of the clearing, experiencing again that strange, unsteady feeling.

A vine had snagged the back hem of Miss Vangelder's elegant bustled walking gown, and she was trying to free herself by poking with the tip of her lace parasol. Any other woman would have seemed ungraceful, but not the heiress. She looked playful, competent and altogether enchanting.

In the wooden voice he used to conceal unseemly feelings, he said, "May I be of assistance?"

The girl looked up with a startled glance, then smiled with relief. "You certainly can! Otherwise, my gown is doomed, and Mr. Worth will be terribly cross with me if he ever finds out."

Justin knelt and began trying to disentangle her hem. "Does it matter what a dressmaker thinks?"

"Mr. Worth is not a dressmaker, but an *artiste*. I'm told that I was singularly fortunate that he condescended to see me personally. After examining me like a prize turkey, he designed every ensemble right down to the last slipper and scarf." She gave a gurgle of laughter. "I was informed in no uncertain terms that any substitutions would be disastrous."

The vine was remarkably tenacious. As Justin tried to loosen it without damaging the heavy ecru silk, he asked, "Do you always do what others wish you to do?"

"Generally," she said with wry self-understanding. "Life is easier when I do."

Her skirt finally came free, and he got to his feet. "I'm Justin Aubrey, by the way."

"I'm Sarah Vangelder, but most people call me Sunny." She offered her hand, and a smile that melted his bones.

She was tall, her eyes almost level with his. He had assumed that they would be blue, but the color was nearer aqua, as deep and changeable as the sea. He drew a shaken breath, then bowed over her hand. Straightening, he said, "You should not be here alone, Miss Vangelder."

"I know," she said blithely, "but I was afraid

that if I didn't take the initiative, I'd leave without having a chance to really see the gardens.''

''Are you rating them for possible future occupancy?'' he said dryly. ''I regret to inform you that my brother is no longer in the marriage mart.''

''I simply like gardens, Lord Justin,'' she said crisply, her aqua eyes turning cool. ''Are you always so rude?''

So the exquisite Miss Vangelder had thorns. Suppressing a smile, he said, ''Always. I took a first in rudeness at Oxford.''

Her expression instantly transformed from reproval to delight. ''You have a sense of humor!''

''Don't spread such a base rumor around. It would utterly ruin my reputation.'' He offered his arm. ''Let me escort you back to the fete.''

As she slipped her hand into the crook of his elbow, she asked, ''Could we take an indirect route? I particularly want to see the famous water garden.''

He knew that he should return her before her chaperon became concerned. Yet when he looked into her glorious eyes, he found himself saying, ''Very well, Miss Vangelder.''

As they started down the pine-needle-carpeted path, he was very aware of the light pressure of her hand on his arm and the luxuriant rustle of her petticoats. And her perfume, a delicate fragrance reminiscent of violets....

He took a deep, slow breath. "I assume you are related to Admiral Vangelder?"

"You've heard of my grandfather?"

"It would be surprising if I hadn't." He held a branch aside so that she could pass without endangering her deliciously frivolous hat. "He was one of the great American success stories."

"Yes, and something of a robber baron, as well, though he was always a darling to me. I miss him." She chuckled. "He liked people to think that he was called Admiral because of his magnificent yachts, but actually, he got the nickname because his first job was tending mules on the Erie Canal."

"Really?" Justin said, amused by her artlessness.

"Really. In fact, there are grave suspicions that his papa was not married to his mama." She bit her lip guiltily. "You're dangerously easy to talk to, Lord Justin. I shouldn't have said so much—my mother would be horrified if the Admiral's dubious parentage became common knowledge." She grinned again. "Her own family has been respectable for at least a generation longer."

"Your secret is safe, Miss Vangelder," he assured her.

She gave him another entrancing smile that struck right to the heart. For a mad instant, he felt as if he was the only person who existed in her world. She had charm, this gilded girl, a quality as unmistakable as it was hard to define. He drew a shaken breath and returned his gaze to the winding path.

Though she had said he was easy to talk to, in fact he found himself talking more than usual as they strolled through the park. He told her about the history of the estate, answered questions about the crops and tenants. Together they stood in the gazebo that was designed like a miniature Greek temple, and when they visited the picturesque ruins of an old monastery he described what the community would have been like in its heyday.

She was a wonderful audience, listening with a grave air of concentration that was occasionally punctuated by an incisive question. After she asked about the effects of the agricultural depression on the farm laborers, he remarked, "You have a wide range of interests, Miss Vangelder."

"Education is something of an American passion, so my father insisted that I have a whole regiment of tutors. Shortly before he died, he had me take the entrance exams to Oxford and Cambridge. He was quite pleased when I passed with flying colors." She sighed. "Of course there was never any question of me actually going to a university. That would have been shockingly bluestocking."

At least she had been well taught. Like most English girls, his own sisters had received the sketchiest of educations. Only Alexandra, who loved to read, had a well-informed mind. The man who married Sunny Vangelder would be lucky in more ways than one.

Justin had chosen a path that brought them out of the park's wilderness area right beside the water garden. It was an elaborate series of pools and channels that descended across three levels of terraces before flowing into the ornamental lake.

Sunny stopped in her tracks with a soft exhalation of pleasure. "Exquisite. The proportions—the way the statues are reflected in the pools—the way the eye is led gradually down to the lake. It's masterful. And the grass surrounding it! Like green velvet. How do the English grow such perfect grass?"

"It's quite simple, really. Just get a stone roller and use it on the lawn regularly for two or three hundred years."

She laughed and gave him a glance that made him feel as if he was the wittiest, handsomest man alive.

His heart twisted, and he knew that he must get away from her before he started to act like an utter idiot. "I really must take you back now."

"I suppose so." She took a last look at the water garden. "Thank you for indulging me, Lord Justin."

Their walk had taken them around three sides of the palace, and it was only a short distance to the Versailles garden where the fete was being held. As they approached the festivities, a tall man saw them and walked over swiftly. It was Paul Curzon, who had gone to Eton with Justin, though they had never been more than acquaintances. Curzon had been active in the most social set, while Justin had paid an unfashionable amount of attention to his studies.

After giving Justin a barely civil nod, Curzon said, "Lady Westron has been wondering what happened to you, Miss Vangelder."

Justin glanced at his companion and saw how her face lit up when Curzon spoke to her.

"I was in no danger, Mr. Curzon," she said, her voice proper but her eyes brimming with excitement. "I'm an avid gardener, you see, and Lord Justin very kindly consented to show me some of the lesser-known parts of the park."

In a careless tone that managed to imply that Justin was scarcely better than an under gardener, Curzon said, "You could not have chosen a better guide, for I'm sure that no one knows more about such matters than Lord Justin." He offered Sunny his arm. "Now I shall take you to Lady Westron."

Sunny turned to Justin and said with sweet sincerity, "Thank you for the tour, my lord. I enjoyed it very much."

Yet as soon as she took Curzon's arm, Justin saw that she forgot his existence. He watched them walk away together—two tall, blond, laughing people. They were like members of some superior race, set apart from the normal run of mankind.

For the first time in his life, Justin found himself resenting Gavin for having been born first. The Sunny Vangelders of the world would always go to men like Gavin or Curzon.

His aching regret was followed by deep, corroding anger. Damning himself for a fool, he turned and headed toward the house. Gavin's fete could progress to its conclusion without him.

Chapter Two

Swindon Palace
Summer 1885

Justin stared out the study window at the dreary landscape, thinking that rain was appropriate for the day he had buried his only brother. After a gray, painful interval, a discreet cough reminded him that he was not alone. He turned to the family solicitor, who had formally read the will earlier in the afternoon. "Why did you ask to speak with me, Mr. Burrell?"

"Though I'm sorry to intrude at such a time, your grace," the solicitor said, "there are several pressing matters that must be addressed without delay."

Justin winced inwardly. Five days of being the ninth Duke of Thornborough was not long enough to accustom him to his new status. "I assume that you are going to tell me that the financial situation is difficult. I'm already aware of that.''

Another little cough, this one embarrassed. ''While you are extremely well-informed about estate matters, there are, ah, certain other items that you might not know of.''

With sudden foreboding, Justin asked, ''Had Gavin run up extensive personal debts?''

''I'm afraid so, your grace. To the tune of... almost a hundred thousand pounds.''

A hundred thousand pounds! How the devil had Gavin managed to spend so much? Justin wanted to swear out loud.

Seeing his expression, Mr. Burrell said, ''It was unfortunate that your brother's death occurred just when it did.''

''You mean the fact that he died while on his way to marry May Russell? It certainly would have been more prudent to have waited until after the wedding,'' Justin said bitterly.

It would have been even more prudent if Gavin had stayed in the private Thornborough railway car. Instead, he had been taken by the charms of a French lady and had gone to her compartment. When the train crashed, the duke and his inamorata had both died, locked in a scandalous embrace. If Gavin had been in his own car, he would have survived the crash with scarcely a bruise.

Oh, damn, Gavin, why did you have to get yourself killed?

Justin swallowed hard. "Obviously drastic measures will be required to save the family from bankruptcy."

"You could sell some land."

"No!" More moderately, Justin said, "The land is held in trust for future generations. It should not be sold to pay frivolous debts."

Burrell nodded, as if he had expected that response. "The only other choice is for you to make an advantageous marriage."

"Become a fortune hunter, you mean?"

"It's a time-honored tradition, your grace," Burrell pointed out with dignity. "You have a great deal to offer a well-dowered bride. One of England's greatest names, and the most magnificent private palace in Great Britain."

"A palace whose roof leaks," Justin said dryly. "Even as we speak, dozens of buckets in the attic are filling with water."

"In that case, the sooner you marry, the better." The solicitor cleared his throat with a new intonation. "In fact, Mrs. Russell hinted to me this morning that if you were interested in contracting an alliance with her, she would look with favor on your suit."

"Marry my brother's fiancée?" Justin said incredulously. He thought of how May had looked earlier at Gavin's funeral, weeping copiously, her beautiful face obscured by her black mourning veil. Perhaps if he had looked more closely, he would have seen a speculative gleam in her eyes. "It's hard to believe that even she would go to such lengths to become a duchess."

"The lady implied that she has a certain fondness for you as well," Burrell said piously.

"The lady has a deficient memory," Justin retorted. It was May Russell who had first called him the Gargoyle. She had been demonstrating her wittiness. Even Gavin had laughed.

"She has a very large fortune under her own control," the solicitor said with regret. "But I suppose you're right—it would be unseemly for you to marry your brother's betrothed. Do you have another suitable female in mind?"

"No. For the last several years, I've been too busy to look for a wife." Justin returned to his position by the window and stared blindly across the grounds. Burrell was right—marriage was the only plausible answer. Justin wouldn't be the first, and certainly not the last, to marry for money.

Even as a younger son, Justin would have had no trouble finding a wife, for he was an Aubrey, had no appalling vices and he had inherited an adequate private income. Yet though Gavin's entertaining had brought a steady stream of polished, fashionable females through Swindon, there had never been one whom Justin had wanted for a wife.

Except...

He closed his eyes, and instantly the memory he had tried to suppress for months crossed his mind—a perfect spring day, a tall, graceful young woman with a smile of such bright sweetness that she was nicknamed for the sun. The image was more real than the foggy landscape outside.

Though Justin had hated himself for his weakness, he had compulsively tracked Sunny Vangelder's triumphant passage through English society. Scarcely an issue of the *Morning Post* had arrived without mentioning her presentation at court, or her glowing appearance at a ball, or the fact that she had been seen riding in Rotten Row. Rumor said that many men had asked for her hand, and daily Justin had steeled himself for an announcement of a brilliant match. Yet at the end of the season, she had left London still unbetrothed.

He drew a painful breath. It was absurd to think of such an incomparable female marrying someone as ordinary as himself. But Gavin had said that she was the greatest heiress ever to cross the Atlantic, which meant that she was exactly the sort of wife Justin needed. And it was also said that her mother wanted to see her a duchess.

Scarcely daring to hope, he asked, "Do you know if Miss Vangelder has contracted a marriage yet?"

"You want to marry the Gilded Girl?" Burrell said, unable to conceal his shock at such effrontery. "Winning her would be quite a coup, but difficult, very difficult. There's a mining heiress from San Francisco who might be a better choice. Almost as wealthy, and I am acquainted with her father. Or perhaps..."

Interrupting the solicitor, Justin said, "I would prefer Miss Vangelder. I met her once, and found her...very amiable."

After a long pause, Burrell said doubtfully, "Of course, you *are* the Duke of Thornborough now. Perhaps it could be done."

Justin smiled humorlessly at the slate-gray pools of the water garden. "How does one go about selling oneself, Burrell? My experience is sadly deficient."

Ignoring the sardonic tone, the solicitor said, "I shall visit Lady Westron. She's the girl's godmother, you know. If she thinks the idea has merit, she can write Augusta Vangelder."

"Very well—call on her ladyship before the roof collapses."

"There is one thing you should consider before proceeding, your grace," Burrell said with a warning note. "Certainly there are more American heiresses than English ones, and they tend to be much more polished, but the drawback of such an alliance is that the families usually drive hard bargains. You would probably have restrictions placed on your control of the dowry, and you might have to return the balance if the marriage ends."

Justin's mouth tightened. "I wouldn't be marrying the girl with the intention of divorcing her, Burrell."

"Of course not," the solicitor said quickly. After a shuffle of papers, he added, "If I may say so, you're very different from your brother."

"Say what you like," Justin said tersely. Yet though he told himself that a rich wife was strictly a practical matter, the possibility of marrying Sunny Vangelder filled him with raw, aching hunger.

If she came to Swindon, there would always be sunshine.

Newport, Rhode Island

Laughing and breathless from the bicycle ride, Sunny waved goodbye to her friends, then skipped up the steps of The Tides, the Vangelder summer home. Like most Newport "cottages," it would have been called a mansion anywhere else. Still, the atmosphere was more informal than in New York, and she always enjoyed the months spent in Newport.

And this summer was the best ever, because the Honorable Paul Curzon was visiting the Astors. He had arrived in Newport three weeks earlier, and the first time they had waltzed together he had confided that he had come to America to see Sunny.

She had almost expired from sheer bliss, for she had been thinking of Paul ever since their first meeting. They had carried on a delicious flirtation throughout the season, and she had sensed that there were deeper feelings on both sides; certainly there had been on her part. It had been a bitter disappointment that he had not offered for her then.

As they danced, he explained that he had not spoken earlier for he had feared that he would not be considered an acceptable suitor. But after weeks of yearning, he had finally decided to come to America and declare his love. Breathlessly she had confessed that she also had tender feelings for him.

Ever since that night, she had been living in an enchanted dream. Each morning she woke with the knowledge that she would see Paul at least once during the day, perhaps more than that. The business of Newport was society, and there was an endless succession of balls and dinner parties and polo matches.

Though the two of them had behaved impeccably in public, on two magical occasions they had had a moment's privacy, and he had kissed her with a passion that made her blood sing through her veins. At night, as she lay in her chaste bed, she remembered those kisses and yearned for more.

His courtship had culminated this morning, in the few minutes when the two of them had cycled ahead of the rest of their party. After declaring his love, he had asked her to marry him. Dizzy with delight, she had accepted instantly.

As Sunny stepped into the cool marble vestibule of The Tides, she tried to calm her expression, for she knew that she was beaming like a fool. It was going to be hard to keep her lovely secret, but she must until the next day, when Paul would ask her mother's permission. It was not to be expected that her mother would be enthralled by the match. However, Sunny was sure that she would come around, for Paul came from a fine family and he had a distinguished career in front of him.

She handed the butler her hat, saying gaily, "It's a beautiful day, Graves."

"Indeed it is, Miss Sarah." Taking the hat, he added, "Your mother has asked that you see her as soon as you return home. I believe that she is in her private salon."

Such summons were not uncommon, so Sunny went upstairs with no premonition of disaster. She knocked on her mother's door and was invited in.

When she entered, Augusta looked up from her desk with triumph in her eyes. "I have splendid news, Sarah. I'll admit I was tempted by some of the offers I received for your hand, but it was right to wait." After a portentous pause, she said, "You, my dear, are going to become the Duchess of Thornborough."

The shock was so stunning that at first Sunny could only say stupidly, "What on earth do you mean?"

"You're going to marry Thornborough, of course," her mother said briskly. "For the last several days cables have been flying back and forth between Newport and England. The essentials have been settled, and Thornborough is on his way to Newport to make you a formal offer.''

"But...but I thought the Duke of Thornborough was going to marry Mrs. Russell.''

"That was Gavin, the eighth duke. Unfortunately he was killed in a train wreck several weeks ago, two days before he was to marry May.'' Augusta smiled maliciously. "I would wager that May tried her luck with his successor, but clearly the ninth duke has better taste than his brother.''

Feeling ice-cold, Sunny sank into a chair. "How can I marry a man whom I've never even met?'' she said weakly.

"Katie Westron said that you did meet him. In fact, you spent a rather indecent amount of time strolling through the Swindon gardens together,'' her mother said tartly. "He was Lord Justin Aubrey then, younger brother to the duke who just died.''

The fete at Swindon was when Sunny had met Paul. Beside that, other events of the day had paled. Dazedly she tried to remember more. The gardens had been superb, and she vaguely recalled being escorted through them by someone. Had that been Lord Justin? She supposed so, though she could remember nothing about him except that he was dark, and quiet, and...unmemorable.

But it didn't matter what he was like, because she wasn't going to marry him. Steeling herself for battle, Sunny said, "I can't marry Thornborough, because I'm betrothed to Paul Curzon."

There was an instant of ominous silence. Then her mother exploded. "I considered putting a stop to that earlier, but I thought it was a harmless flirtation. I couldn't *believe* that you would be so foolish as to entertain thoughts of marrying such a man." Her eyes narrowed. "I trust that at least you've had the sense not to tell anyone about this so-called engagement?"

Sunny shook her head. "Paul only asked me this morning."

"I shall send him a note saying that he is never to call on you, or speak to you, again. That will put an end to this nonsense." Augusta drummed her fingers on the elaborate desk as she thought. "Thornborough will be here in nine days. I shall give a ball in his honor a week later, and we can announce the betrothal then. The wedding should take place in October, I think. It will take that long to make suitable arrangements."

Knowing that she faced the fight of her life, Sunny wiped her damp palms on her skirt, then said evenly, "You must cable the duke and stop him from coming, Mother. Paul Curzon and I love each other, and I am going to marry him."

It was the first time she had ever defied her mother, and Augusta's jaw dropped in shock. Recovering quickly, she said in a low, furious voice, "You are a Vangelder, my girl, and I've devoted my life to training you to be worthy of the highest station. I will never permit you to throw yourself away on a worthless, fortune-hunting younger son.''

"Paul is no fortune hunter! He said that if you refused permission, we could live on his income,'' Sunny said hotly. "And he isn't worthless! He's a British aristocrat, exactly what you wanted for me, and he has a great future in British politics. He was recently made a junior minister, and he says that with me by his side he'll soon be in the Cabinet.''

"Your money would certainly help his career,'' Augusta said grimly, "but he'll have to find himself another heiress, because I will never give my consent.''

"I don't need your consent!'' Sunny said fiercely. "I'm of legal age and can marry whomever I wish. And I *will!*''

"How dare you speak to your mother this way!'' Augusta grabbed Sunny's elbow, then marched her down the hall to her bedroom and shoved her inside. "If you think a humble life is so splendid, you can stay locked in here and live on bread and water until you change your mind.''

As the key turned in the lock, Sunny collapsed, shaking, on the bed. She had never dreamed how painful defiance could be. Yet she could not surrender, not when her whole life's happiness was at stake.

She must see Paul; he would know what to do.

The thought steadied her churning emotions, and she began to consider what to do. Her bedroom opened onto the roof of one of the porches, and her older brother Charlie had showed her how to climb to the ground. Her mother had never dreamed that her well-bred daughter would behave in such a hoydenish fashion.

Paul was staying at Windfall, which was only a mile away. Would he be there this evening? Yes, he had mentioned that the Astors were giving a dinner party. She would wait until her mother retired, then escape and walk to Windfall. With a veil over her face, no one would recognize her even if she was seen. She'd go to the servants' entrance and ask for the butler. He knew her, and she thought that for a suitable consideration he would summon Paul and let them have a few minutes of privacy.

Once they were together, everything would be all right.

Sunny's plan went smoothly, and by ten o'clock that evening she was pacing nervously around the Windfall servants' sitting room. She hoped that Paul would be able to slip away quietly when the butler delivered her message. But what if the butler betrayed her to Mrs. Astor? Or if Mrs. Astor suspected that something was amiss and decided to investigate?

The door opened and she whirled around, ready to jump from her skin. With a wave of relief, she saw that it was Paul, devastatingly attractive in his evening dress. Coming toward her with concern on his face, he said, "Darling, you shouldn't risk your reputation like this—but it's wonderful to see you."

He opened his arms, and she went into them eagerly. She loved his height, which made her feel small and feminine. It was the first time they had real privacy, and his kiss far surpassed what they had shared before. Her resolve strengthened. She would never give up his love for the dubious pleasure of marrying a nondescript duke. *Never.*

Remembering the reason for her visit, she reluctantly ended the kiss. "Oh, Paul, something dreadful has happened!" she said miserably. "Today my mother told me that she has arranged for me to marry someone else. I told her about our betrothal, but she won't hear of it. She locked me in my room and swore I'd stay there on bread and water until I changed my mind."

"How dare she treat you in such a way!" Paul exclaimed. "I won't permit it."

"I refused to agree to her wishes, of course, but it was so difficult. I...I think we should elope. Tonight."

"Right now?" he said, startled. "That's not what I want for you, darling. You deserve the grandest wedding of the century, not a furtive, hole-in-corner affair.''

"What does that matter?" she said impatiently. "I'm trying to be strong, but my mother is...is not easy to resist."

"Who does she want you to marry?"

"The new Duke of Thornborough, Justin Aubrey. His brother, Gavin, just died, and Justin needs a rich wife."

Before she could say more, Paul said in a stunned voice, "The Duke of Thornborough! You would be one of the most influential women in England."

"And one of the unhappiest." Tears welled in her eyes, and she blinked them back angrily. "I need to be with you, Paul."

"We must reason this out." He stroked her back soothingly. "Your mother flatly refused to consider me as a suitor?"

"She said that it was unthinkable that I should marry a nobody." Sunny relaxed again, comforted by his touch. "Such nonsense! Titles mean nothing. What matters is being a gentleman, and no one is more gentlemanly than you."

There was a long pause. Then Paul said gravely, "Sunny, I can't marry you against your mother's wishes. Though I knew that she would not be enthusiastic about my suit, I thought I would be able to persuade her. But to be Duchess of Thornborough! With that in prospect, she will never accept me.''

A tendril of fear curled through Sunny. ''It is not my mother's place to choose my husband,'' she said sharply. ''It's mine, and you are my choice. That's all that matters.''

''If only it were that simple!'' He sighed. ''But it's not, my dear. You are not simply my own sweet love, but a national treasure—one of America's princesses. What kind of cad would I be to take advantage of your innocence to keep you from a glorious future?''

Sunny stared at him, thinking that this scene couldn't be real. Perhaps she had fallen off her bicycle and injured her head, and everything that had happened since was only a bad dream. Very carefully she said, ''You're saying that you don't want to marry me?''

''Of course I do, but clearly that is impossible. If you marry me, you will become estranged from your family. I don't want to be the cause of that.'' He gazed lovingly into her eyes. ''This won't be so bad, darling. In fact, one could see it as a piece of good fortune. With your influence to further my career, I'll be in the Cabinet in no time.''

''Is that what matters most—your career?'' she said brittlely.

''Of course not!'' He pulled her close again. ''The most important thing is our love, and your mother can't take that away from us. After you've given Thornborough an heir and a spare, we'll be free to love each other as we were meant to.''

She went rigid, unable to believe what he was saying.

Feeling her withdrawal, he said tenderly, "I don't want to wait, either. If we're discreet, we can be together as soon as you're back from your honeymoon. Believe me, I would like nothing better! We'll have to be careful, of course—it wouldn't do to foist a bastard on Thornborough." He gave a wicked chuckle. "Though if the Gargoyle is unable to perform his duty, I'll be happy to help him. I look more like an Aubrey than he does."

"In other words, I make you a Cabinet minister, and my reward is adultery in the afternoon," she said numbly. "No, thank you, Mr. Curzon." Knowing that she would break down in tears if she stayed any longer, she headed for the door.

He followed her and caught her shoulders. "Don't look at it that way, darling. I promise you that this will turn out all right. We'll be able to enjoy the very cream of love, with none of the dreariness of daily living that kills romance."

He turned her around so that she was facing him. He was as heart-stoppingly handsome as ever, his golden hair glowing in the gaslight, his blue eyes limpid with sincerity.

She drew a shuddering breath. How could she have been such a fool?

His voice richly confident, he said, "Trust me,

darling.'' Then he started to pull her toward him for another kiss.

She slapped him with all her strength. ''You're right that this is a fortunate turn of events, because it's given me a chance to see what a swine you are,'' she said, her voice trembling. ''I hope I never see you again, though I don't suppose I'll be so lucky. Goodbye, Mr. Curzon, and good riddance.''

As he gaped with shock, the imprint of her hand reddening on his face, she spun on her heel and raced from the room. When she was outside the cottage, she took refuge in the shadowy lee of a huge hedge. There she fell to her knees, heart hammering and tears pouring down her face.

Ever since her childhood, she had dreamed of finding a man who would love her forever. She had wanted a marriage different from the carefully concealed hostility between her parents, or the bored civility common between many other fashionable couples. In Paul, she thought she had found the man she was seeking.

But she had been wrong, so wrong. Oh, he desired her body, and he lusted after her family's money and influence, but that wasn't love—she doubted that he knew what love was. Obviously she didn't know much about it, either. Perhaps the love she craved had never been more than a romantic girl's futile fantasy.

Blindly she stumbled to her feet and began the

slow walk to The Tides. After Paul's betrayal, there was no reason to go anywhere else.

The next morning, when a maid delivered a half loaf of freshly baked bread and a crystal pitcher of water on a tray decorated with a fresh rosebud, Sunny summoned her mother and said that she would accept the Duke of Thornborough's offer.

Chapter Three

Justin found America a mixture of the sublime and the ridiculous. He liked the bustling energy of New York City and the cheerful directness of the average citizen. Yet in what was supposedly a nation of equals, he found people whose craven fawning over his title would have shamed a spaniel.

Newport society, which considered itself the *crème de la crème* of America, apparently wanted to out-Anglo the English when it came to formality and elaborate rules. Augusta Vangelder was in her element as she escorted him to an endless series of social events. She invariably referred to him as her "dear duke." He bore that stoically, along with all the other absurdities of the situation.

But the habits of the natives were of only minor interest; what mattered was Sunny Vangelder. He had hoped that she would greet him with the same sweet, unaffected good nature that she had shown at Swindon, perhaps even with eagerness.

Instead, she might have been a different person. The laughing girl had been replaced by a polished, brittle young woman who avoided speaking with him and never once met his gaze. Though he tried to revive the easy companionship they had so briefly shared, he had no success. Perhaps her stiffness was caused by her mother's rather repressive presence, but he had the uneasy feeling that there was a deeper cause.

His fifth morning in Newport, he happened to find Sunny reading in the library during a rare hour when they were at home. She didn't hear him enter, and her head remained bent over her book. The morning light made her hair glow like sun-struck honey, and the elegant purity of her profile caught at his heart.

It was time to make his formal offer of marriage. A flurry of images danced through his mind: him kneeling at her feet and eloquently swearing eternal devotion; Sunny opening her arms and giving him that wonderful smile that had made him feel as if he were the only man in the world; a kiss that would bring them together forever.

Instead, he cleared his throat to get her attention, then said, "Miss Vangelder—Sunny—there is something I would like to ask you. I'm sure you know what it is."

Perhaps she had known that he was there, for there was no surprise on her face when she lowered her book and looked up.

"All of Newport knows," she said without inflection.

She wasn't going to make this easy for him. Wishing that he was skilled at spinning romantic words, he said haltingly, "Sunny, you have had my heart from the first moment I saw you at Swindon. There is no one else..."

She cut him off with an abrupt motion of her hand. "You needn't waste our time with pretty lies, Duke. We are here to strike a bargain. You need a fortune and a wife who knows what to do with a dinner setting that includes six forks. I need a husband who will lend luster to my mother's position in society, and who will confirm our fine American adage that anything can be bought. Please get on with the offer so I can accept and return to my book."

He rocked back on his heels, feeling as if he had been punched in the stomach. Wanting to pierce her contemptuous calm, he said with uncharacteristic bluntness, "We're talking about a marriage, not a business. The first duty of a nobleman's wife is to produce an heir, and knowledge of which fork to use will not help you there."

"I've heard that begetting children is a monstrously undignified business, but didn't the Queen tell her oldest daughter that a female needs only to lie there and think of England?" Sunny's lips twisted. "I should be able to manage that. Most women do."

Damning the consequences to Swindon, he said tightly, "There will be no offer, Miss Vangelder, for I will do neither of us a favor by marrying a woman who despises me."

Sunny caught her breath, and for the first time since he had arrived in Newport looked directly at him. He was shocked by the haunted misery in her aqua eyes.

After a moment she bent her neck and pressed her slim fingers to the center of her forehead. "I'm sorry, your grace. I didn't mean to imply that I despise you," she said quietly. "I recently...suffered a disappointment, and I'm afraid that my temper is badly out of sorts. Still, that does not excuse my insufferable rudeness. Please forgive me."

He guessed that only a broken heart would cause a well-mannered young lady to behave so brusquely. He had heard that Paul Curzon had been in Newport until the week before. Could Sunny have fallen in love with Curzon, who had as many mistresses as the Prince of Wales? Recalling how she had looked at the man when she was at Swindon, Justin knew it was all too likely.

The disappointment was crushing. When he had received Augusta Vangelder's invitation, he had assumed that she had obtained her daughter's agreement to the marriage. He should have known that he would never have been Sunny's choice. It was Augusta, after all, who was enthralled by the idea of a dukedom; Sunny was obviously unimpressed by the prospect.

In a voice of careful neutrality, he said, "You're forgiven, but even if you don't despise me, it's clear that this is not a match that you want." His throat closed, and it took an immense effort to add, "I don't want an unwilling bride, so if there is someone else whom you wish to marry, I shall withdraw."

She stared at her hands, which were locked tightly on her book. "There is no one I would prefer. I suppose that I must marry someone, and you'll make as good a husband as any."

He studied the delicate line of her profile, his resolve to do the right thing undermined by his yearning. Then she raised her head, her gaze searching. He had the feeling that it was the first time she had truly looked at him as an individual.

"Perhaps you would be better than most," she said after a charged silence. "At least you are honest about what you want."

It was a frail foundation for a lifetime commitment, but he could not bear to throw away this chance. "Very well," he said formally. "I would be very honored, and very pleased, if you would consent to become my wife."

"The honor is mine, your grace," she said with equal formality.

If this was a normal engagement, he would kiss his intended bride now, but Sunny's expression was unwelcoming, so he said only, "My name is Justin. It would please me if you used it."

She nodded. "Very well, Justin."

An awkward silence fell. Unhappily he wondered how achieving the fondest hope of his heart could feel so much like ashes. "Shall we go and inform your mother of our news?"

"You don't need me for that. I know that she is interested in an early wedding, perhaps October. You need only tell her what is convenient for you." Rubbing her temples, she set aside her book and got to her feet. "If you'll excuse me, I have a bit of a headache."

"I hope that you feel better soon."

"I'm sure I shall." Remembering that she had just agreed to give her life, her person and her fortune into this stranger's keeping, she attempted a smile.

It must not have been a very good attempt, because the duke's face remained grave. His thoughtful eyes were a clear, light gray, and were perhaps his best feature.

"I don't wish to seem inattentive," he said, "but my brother left his affairs in some disarray, and I must return to London the day after your mother's ball. I probably won't be able to return until a few days before the wedding."

"There is no need for romantic pretenses between us." She smiled, a little wryly, but with the first amusement she had felt since discovering

Paul's true character. "It will be best if you aren't here, because there will be a truly vulgar amount of publicity. Our marriage will inevitably be deemed the Wedding of the Century, and there will be endless stories about you and me, your noble ancestors and my undistinguished ones, my trousseau, my flowers, my attendants and every other conceivable detail. And what the reporters can't find out, they will invent."

His dark brows arched. "You're right. It will be better if I am on the other side of the Atlantic."

He opened the door for her. When she walked in front of him, on impulse she laid her hand on his arm for a moment. "I shall do my best to be a duchess you will be proud of."

He inclined his head. "I'm sure you will succeed."

As she went upstairs to her room, she decided that he was rather attractive, in a subdued way. Granted, he wasn't much taller than she, but she was a tall woman. The quiet excellence of British tailoring showed his trim, muscular figure to advantage, and his craggy features had a certain distinction.

The words echoed in her mind, and as she entered her room and wearily lay on the bed, she realized that she had had similar thoughts when she first saw him at Swindon Palace.

That memory triggered others, and gradually fragments of that day came back to her. Lord Justin had been quiet but very gentlemanly, and knowledgeable about the gardens and estate. He had even showed signs of humor, of a very dry kind. It had been a pleasant interlude.

Yet he was still almost entirely a stranger, for she knew nothing of his mind or emotions. He didn't seem to be a man of deep feelings; it was his duty to marry well, so he was doing so, choosing a wife with his head rather than his heart.

Her eyes drifted shut. Perhaps this marriage would not be such a bad thing; she had heard that arranged marriages were happy about as often as love matches. She and the duke would treat each other with polite respect and not expect romance or deep passion. God willing, they would have children, and in them she might find the love she craved.

Certainly the duke had one great advantage: he could hardly have been more different from charming, articulate, false-hearted Paul Curzon.

The maid Antoinette made a last adjustment to the train of Sunny's ball gown. "You look exquisite, mademoiselle. *Monsieur le Duc* will be most pleased."

Sunny turned and regarded herself in the mirror. Her cream-colored gown was spectacular, with sumptuous embroidery and a décolletage that set off her bare shoulders and arms perfectly. After her hair had been pinned up to expose the graceful length of her neck, fragile rosebuds had been woven into the soft curls. The only thing her appearance lacked was animation. "Thank you, Antoinette. You have surpassed yourself."

The maid permitted herself a smile of satisfaction before she withdrew. Sunny glanced at the clock and saw that she had a quarter of an hour to wait before making her grand entrance at the ball. The house hummed with excitement, for tonight Augusta's triumph would be announced. All of Newport society was here to fawn over Thornborough and cast envious glances at Sunny. There would also be sharp eyes watching to see how she and the duke—Justin—behaved with each other. Antoinette, who was always well-informed, had passed on several disturbing rumors. It was said that Sunny had at first refused to marry the duke because of his licentious habits, and that Augusta had beaten and starved her daughter into accepting him.

Even though there was a grain of truth in the story about her mother, Sunny found the gossip deeply distasteful. She must make a special effort to appear at ease with her mother and her fiancé. She looked in the mirror again and practiced her smile.

The door opened and a crisp English voice said, "How is my favorite goddaughter?"

"Aunt Katie!" Sunny spun around with genuine

pleasure. "I had no idea that you were coming for the ball."

"I told Augusta not to mention the possibility since I wasn't sure I would arrive in time." Laughing, Lady Westron held Sunny at arm's length when her goddaughter came to give her a hug. "Never crush a Worth evening gown, my dear! At least, not until the ball is over."

After a careful survey, she gave a nod of approval. "I'm madly envious. Even Worth can't make a short woman like me look as magnificent as you do tonight. The Newport cats will gnash their teeth with jealousy, and Thornborough will thank his stars for his good fortune."

Sunny's high spirits faded. "I believe he feels that we have made a fair bargain."

Katie cocked her head. "Are you unhappy about the match?"

Sunny shrugged and began carefully drawing an elbow-length kid glove onto her right hand. "I'm sure that we'll rub along tolerably well."

Ignoring her own advice about crushing a Worth evening gown, Katie dropped into a chair with a flurry of satin petticoats. "I made inquiries about Thornborough when his solicitor first approached me about a possible match. He'll make you a better husband than most, Sunny. He's respected by those who know him, and while he isn't a wit like his brother was, and he's certainly not fashionable, he's no fool, nor is he the sort to humiliate you by flaunting his mistress.''

Sunny stiffened. "Thornborough has a mistress?"

"Very likely—most men do." Katie's lips curved ruefully. "There's much you need to learn about English husbands and English houses. Living in Britain is quite unlike being a visitor, you know.''

Sunny relaxed when she found that her godmother had been talking in general rather than from particular knowledge. Though she knew that fashionable English society was very different from what she was used to, she disliked the idea of Thornborough with a mistress. Acutely.

She began the slow process of putting on her left glove. "Perhaps you had better educate me about what to expect.''

"Be prepared for the fact that English great houses are *cold*." Katie shuddered. "Forget your delicate lace shawls—to survive winter in an English country house, your trousseau should include several wraps the size and weight of a horse blanket. You must have at least one decent set of furs, as well. The houses may be grand, but they're amazingly primitive—no central heating or gaslights, and no hot running water. And the bathrooms! A tin tub in front of the fire is the best you'll do in most houses.''

Surprised and a little amused, Sunny said,

"Surely Swindon Palace can't be that bad. It's said to be the grandest private home in Great Britain."

Katie sniffed. "A palace built almost two hundred years ago, and scarcely a pound wasted on modernization since then. But don't complain to Thornborough—English husbands, as a rule, are not solicitous in the way that American husbands are. Since the duke will not want to hear about your little grievances, you must learn to resolve matters on your own. I recommend that you take your own maid with you. That way you can count on at least one person in the household being on your side."

Sunny put a hand up. "If you say one sentence more, I will go downstairs and cancel my betrothal," she said, not knowing whether to laugh or cry. "I'm beginning to wonder why any woman would want to marry an English lord, particularly if she isn't madly in love with him."

"I didn't mean to terrify you," Katie assured her. "I just want to make sure that you won't be disillusioned. Once a woman gets past the discomforts, she may have more freedom and influence than she would in America. Here, a woman rules her home, but nothing outside. An English lady can be part of her husband's life, or develop a life of her own, in a way most unusual in America."

Since frankness was the order of the day, Sunny asked, "Are you sorry you married Lord Westron?"

Katie hesitated a moment. "There are times when I would have said yes, but we've come to understand each other very well. He says that I've been invaluable to his political career, and through him, I've been able to bring a little American democracy to some hoary bits of British law." She smiled fondly. "And between us, he and I have produced three rather splendid children, even if I shouldn't say so myself."

Sunny sighed; it was all very confusing. She was glad when a knock sounded on her door. "Your mother says that it is time to come down, Miss Sarah," the butler intoned.

"Don't forget your fan. It's going to be very warm on the dance floor," Katie said briskly. "I'll be down after I've freshened up."

Sunny accepted the fan, then lifted her train and went into the corridor. At the top of the sweeping staircase, she carefully spread the train, then slowly began descending the stairs, accompanied by the soft swish of heavy silk. She had been told that she walked with the proud grace of the Winged Victory. She ought to; as a child, she had been strapped into an iron back brace whenever she did her lessons. Perfect posture didn't come easily.

The hall below opened into the ballroom, and music and guests wafted through both. As she came into view, a hush fell and all eyes turned toward her. The cream of American society was evaluating the next Duchess of Thornborough.

When she was three-quarters of the way down, she saw that her fiancé was crossing the hall to the staircase. The stark black of formal evening wear suited him.

When she reached the bottom, he took her hand. Under his breath, he said, "You look even more beautiful than usual." Then he brushed a courtly, formal kiss on her kid-covered fingers.

She glanced at him uncertainly, not sure if he truly admired her or the compliment was mere formality. It was impossible to tell; he was the most inscrutable man she had ever met.

Then he smiled at her and looked not merely presentable, but downright handsome. It was the first time she had seen him smile. He should do so more often.

Her mother joined them, beaming with possessive pride. "You look splendid, Sarah."

A moment later they were surrounded by chattering, laughing people, particularly those who had not yet met the duke and who longed to rectify the omission. Sunny half expected her fiancé to retreat to a corner filled with men, but he bore up under the onslaught very well. Though he spoke little, his grave courtesy soon won over even the most critical society matrons. She realized that she had underestimated him. Thornborough's avoidance of the fashionable life was obviously from choice rather than social ineptitude.

When she finally had a chance to look at her

dance card, she saw that her fiancé had put himself down for two waltzes as well as the supper dance. That in itself was a declaration of their engagement, for no young lady would have more than two dances with one man unless intentions were serious.

When the orchestra struck up their first waltz, Thornborough excused himself from his admirers and came to collect her.

She caught her train up so that she could dance, then took his hand and followed him onto the floor. "It will be a pleasure to waltz," she said. "I feel as if I've been talking nonstop for the last hour."

"I believe that you have been," he said as he drew her into position, a light hand on her waist. "It must be fatiguing to be so popular. In the interests of allowing you to recover, I shan't require you to talk at all."

"But you are just as popular," she said teasingly. "Everyone in Newport wants to know you."

"It isn't me they're interested in, but the Duke of Thornborough. If I were a hairy ape from the Congo, I'd be equally in demand, as long as I was also a duke." He considered, then said with good-natured cynicism, "More so, I think. Apes are said to be quite entertaining."

Though Sunny chuckled, his remark made her understand better why he wanted her to call him Justin. Being transformed overnight from the Gargoyle to the much-courted Duke of Thornborough must have been enough to make anyone cynical.

It came as no surprise to learn that he danced well. She relaxed and let the voluptuous strains of music work their usual magic. The waltz was a very intimate dance, the closest a young woman was allowed to come to a man. Usually it was also an opportunity to talk with some privacy. The fact that she and Justin were both silent had the curious effect of making her disturbingly aware of his physical closeness, even though he kept a perfectly proper twelve inches between them.

Katie had been right about the heat of the ballroom; as they whirled across the floor, Sunny realized that a remarkable amount of warmth was being generated between their gloved hands. It didn't help that their eyes were almost level, for it increased the uncomfortable sense of closeness. She wished that she knew what was going on behind those enigmatic gray eyes.

A month before, she had waltzed like this with Paul Curzon and he had told her that his heart had driven him to follow her to America. The memory was jarring and she stumbled on a turn. If Justin hadn't quickly steadied her, she would have fallen.

His dark brows drew together. "Are you feeling faint? It's very warm—perhaps we should go onto the porch for some air."

She managed a smile. "I'm fine, only a little dizzy. It's absurd that we can turn only one direction during a waltz. If we could spin the other way now and then, it would be much easier.''

"Society thrives on absurdity," he observed. "Obscure rules are necessary so that outsiders can be identified and kept safely outside."

While she pondered his unexpected insight, the waltz ended and another partner came to claim her. The evening passed quickly. After the lavish supper was served, the engagement was formally announced. Augusta was in her element as even her most powerful social rivals acknowledged her triumph.

Sunny felt a pang as she accepted the good wishes of people she had known all her life. This was her last summer in Newport. Though she would visit in the future, it would not be the same; already her engagement to an Englishman was setting her apart.

The first phase of her life was ending—and she had no clear idea what the next phase would be like.

It was very late when the last of the guests left. As her official fiancé, Thornborough was allowed to escort Sunny to her room. When they reached her door, he said, "My train leaves rather early tomorrow, so I'll say goodbye now."

"I'm sorry that you'll have to travel without a proper night's sleep." Almost too tired to stand, she masked a yawn with her hand. "Have a safe and pleasant journey, Justin."

His gaze caught hers, and she couldn't look away. The air between them seemed to thicken. Gently he curved his hand around her head and drew her to him for a kiss.

Because she didn't love him she had been dreading this moment, yet again he surprised her. His lips were warm and firm. Pleasant. Undemanding.

He caressed her hair, disturbing the rosebuds, and scented petals drifted over her bare shoulder in a delicate sensual caress. She gave a little sigh, and his arms went around her.

The feel of his broad chest and his hand on the small of her back triggered a vivid memory of her last kiss, in Paul Curzon's embrace. All the anger and shame of that episode flooded back. She stiffened and took an involuntary step backward.

He released her instantly. Though his eyes had darkened, his voice was mild when he said, "Sleep well. I shall see you in October."

She opened her door, but instead of entering her room she paused and watched his compact, powerful figure stride down the hall to his own chamber. In spite of the warmth of the night, a shiver went down her spine. Her feelings about Justin were confused, but one thing was certain: it would be disastrous to continue to let the shadow of Paul Curzon come between her and her future husband.

Yet she didn't know how to get rid of it.

Chapter Four

New York City
October 1885

The Wedding of the Century.

Justin stared at the blaring headline in one of the newspapers that had just been delivered to his hotel room. It was a rude shock for a man who had disembarked in New York City only two hours earlier.

Below the headline were drawings of Sunny and himself. The likeness of him was not flattering. Were his brows really so heavy and threatening? Perhaps.

He smiled wryly as he skimmed the story; it was every bit as bad as Sunny had predicted. Apparently Americans had a maniacal interest in other people's private business. There was even a breathless description of the bride's garters, which were allegedly of gold lace with diamond-studded clasps. The item must have been invented, since he could not imagine Sunny discussing her garters with a reporter.

The thought of Sunny in her garters was so distracting that he swiftly flipped to the next newspaper. This one featured a cartoon of a couple getting married by a blindfolded minister. The tall, slim bride wore a martyred expression as she knelt beside a dissolute-looking groom who was half a head shorter.

The accompanying story implied rather strongly that the Duke of Thornborough was a corrupt specimen of European cadhood who had come to the New World to coldly steal away the finest, freshest flower of American femininity. At the same time, there was an unmistakable undercurrent of pride that one of New York's own was to become a duchess. Apparently the natives couldn't decide whether they loathed or loved the trappings of the decadent Old World.

Disgusted, he tossed the papers aside and finished dressing for the dinner that Augusta Vangelder was giving in his honor. Afterward, the marriage settlements would be signed. Yet though that would make him a far wealthier man, what made his heart quicken was the fact that after three long months, he would see Sunny again. And not only see, but touch...

After his Newport visit they had written each

other regularly, and he had enjoyed her whimsical anecdotes about the rigors of preparing for a wedding. If she had ever expressed any affection for him, he might have had the courage to tell her his own feelings, for it would be easier to write about love than to say the words out loud.

But her letters had been so impersonal that anyone could have read them. He had replied with equal detachment, writing about Swindon and acquainting her with what she would find there. He had debated telling her about some of the improvements he had ordered, but decided to keep them as a surprise.

He checked his watch and saw that the carriage the Vangelders were sending should be waiting outside the hotel. Brimming with suppressed excitement, he went downstairs.

As he crossed the lobby, a voice barked, "There he is!"

Half a dozen slovenly persons, obviously reporters, bolted across the marble floor and surrounded him. Refusing to be deterred, he kept walking through the babble of questions that came from all sides.

The loudest speaker, a fellow with a red checked vest, yelled, "What do you think of New York, Duke?"

Deciding it was better to say something innocuous rather than to ignore them entirely, Justin said, "A splendid city."

Another reporter asked, "Any of your family coming to the wedding, Duke?"

"Unfortunately that isn't possible."

"Is it true that Sunny has the largest dowry of any American girl to marry a British lord?"

The sound of her name on the man's lips made Justin glad that he wasn't carrying a cane, for he might have broken it across the oaf's head. "You'll have to excuse me," he said, tight-lipped, "for I have an engagement."

"Are you going to visit Sunny now?" several chorused.

When Justin didn't answer, one of the men grabbed his arm. Clamping onto his temper, Justin looked the reporter in the eye and said in the freezing accents honed by ten generations of nobility, "I beg your pardon?"

The man hastily stepped back. "Sorry, sir. No offense meant."

Justin had almost reached the door when a skinny fellow jumped in front of him. "Are you in love with our Sunny, your dukeship, or are you only marrying her for the money?"

It had been a mistake to answer any questions at all, Justin realized; it only encouraged the creatures. "I realize that none of you are qualified to understand gentlemanly behavior," he said icily, "so you will have to take my word for it that a gentleman never discusses a lady, and particularly not in the public press. Kindly get out of my way."

The man said with a leer, "Just asking what the American public wants to know, Thorny."

"The American public can go hang," Justin snapped.

Before the reporters could commit any further impertinence, several members of the hotel staff belatedly came to Justin's rescue. They swept the journalists aside and escorted him outside with profuse apologies and promises that such persons would never be allowed in the hotel again.

In a voice clipped by fury, Justin told the manager, "I hope that is true, because if there is another episode like this I shall move to quieter quarters."

Temper simmering, he settled into the luxurious Vangelder carriage. The sooner this damned wedding was over and he could take his wife home, the better.

Sunny was waiting in the Vangelder drawing room. She came forward with her hands outstretched, and if her smile wasn't quite as radiant as he would have liked, at least it was genuine.

"It's good to see you, Sunny." He caught her hands and studied her face hungrily. "You were right about the publicity surrounding the wedding. I'm afraid that I was just rather abrupt with some members of the press. Has it been hard on you?"

She made a face. "Though it's been dreadful, I'm well protected here. But everyone in the household has been offered bribes to describe my trousseau.''

''Gold-lace garters with diamond-studded clasps?''

''You saw that?'' she said ruefully. ''It's all so *vulgar!*''

She looked utterly charming. He was on the verge of kissing her when the door swung open. Justin looked up to see a tall, blond young man who had to be one of Sunny's older brothers.

''I'm Charlie Vangelder,'' the young man said cheerfully as he offered his hand. ''Sorry not to meet you in Newport, Thornborough, but I was working on the railroad all summer. Have to learn how to run it when my uncle retires, you know.''

So much for being alone with his intended bride. Suppressing a sigh, Justin shook hands with his future brother-in-law. A moment later, Augusta Vangelder swooped in, followed by a dozen more people, and it became clear that the ''quiet family dinner'' was an occasion for numberless Vangelders to meet their new relation by marriage.

The only break was the half hour when Justin met with the Vangelder attorneys to sign the settlement papers. His solicitor had bargained well; the minute that Justin married Sunny, he would come into possession of five million dollars worth of railway stock with a guaranteed minimum income of two hundred thousand dollars a year.

There would also be a capital sum of another

million dollars that Justin would receive outright, plus a separate income for Sunny's personal use so that she would never have to be dependent on her husband's goodwill for pin money. As an incentive for Justin to try to keep his wife happy, the stock would revert to the Vangelder family trust if the marriage ended in divorce.

Gavin would have been amused to know that the value of the Thornborough title had risen so quickly. May Russell would have brought only half as much to her marriage.

Impassively Justin scrawled his name over and over, hating every minute of it. He wished that he could marry Sunny without taking a penny of her family money, but that was impossible; without her wealth and his title, there would be no marriage.

As he signed the last paper, he wondered if Sunny would ever believe that he would have wanted her for his wife even if she had been a flower seller in Covent Garden.

When her daughter entered the breakfast parlor, Augusta said, "Good morning, Sarah." She took a dainty bite of buttered eggs. "There's a letter here for you from England."

Sunny tried unsuccessfully to suppress a yawn as she selected two muffins from the sideboard. The dinner party for Thornborough had gone on very late, and she had smiled at so many cousins that her jaw ached this morning.

She wished that she had had a few minutes alone with her future husband; she would have liked to tell him how much she had enjoyed his letters. She didn't know if it had been a deliberate effort on his part, but his descriptions of life at Swindon Palace had made her future seem less alien. His dry wit had even managed to make her smile.

She slit open the envelope that lay by her plate and scanned the contents. "It's from Lady Alexandra Aubrey, Thornborough's youngest sister. A charming note welcoming me to the family."

Uncomfortably Sunny remembered that Katie had said the girl had been nicknamed the Gargoylette. Her lips compressed as she returned the note to the envelope. The girl might be small, shy and seventeen, but she was the only Aubrey to write her brother's bride, and Sunny looked forward to meeting her.

"Are you only going to have muffins for breakfast?" Augusta said with disapproval.

"After the dinner last night, it's all I have room for." Sunny broke and buttered one of the muffins, wondering why her mother had requested this private breakfast.

Expression determined, Augusta opened her mouth, then paused, as if changing her mind about what she meant to say. "Look at the morning paper. Thornborough was intemperate."

Obediently Sunny lifted the newspaper, then

blinked at the screaming headline. *Duke Tells American Public to Go Hang!*

"Oh, my," she said weakly. The story beneath claimed that Thornborough had bodily threatened several journalists, then bullied the hotel manager in a blatant attempt to infringe on the American public's constitutional right to a free press. "He mentioned yesterday that he'd been abrupt with some reporters, but surely this story is exaggerated."

"No doubt, but someone should explain to Thornborough that it's a mistake to pick fights with men who buy ink by the barrel." Augusta neatly finished the last of her meal. "A good thing that he was in England until now. Heaven knows what trouble he would have gotten into if he had been here longer."

Feeling oddly protective, Sunny said, "He's a very private man. He must find this vulgar publicity deeply offensive."

"Unfortunately, wealth and power always attract the interest of the masses."

Sunny poured herself coffee without comment. Her mother might say that public attention was unfortunate, but she would not have liked to be ignored.

Augusta began pleating her linen napkin into narrow folds. "You must be wondering why I wanted to talk to you this morning," she said with uncharacteristic constraint. "This will be difficult for both of us, but it's a mother's duty to explain to her daughter what her...her conjugal duties will be.''

The muffin turned to sawdust in Sunny's mouth. Though she didn't want to discuss such a horribly embarrassing subject, there was no denying that information would be useful. Like all well-bred young ladies, her ignorance about marital intimacy was almost total.

Briskly Augusta explained the basics of male and female anatomy. Then, rather more slowly, she went on to describe exactly what a husband did to his wife.

Sunny choked on her coffee. "That's disgusting!" she said after she stopped coughing. She had heard whispered hints and giggles about the mysterious *something* that happened between men and women in the marriage bed, but surely it couldn't be what her mother was describing.

"It *is* disgusting," Augusta agreed, "as low and animal as the mating of hogs. It's also uncomfortable and sometimes painful. Perhaps someday scientific progress will find a better, more dignified way to make babies, but until then, women must suffer for the sins of Eve."

She took a piece of toast and began crumbling it between nervous fingers. "Naturally women of refinement are repulsed by the marital act. Unfortunately, men enjoy it. If they didn't, I suppose there would be no such thing as marriage. All a woman can do is lie there very quietly, without moving, so that the man will please himself quickly and leave her alone.''

Lie there and think of England, in other words. Sunny's stomach turned. Had her tall, athletic father actually done such things to her delicate mother? Was this what Paul Curzon had wanted when he was kissing her? And dear God, must she really allow Thornborough such liberties? Her thighs squeezed together as her body rejected the thought of such an appalling violation.

Seeing her expression, Augusta said reassuringly, ''A gentleman will not visit your bed more than once or twice a week. You also have the right to refuse your husband once you are with child, and for at least three months after you deliver.'' She glanced down at the pile of crumbs she had created. ''Last night, after the settlements were signed, I took the duke aside and reminded him that you are gently bred, and that I would not permit him to misuse you.''

''You spoke to Thornborough about this?'' Sunny gasped, so humiliated that she wanted to crawl under the table and never come out. ''How did he reply?''

''He gave me the oddest look, but said that he understood my concern for your welfare, and assured me that he would be mindful of your innocence.'' Augusta gave a wintry smile. ''It was very properly said. He is, after all, a gentleman.''

Sunny's mind was a jumble of chaotic thoughts. The marriage bed sounded revolting—yet she had enjoyed Paul Curzon's kisses, and kissing was supposed to be a prelude to doing *it*. Surely the women who carried on flagrant affairs wouldn't do so if they found the whole business distasteful. Timidly she asked, "Do all women dislike the marital act?"

"I wish that I could say that was so, but there is no denying that there are some women of our order who are a disgrace to their sex—low-bred creatures who revel in their animal nature like barmaids. I know that you are not like that, but you will meet women who are." Leaning forward, Augusta said earnestly, "I cannot emphasize enough that it is fatal to seem to take pleasure in a gentleman's embrace. If you do, he will instantly lose all respect for you. A woman who acts like a prostitute will be treated like one. Always strive to maintain your dignity, Sarah—ultimately it is all that a lady has."

With horror, Sunny remembered that when Paul had taken liberties, she had responded eagerly. Was that why he had made his degrading suggestion that she marry Thornborough, then have an affair with him? She still thought his behavior despicable—but perhaps she had brought it on by her wantonness. Paul had seen her acting like a slut, so he had treated her like one. It was exactly what her mother was warning her about.

Apparently a woman who gave in to her animal nature also risked unleashing a man's worst traits. That had been bad enough in the case of Paul Curzon, but Thornborough was going to be her husband; if he didn't respect her, the marriage would be hellish.

Feeling ill, Sunny said, "I shall remember all you have said and I will strive to behave in a manner that you would approve."

"I'm sure you will not disgrace your upbringing." Augusta bit her lip, her usual confidence gone. "Oh, Sarah, I'm going to miss you dreadfully. You'll be so far away."

Sunny resisted the temptation to point out that her mother should have thought of that before accepting the proposal of a foreigner. "I'll miss you, too. You must visit us at Swindon soon."

Augusta shook her head. "Eventually, but not right away. I know that I'm a strong-minded woman, and I don't want to cause trouble between you and your husband. Marriage is a difficult business, and you and he must have time together with as little interference as possible."

At moments like this, Sunny loved her mother with painful intensity. It was true that Augusta was often domineering—yet her love for her children was very real. She was a woman of formidable energy; if she had a railroad or a bank to run, she might have been less absorbed in her daughter's life.

"I'll be fine," Sunny said with determined optimism. "Thornborough is a gentleman, and I am a lady. I'm sure that we can contrive a civilized marriage between us."

She wished that she was certain that was true.

Chapter Five

Tears flowing down her face, Sunny stood patiently while her maid laced up her white brocade bridal corset. Then Antoinette dropped the wedding gown over her head. It was magnificent, with foaming layers of Brussels lace and billows of white satin spangled with seed pearls and silver thread. Augusta had been so confident of her daughter's future triumph that she had ordered the gown from Worth when they visited Paris in March, before Sunny had ever set foot in London.

When the gown was fastened, Antoinette lifted the tulle veil and carefully draped it over the intricate coils of Sunny's hair. As the gauzy fabric floated down to her knees, the bride bleakly wondered if it was dense enough to conceal her tears.

Antoinette secured the veil with a coronet of orange blossoms, saying soothingly, ''Don't fret, mademoiselle. Every girl is nervous on her wedding day. *Monsieur le Duc* is a fine gentleman, and he will make you very happy.''

Sunny's shoulders began shaking with the force of her sobs. Antoinette frowned and gave her a handkerchief, muttering, "Madame Vangelder should not have gone ahead to the church. A girl needs her mother at a time like this.''

As Sunny wept into the crumpled muslin square, a knock sounded at the door. Antoinette answered and returned with a large white flower box. ''For you, mademoiselle.''

''You can open it if you like,'' Sunny said drearily.

Less jaded than her mistress, Antoinette opened the package, disclosing an exquisite orchid bouquet nestled in layers of tissue paper. ''There is a card for you, mademoiselle.''

Sunny's puffy eyes widened when she read, *These flowers are from the Swindon greenhouse. If they are suitable, perhaps you might wish to carry them. Fondly, Justin.*

Oblivious to the fate of her five-yard-long train, Sunny dropped into a chair and wept even harder.

''Oh, mam'zelle,'' Antoinette said helplessly. ''What about the orchids makes you weep? They are very lovely.''

''Yes, they are.'' Sunny made a desperate effort to collect herself. ''I was...touched by Thornborough's thoughtfulness in having them sent all the way from England.''

Though it was not something she could say to her maid, she was even more moved by the fact that he was actually letting her choose whether or not to carry them. Every other detail of the wedding—the trousseau, the decorations, the extravagant reception—had been determined by her mother. Even the eight bridesmaids—including two Vangelder cousins, a Whitney, a Jay and an Astor—had been selected by Augusta for reasons of her own. Sunny had been swept along like a leaf in a torrent.

But Justin had given her a choice. Surely with such a considerate man, she could be happy. Unsteadily she said, "I must look like a fright. Please bring me some cold water and a facecloth." She glanced at the enormous bouquet Augusta had ordered. "You can set that aside. I will carry the orchids."

"But..." After the beginning of a protest, the maid nodded. "Yes, mademoiselle. An excellent choice."

As Antoinette went for the cold water, Sunny found herself wondering if the maid had ever endured the grotesquely undignified process of mating that Augusta had described. The thought almost sent her off in tears again.

For the last two days, at the most awkward moments, she had wondered the same thing about others: her brother Charlie, who was very fond of female company; the wife of the Anglican bishop

who was going to perform the ceremony; Thornborough himself. Her morbid imaginings were
turning her into a nervous wreck.

Antoinette returned with a basin of water and a
cloth, then flipped the veil back over Sunny's head
so that her face was bare. "You must hurry, mademoiselle, or you will be late."

As she sponged her stinging eyes with the cool,
moist cloth, Sunny snapped, "They can all *wait*."

The day became increasingly unreal. Fifth Av-
enue was lined on both sides with policemen assigned to prevent the thousands of spectators from
breaking through. The wedding was to be at St.
Thomas's Anglican church. Though the Vangelders didn't usually worship there, it was the only
fashionable church with enough space for the sev-
enty-voice choir Augusta had chosen.

Inside the church, huge arches of orange blossoms spanned the aisle, and banks of palms and
chrysanthemums seemed to cover every vertical
surface. Twenty-five excruciating minutes behind
schedule, Sunny waited for her entrance, one icy
hand clenched around her orchid bouquet and the
other locked on her brother Charlie's arm. Though
she could not see the guests clearly in the dim
light, every pew seemed to be filled.

As the bridesmaids marched smartly down the
aisle to the music of the sixty-piece orchestra,
Charlie whispered, "Buck up, Sunny. Show them

that an American girl is every bit the equal of any European princess.''

The wedding march began, and Sunny started the long walk to the altar. If it hadn't been for her brother's firm support, the ''American princess'' might have fallen flat on her face.

With hysterical precision, she calculated that in the months since she had met Thornborough, they had seen each other for ten days, and been alone together for less than an hour. *Why was she marrying a stranger?* If it hadn't been for the five-yard train, she might have turned and bolted.

The dark figure of her fiancé waited impassively at the altar. Next to him was his best man, a pleasant fellow called Lord Ambridge, an old school friend of Justin's who was currently serving in the British Embassy in Washington.

As Sunny drew closer to her future husband, she saw that his expression was grim. Then she looked into his eyes and realized that he was as nervous as she. Her lateness must have made him wonder if she had changed her mind.

Dear God, how humiliating those long minutes of waiting must have been for him. As Charlie handed her over, she gave Thornborough an unsteady smile of apology.

His expression eased. He took her hand, and the warmth of his clasp was the most real thing she had experienced all day.

They turned to face the bishop, and the ancient,

familiar words transformed the stranger beside her into her husband.

The wedding night was a disaster. Later Justin realized that it had been foolish of him to think it could have been otherwise, yet he had had the naive hope that once he and his bride were alone together, they would be able to relax. To become friends.

Instead, the "wedding breakfast" had proved to be a huge reception that seemed as if it would never end. By the time they reached their hotel suite, Sunny's face was gray with fatigue.

He wanted to hold her but restrained himself, for she looked as if she would shatter at a touch. They had a lifetime ahead of them; it would be foolish to rush matters now.

She mutely followed his suggestion that she relax with a long bath. Much later, after Sunny's maid had finished her ministrations and left for the night, he joined his wife in the spacious bedchamber. He expected to find her in the canopied bed, perhaps already asleep. Instead, she stood by the window, gazing out on the lights of New York.

He found her a far more interesting sight than the city. The glossy, honey-gold hair that flowed over her shoulders was even lovelier than he had imagined, and he longed to bury his face among the silken strands. Her white negligee frothed with lace and delicate embroidery, and was so translucent that he could see the lithe shape of her body beneath. It must be another Worth creation; only a master could make a woman look simultaneously pure and provocative.

His wife. He was still awed by the miracle of it.

Justin had been introduced to the dark mysteries of passion when he was sixteen. Deciding it was time his young brother became a man, Gavin had taken Justin to a courtesan. With his usual careless kindness, Gavin had chosen the woman well. Lily was a warmhearted, earthily sensual Frenchwoman who had known exactly how to initiate a shy youth half her age.

Justin's shamed embarrassment had been gone by the end of his first afternoon with Lily. With her he had discovered not only passion, but kindness and mutual affection. He had visited her many times over the ensuing years. When her looks faded and she could no longer support herself as a courtesan, he had quietly bought her a cottage in the south of France so that she could retire in comfort. They still corresponded occasionally.

Because of Lily, he was now able to give his wife the gift of passion. Praying that desire would not make him clumsy, he went to join her by the window. Her delicate violet scent bewitched him, and his hands clenched with the effort of not touching her. Needing a safe, neutral topic, he said, "New York is lovely in a way quite distinct from London or Paris."

"I shall miss it," she whispered.

He glanced over and saw tears trembling in her eyes. "It must be hard to leave one's home," he said quietly, "but you can come back whenever you wish."

"Yes." She drew an unsteady breath. "Still, it hurts knowing that I am no longer an American. Though I understood that marrying a foreigner meant that I would lose my citizenship, I didn't expect to feel it so much."

"The law might say that you are now an Englishwoman, but it can't change what you are in your heart. America made you, and nothing can take that away."

After a long pause, she said in a low voice, "Thank you. I needed to be reminded of that."

Thinking the time was finally right, he put an arm around her waist. For the barest instant, she was pliantly yielding. Then she went rigid, like a small woodland creature holding still in the desperate hope that it would escape a predator's notice.

He turned her toward him and pulled her close, stroking her back in the hope that she would relax, but he was unsuccessful. Though she submitted without protest, her body remained as stiff as a marble statue.

Shyness or nerves were to be expected, but her reaction seemed extreme. He put his hands on her shoulders and held her away from him. "Sunny, are you afraid of me?"

"Not...not of you, really," she said, her eyes cast down.

It wasn't a heartening answer for an eager bridegroom. Patiently he said, "Then are you afraid of...marital intimacy?"

"It's more than that, Justin. I don't know quite how to explain." She pressed her hands to her temples for a moment, then looked into his eyes for the first time in days. "I was raised to be a wife. In the whole of my life, there was never any thought that I would ever be anything else." She swallowed hard. "Only now, when it's too late, does it occur to me that I don't really want to be married to anyone."

Though she claimed that he was not the problem, it was hard not to take her comments personally. Feeling a chill deep inside, he lowered his hands and said carefully, "What do you want me to do—set you up in a separate establishment so that you never have to see me? File for an annulment on the grounds that your mother coerced you into marriage against your will?"

She looked shocked. "Oh, no, of course not. I pledged my word today, and that can't be undone. I will do my best to be a good wife to you—but I don't know if I will succeed."

Some of the pain in his chest eased. As long as

they were together, there was hope for building a loving marriage.

Though he had been counting the hours until they could be together, he said, ''We needn't share a bed tonight, when you're so tired. It might be better to wait a few days until you're more at ease with me.''

She hesitated, clearly tempted, before she shook her head. ''I think it will be best to get it over with. Waiting will only give me more time to worry.''

He wanted to make love to his wife, and she wanted to ''get it over with,'' like a tooth extraction. Dear God, this was not what he had dreamed of. Yet perhaps she was right. Once she learned that intercourse was not as bad as she feared, she could relax and find pleasure in physical intimacy.

Yet he could not quite suppress the fear that his wife might never come to welcome his touch. He had been concerned ever since Augusta had ordered him to try to control his beastly animal nature. Obviously Augusta had loathed her own marital duties, and there was a strong possibility that she had passed her distaste on to her daughter.

His mouth tightened. Brooding would solve nothing. If his wife wanted the marriage consummated tonight, he would oblige—partly because it might be the wisest course, but more because he wanted her with an intensity that was painful.

''Come then, my dear.'' He untied the ribbons

of her negligee and pushed it from her shoulders so that she was clad only in a sheer silk nightgown that revealed more of her tantalizing curves than it concealed. He drew a shaky breath. It was how he had dreamed of her—and at the same time, it was utterly wrong, for she looked at him with the despairing eyes of a wounded doe.

She colored under his hungry gaze and glanced away. "Could you...would you turn the lamps out?"

Though he yearned to see her unclothed, he said, "As you wish."

As he put out the lights, she drew the curtains so that the windows were covered and the room became suffocatingly dark. Then she climbed into the bed with a faint creak of springs.

After removing his robe, he located the bed by touch and slid in beside her. He would have liked to take his nightshirt off, as well, but a man's naked body might upset her more, even in the dark and under blankets.

He drew her into his arms and kissed her with all the tenderness he had been yearning to lavish on her. Though she did not reject him, her mouth was locked shut and her whole frame was tense and unyielding. No amount of patient skill on his part could soften her; in fact, his feather kisses and gentle stroking seemed to make her more rigid. He felt as if he was trying to ravish a vestal virgin.

Despairing, he pushed himself up with one arm and said hoarsely, "This isn't right."

"Please, just *do* it," she said, an edge of hysteria in her voice.

His better nature surrendered, for despite his doubts, his body was hotly ready, burning for completion. He reached for the lotion he had provided to ease this first union.

She gasped when he raised the hem of her gown, separated her legs and touched her intimately. He hoped that she might respond positively to his sensual application of the lotion, but there was no change. She simply endured, her limbs like iron, her breath coming in short, frightened gulps.

Though his blood pounded in his temples, he forced himself to go slowly when he moved to possess her. Her body resisted and he heard the scratch of her nails digging into the sheets, but she made no protest.

When the frail membrane sundered and he thrust deeply into her, she gave a sharp, pain-filled cry. He held still, waves of exquisite sensation sweeping through him, until her breathing was less ragged.

Then he began to move, and his control shattered instantly. He loved her and she was his, and he groaned with delirious pleasure as he thrust into her again and again.

His mindless abandon had the advantage of swiftness, for he could not have prolonged their coupling even if he tried. After the fiery culmination, he disengaged and lay down beside her, trembling with reaction. He yearned to hold her close and soothe her distress, but hesitated to touch her. "I'm sorry I hurt you," he panted. "It won't be this painful again."

"I'm all right, Justin," she said, voice shaking. "It...wasn't as bad as I expected."

It was a lie, but a gallant one. No longer able to restrain his impulse to cradle her in his arms, he reached out. If she would let him comfort her, something good would come of this night. But she rolled away into a tight little ball, and his searching fingers found only her taut spine.

The silence that descended was broken by the anguished sound of her muffled sobs. He lay still, drenched with self-loathing at the knowledge that he had found intoxicating pleasure in an act that had distressed her so profoundly.

After a long, long time, her tears faded and her breathing took on the slow rhythm of sleep. Quietly he slid from the bed and felt his way to the door that led to the sitting room, cracking his shin on a stool as he went.

A gas lamp burned in the sitting room, and he saw his haunted reflection in a mirror on the far wall. He turned away, unable to bear the sight of his own misery.

The suite was the most luxurious in the hotel, though not as richly furnished as the Vangelder houses. A porcelain bowl filled with potpourri sat on a side table. He sifted it through his fingers, and the air filled with a tangy fragrance.

He had reached for heaven and landed in hell. Their disastrous wedding night had not been the result of anything simple, like shyness on her part or ineptness on his; it had been total rejection. The woman of his dreams couldn't bear his touch, and there seemed little chance that she would change in the future.

Vases of flowers were set all over the room. Some he had ordered, others were courtesy of the hotel, which was embarrassingly grateful to have the Duke and Duchess of Thornborough as guests. He pulled a white rose from an elegant cut-glass vase. It was just starting to open, at the perfect moment when promise met fulfillment.

Inevitably, he thought of Sunny when he had first seen her at Swindon. Exquisite, laughing, without flaw.

And now she lay weeping in the next room, her bright gaiety gone. He supposed that part of the blame for that could be laid to a false lover, and part to Augusta, who loved her daughter with utter ruthlessness. But most of the fault was his. By the simple act of wanting to marry her, he might have destroyed her blithe sweetness forever.

He began plucking out the satiny white petals, letting them drop one by one. She loved him, she loved him not, over and over, like a litany, as the scent of rose wafted around him.

The last petal drifted to the floor. She loved him not.

He lifted the vase and studied the artistry of the cut glass. Then, in one smooth, raging gesture, he hurled it across the room, where it shattered into a thousand pieces.

She loved him not.

Chapter Six

Justin glanced out the train window at the rolling English landscape. "We'll reach Swindon station in about five minutes."

Sunny lifted her hat from the opposite seat and secured it to her coiled hair with a pearl-headed hat pin. Since they were traveling in the luxurious solitude of the Thornborough private car, she had had ample space for her possessions.

As she prepared for their arrival, she surreptitiously studied her husband. His expression was as impassive as always, even though he was bringing his bride home for the first time. Didn't he ever feel anything? In three weeks of marriage, he had never been anything but unfailingly polite. Civil. Kind. As remote as if he were on the opposite side of the earth.

Not that she should complain, for his calm detachment had made it possible to reach a modus vivendi very quickly. In public, she took his arm and smiled so that they presented a companionable picture to the world.

Naturally neither of them ever referred to what happened in the silence of the night. Justin always ordered suites with two bedrooms so they could sleep separately. Every three or four days, with his gaze on the middle distance, he would ask if it was convenient for him to visit her.

She always gave her embarrassed assent, except for once when she had stammered that she was "indisposed." She would have died of mortification if he had asked what was wrong, but he had obviously understood. Five days passed before he asked again, and by then she was able to give him permission to come.

As he had promised, there had been no pain after the first occasion, and soon her fear had gone away. Dutifully she obeyed her mother's dictum and lay perfectly still while her husband did what husbands did. The marital act took only a few minutes, and he always left directly after.

Once or twice, she had felt his fingers brush through her hair before he climbed from the bed. She liked to think that it was a gesture of affection, though perhaps it was mere accident, a result of fumbling in the dark.

But her mother had been right; passive acceptance of her wifely role had won Justin's respect. Besides treating her with the utmost consideration, he also encouraged her to speak her opinions. That was certainly an unusual sign of respect, as well as a pleasure few wives had.

They discussed a wide variety of topics—British and American politics, art and music, architecture and history. Though Justin was never talkative, his observations were perceptive and he seemed to genuinely enjoy listening to her chatter. Best of all, the conversations were slowly building a rapport between them. It wasn't love—but perhaps someday it might be.

She prayed that that would happen, for living without love was a sad business.

Getting to her feet, she pulled on her sable-lined coat. Though it would warm her on the raw November day, that practical use was secondary. Before they left New York, her mother had emphasized that it was essential to wear her furs as a sign of wealth when she was first introduced to her new home and family. A good thing it wasn't August. Unable to see all of herself in the mirror, she asked, "Do I look all right?"

Her husband studied her gravely. "You look very lovely. Exactly as a duchess should, but seldom does."

The train squealed to a halt, and she glanced out to see a bunting-draped platform. "Good heavens," she said blankly. "There are hundreds of people out there."

"I did warn you." He stood and walked to the carriage door. "It's probably the entire population of Swindon Minor and everyone for five miles around. The schools will have given a holiday so that the pupils can come and wave flags at you.''

''It's different actually seeing them.'' Observing her husband's closed expression, she said, ''You don't look very enthusiastic.''

''Gavin was much better at this sort of thing.''

Perhaps that was true, but when Justin opened the door and stepped onto the platform, a roar of welcome went up. He gave a nod of acknowledgment, then turned to help Sunny step down. Another cheer went up, so she gave a friendly wave.

She met a blur of local dignities, all of whom gave speeches of welcome. Luckily she was good at smiling graciously, and the sables kept her from freezing in the damp air.

The only part that stood out in her mind was the little girl who was pushed forward, clutching a bouquet in her tiny hands. ''Give the posies to the duchess, Ellie,'' her mother hissed.

Unclear on the theory, Ellie swept the bouquet around in circles. With a grin, Sunny intercepted it, then dropped a kiss on the child's soft brown curls. ''Thank you, Ellie.''

Another cheer arose. Sunny blushed; her gesture had not been calculated, but apparently kissing babies was good policy everywhere.

The mayor of the borough assisted her into the waiting carriage and Justin settled beside her.

However, instead of starting for the palace, there was a delay while the horses were unhitched. A dozen men seized the shafts and began pulling the carriage up the village high street as the church bell began to ring clamorously. Sunny gave her husband a doubtful glance. "This seems dreadfully feudal."

He lifted his hand in response to a group of exuberant uniformed schoolchildren. "This isn't really for you, or for me, either. It's a celebration of continuity—of a life lived on this land for centuries. Swindon Palace belongs as much to the tenants as it does to the Aubreys."

She supposed he was right, and certainly the crowd seemed to be having a very jolly time. Nonetheless, her democratic American soul twitched a bit. Trying to look like a duchess, she smiled and waved for the slow two miles to Swindon Palace.

Another crowd waited in the courtyard. After the newlyweds had climbed the front steps, Justin turned and gave a short thank-you speech in a voice that carried easily to everyone present. Gavin might have had a talent for grand gestures, but the tenants had had more daily contact with Justin, and they seemed to heartily approve of him.

After one last wave, she went inside with her husband. The greetings weren't over yet, for a phalanx of Aubrey relations waited with a sea of servants behind them.

As she steeled herself for more introductions and smiles, two huge wolfhounds galloped toward the door, nails scrabbling on the marble floor. The sight of the enormous dogs charging full speed at her made Sunny give a small squeak of alarm.

Before the beasts could overrun them, Justin made a quick hand gesture and commanded, "Sit!"

Instantly the wolfhounds dropped to their haunches, though they wriggled frantically for attention. Justin stroked the sleek aristocratic heads, careful not to neglect either. "These were Gavin's dogs. They miss him dreadfully."

To Sunny, it looked as if the wolfhounds were perfectly satisfied with the new duke. It took a moment to realize that Justin's comment was an oblique admission of his own grief. She was ashamed of the fact that she had not really considered how profoundly he must feel his brother's death. Though the two men had been very different, the first time she had seen them they had been standing side by side. They must have been close, or Justin would not have chosen to manage the family property when he could have done many other things.

While she was wondering if she should say something to him, the relatives descended. First in consequence was the dowager duchess, Justin's mother, who wore mourning black for Gavin. Her forceful expression reminded Sunny of her own mother, though Augusta was far more elegant.

After a fierce scrutiny of the colonial upstart, the dowager said, "You look healthy, girl. Are you pregnant yet?"

As Sunny flushed scarlet, Justin put a protective arm around her waist. "It's a little early to think about that since we've been married less than a month, Mother," he said calmly. "Sunny, I believe you already know my older sisters, Blanche and Charlotte, and their husbands, Lord Alton and Lord Urford."

Sunny had met all four in London during the season. The sisters were in the same mold as Gavin: tall, blond, handsome Aubreys whose self-absorption was tempered by underlying good nature. They examined Sunny's furs with frank envy, but their greetings were friendly. After all, it was her money that would keep up the family home.

Next in line was Lady Alexandra, the Gargoylette. She hung back until Justin pulled her into a hug. It was the most affectionate Sunny had ever seen him. "I don't believe you've met my little sister, Alexandra."

He accompanied his introduction with a speaking look at his wife. Sunny guessed that if she was dismissive or abrupt, he would not easily forgive her.

Alexandra stammered a greeting, too bashful to meet her new sister-in-law's eyes. Dark and inches shorter than the older girls, she looked very like Justin. There was nothing wrong with her appearance except that her mother dressed her very badly.

Following her instinct, Sunny also hugged her smallest sister-in-law. "Thank you so much for your letter," she said warmly. "It was good to know that I would have a friend here."

Alexandra looked up shyly. Her gray eyes were also like Justin's, but where he was reserved, she was vulnerable. "I'm glad you're here," she said simply. "I saw you when you came to the garden fete last spring, and thought you were the loveliest creature in the world."

A little embarrassed at such frank adoration, Sunny said lightly, "It's amazing what a good dressmaker can do."

Then it was onward to sundry Aubrey cousins and shirttail relations. After that, the butler and housekeeper—two *very* superior persons—welcomed her as their new mistress and presented her with a silver bowl as a wedding gift from the household. While Sunny wondered how much the poor servants had been forced to contribute, she was paraded past ranks of maids and footmen as if she were a general reviewing troops.

Finally it was time to go upstairs to prepare for dinner. Justin escorted her to her new rooms.

The duchess's private suite was rather appallingly magnificent. Eyeing the massive, velvet-hung four-poster bed, Sunny asked, "Did Queen Elizabeth sleep there?"

"No, but Queen Anne did." The corner of Justin's mouth quirked up. "I know it's overpowering, but I didn't order any changes because I thought you'd prefer to make them yourself."

Sunny thoughtfully regarded a tapestry of a stag being torn apart by a pack of dogs. "I don't care if it is priceless—that tapestry will have to go. But I can bear it for now. How long do I have until dinner?"

"Only half an hour, I'm afraid. There's more to be seen, but it can wait." He gestured to a door in the middle of one wall. "That goes directly to my bedchamber. Don't hesitate to ask if there's anything you need."

"I'm too confused to know what I need, but thank you." Sunny took off her hat and massaged her throbbing temples. "Should you and I go down together for dinner?"

"Definitely," he replied. "Without a guide to the dining room, you'd probably get lost for a week."

After Justin left, Antoinette emerged from the dressing room. "While everyone was welcoming you, madame, I had time to unpack your clothing. What do you wish to wear tonight? Surely something grand to impress the relations."

"The butter-cream duchesse satin, I think." Sunny considered. "I suppose I should also wear the pearl and diamond dog collar, even though it chafes my neck.''

The maid nodded with approval. ''No one will be your equal.''

After Antoinette disappeared to prepare the gown, Sunny sank into a brocade-covered chair. It was hideously uncomfortable, which was fortunate, because otherwise she might fall asleep.

It was pleasant to have a few minutes alone. In spite of the wretched chair, she was dozing when Antoinette bustled back. ''Madame, I have found something wonderful! You must come see.''

Sunny doubted that anything was worth such enthusiasm, but she obediently rose and followed her maid into the dressing room. Two doors were set into the opposite wall. Antoinette dramatically threw open the right-hand one. ''Voilà!''

Sunny's eyes widened. It was a bathroom that would have impressed even Augusta Vangelder. The mahogany-encased tub was enormous, and the floor and walls had been covered in bright, exquisitely glazed Spanish tiles. ''You're right—it's the most gorgeous bathroom I've ever seen.''

''And the next room over—'' the maid pointed ''—is a most splendid water closet. The chambermaid who brought in the towels said that *Monsieur le Duc* had all this done for you after the betrothal was announced.''

Amused and touched, Sunny stroked a gleaming tile. It appeared that she would not have to suffer the country house horrors that Katie Westron had warned her about. "Perhaps later tonight I will take advantage of this."

Wanting to give credit where credit was due, she went to her bedchamber and opened the connecting door to the duke's suite. "Justin, I have found the bathing room and—"

In the middle of the sentence, her gaze found her husband and she stopped dead. She had caught him in the middle of changing his clothing. He had just taken off his shirt, and she blushed scarlet at the sight of his bare chest.

Though his brows rose, he did not seem at all discomposed. "Having seen the wonders of modern American plumbing, I knew that you would find Swindon rather primitive," he said. "Making some improvements seemed like a more useful wedding gift than giving you jewels."

Though she tried to look only into his eyes, her gaze drifted lower. He was broad-shouldered and powerfully muscled, which was why he didn't have a fashionable look of weedy elegance. She wondered how the dark hair on his chest would feel to her touch. Blushing again, she said hastily, "Your idea was inspired. I've always loved long baths, and I'd resigned myself to having to make do with a tin tub in front of the fire."

"Speaking of fires, I decided that it was also time to install central heating." Justin casually pulled on a fresh shirt, though he didn't bother to button it. "It will be a long time until the whole building is completed, but I had the workers take care of this wing first, so you would be comfortable. I know that Americans like their houses warm."

Only then did she notice that the rooms were much warmer than she should have expected. "Thank you, Justin. I think you must be the most considerate husband on earth." She crossed the room to her husband's side and gave him a swift kiss.

It was the first time she had ever done such a thing, and she wondered belatedly if he would think her too forward. But he didn't seem to mind. His lips moved slowly under hers, and he raised his hand and massaged the back of her neck. He had a tangy masculine scent that was distinctly his own. Succumbing to temptation, she let her fingers brush his bare chest as if by accident. The hair was softer than she had expected, but she felt unnerved when his warm flesh tensed at her touch. Hastily she lowered her hand.

But the kiss continued, and she found that she was in no hurry to end it. Very gently, his tongue stroked her lips. It was a new sensation, but pleasant. Very pleasant....

The clamor of a bell reverberated brassily through the corridors. Both of them jumped as if they had been caught stealing from the church poor box.

After he had caught his breath, Justin said, "The predinner bell. We must be downstairs in ten minutes."

"I barely have time to dress." Embarrassed at how she had lost track of time, Sunny bolted to her own room. As soon as the connecting door was closed, Antoinette started unfastening her traveling dress so that the duchesse satin could be donned.

Yet as her maid swiftly transformed her, Sunny's mind kept returning to the kiss, and her fingertips tingled with the memory of the feel of her husband's bare body.

Dinner was another strain. Sunny sat at the opposite end of the table from her husband, so far away that she could barely see him. Before the first course had been removed, it was obvious that the dowager duchess was a tyrant, with all the tact of a charging bull. She made a string of remarks extolling Gavin's noble spirit and aristocratic style, interspersed with edged comments about the deficiencies of "poor dear Justin."

Charlotte tried to divert the conversation with a cheerful promise to send Sunny a copy of the table of precedence so that she would never commit the cardinal crime of seating people in the wrong order. That inspired the dowager to say, "There are about two hundred families whose history and relationships you must understand, Sarah. Has Justin properly explained all the branches of the Aubreys and of my own family, the Sturfords?''

"Not yet, Duchess," Sunny said politely.

"Very remiss of him. Since he wasn't raised to be a duke, he hasn't a proper sense of what is due his station." The dowager sniffed. "So sad to see poor dear Justin in his brother's place—such a comedown for the family. You must be quick about having a child, Sarah, and make sure it's a boy."

Sunny was tempted to sling the nearest platter of veal collops at her mother-in-law, but it seemed too soon to get into a pitched battle. A quick glance at her husband showed that he had either not heard his mother, or he chose to ignore her. Clearly Alexandra had heard, for she was staring at her plate.

Carefully Sunny said, "The eighth duke's death was a great tragedy. You all have my sympathies on your loss."

The dowager sighed. "Gavin should have betrothed himself to you, not that Russell woman. If he had, he might be alive now, in his proper place."

Sunny had heard enough gossip to know that the fatal problem had not been Gavin's fiancée, but his inability to keep his hands off other women, even when on the way to his own wedding. Hoping to end this line of discussion, she said piously, "It is not for us to question the ways of heaven."

"A very proper sentiment," the dowager said.

"You have pretty manners. One would scarcely know you for an American."

Did the woman suppose that she was giving a compliment? Once more Sunny bit her tongue.

Yet in spite of her good intentions, she was not to get through the evening peacefully. The gauntlet was thrown down at the end of the lengthy meal, when it was time for the ladies to withdraw and leave the gentlemen to their port. Sunny was about to give the signal when the dowager grandly rose to her feet and beat Sunny to it.

As three women followed the dowager's lead, Sunny's blood went cold. This was a direct challenge to her authority as the new mistress of the household. If she didn't assert herself immediately, her mother-in-law would walk all over her.

The other guests hesitated, glancing between the new duchess and the old. Sunny wanted to whimper that she was too *tired* for this, but she supposed that crises never happened at convenient times. Though her hands clenched below the table, her voice was even when she asked, "Are you feeling unwell, Duchess?"

"I am in splendid health," her mother-in-law said haughtily. "Where did you get the foolish idea that I might be ailing?"

"I can think of no other reason for you leaving prematurely," Sunny said with the note of gentle implacability that she had often heard in her mother's voice.

For a moment the issue wavered in the balance. Then, one by one, the female guests who had gotten to their feet sank back into their seats with apologetic glances at Sunny. Knowing that she had lost, the dowager returned to the table, her expression stiff with mortification.

As she waited for a decent interval to pass before leading the ladies from the table, Sunny drew in a shaky breath. She had won the first battle—but there would be others.

The evening ended when the first clock struck eleven. Accompanied by the bonging of numerous other clocks, Justin escorted his wife upstairs. When they reached the door of her room, he said, "I'm sorry that it's been such a long day, but everyone was anxious to meet you."

She smiled wearily. "I'll be fine after a night's sleep."

"You were a great success with everyone." After a moment of hesitation, he added, "I'm sorry my mother was so…abrupt. Gavin was her favorite, and she took his death very badly."

"You miss him, too, but it hasn't made you rude." She bit her lip. "I'm sorry, I didn't mean to sound impertinent."

"My mother is a forceful woman, and I don't expect that you'll always agree. Blanche and Charlotte used to have terrible battles with her. Just remember that you are my wife, and the mistress of Swindon.''

''I shall attempt to be tactful while establishing myself.'' She made a rueful face. ''But I warn you, I have trouble countenancing unkind remarks about other people.''

That sensitivity to others was one of the things he liked best about her. A volatile mix of tenderness and desire moved through him, and he struggled against his yearning to draw her into his arms and soothe her fatigue away.

He might have done so if he hadn't been aware that the desire to comfort would be followed by an even more overwhelming desire to remove her clothing, garment by garment, and make slow, passionate love to her. With the lamps lit, not in the dark.

Innocently she turned her back to him and said, ''Could you unfasten my dog collar? It's miserably uncomfortable.''

The heavy collar had at least fifteen rows of pearls. As he undid the catch and lifted the necklace away, he saw that the diamond clasp had rubbed her tender skin raw. He frowned. ''I don't like seeing you wearing something that hurts you.''

She sighed. ''Virtually every item a fashionable woman wears is designed to hurt.''

He leaned forward and very gently kissed the raw spot on her nape. ''Perhaps you should be less stylish.''

She tensed, as she did whenever he touched her in a sensual way. "A duchess is supposed to be fashionable. I would be much criticized if I didn't do you credit." Eyes downcast, she turned and took the jeweled collar, then slipped into her room.

He felt the familiar ache as he watched her disappear. Who was it who said that if a man wanted to be truly lonely, he should take a wife? It was true, for he didn't recall feeling lonely before he married.

But now that he had a wife, his life echoed with loneliness. The simple fact was that he wanted more of her. He wanted to hold her in his arms all night while they slept. He wanted her to sigh with pleasure when he made love to her. He wanted to be with her day and night.

He drew a deep breath, then entered his room and began undressing. He had hoped that with time she might come to enjoy intimacy more, but every time he came to her bed, she became rigid. Though she never complained, or spoke at all, for that matter—it was clear that she could scarcely endure his embraces.

Yet she didn't seem to dislike him in other ways. She talked easily and was willing to share her opinions. And she had given him that shy kiss earlier. In her innocence, she had not understood that she set the blood burning through his veins. But even going to her bed would not have quenched the fire, for he had found that quick, furtive coupling was more frustrating than if he had never touched her.

As he slid into his bed, he realized how foolish it was of him to object to a necklace that chafed her neck when his conjugal demands disturbed her far more. He despised himself for taking that which was not willingly given—yet he was not strong enough to prevent himself from going to her again and again. His twice weekly visits were his compromise between guilt and lust.

He stared blindly into the darkness, wondering if he would be able to sleep.

If you would be lonely, take a wife.

Chapter Seven

Swindon
February 1886

Sunny abandoned her letter writing and went to stand at her sitting room window, staring out at the gray landscape. In the distance was a pond where long ago a footman had drowned himself in a fit of melancholy. As the dreary winter months dragged by, she had come to feel a great deal of sympathy for the poor fellow.

The loudest sound was the ticking of the mantel clock. Swindon was full of clocks, all of them counting out the endless hours. She glanced at the dog curled in one of the velvet-covered chairs. "Daisy, how many of the women who envied my glamorous marriage would believe how tedious it is to winter on an English country estate?"

Daisy's floppy-eared head popped up and she

gave a sympathetic whimper. Unlike the beautiful but brainless wolfhounds, Daisy, a small black-and-tan dog of indeterminate parentage, was smart as a whip. Sunny liked to think that the dog understood human speech. Certainly she was a good listener.

Sunny's gaze went back to the dismal afternoon. Custom decreed that a bride should live quietly for a time after her wedding, and at Swindon, that was very quietly indeed. Apart from the newlyweds, Alexandra and the dowager were the only inhabitants of the vast palace. There were servants, of course, but the line between upstairs and downstairs was never crossed.

The best part of the daily routine was a morning ride with Justin. Sunny never missed a day, no matter how vile the weather, for she enjoyed spending time with her husband, though she couldn't define the reason. He was simply... comfortable. She only wished that she understood him better. He was like an iceberg, with most of his personality hidden from view.

After their ride, she usually didn't see him again until dinner, for estate work kept him busy. Occasionally he went to London for several days to attend to business. He was gone now, which made the hours seem even longer.

The high point of country social life was making brief calls on neighbors, then receiving calls in turn. Though most of the people Sunny met were pleasant, they lived lives as narrow and caste-ridden as Hindus. Luckily even the most conventional families usually harbored one or two splendid eccentrics in the great British tradition. There was the Trask uncle who wore only purple clothing, for example, and the Howard maiden aunt who had taught her parrot all the basic social responses so that the bird could speak for her. Such characters figured prominently in Sunny's letters home, since little else in her life was amusing.

A knock sounded at the door. After Sunny called permission to enter, her sister-in-law came into the sitting room. "A telegram arrived for you, Sunny, so I said I'd bring it up." Alexandra handed it over, then bent to scratch Daisy's ears.

Sunny opened the envelope and scanned the message. "Justin finished his business early and will be home for dinner tonight."

"That's nice. It's so quiet when he's away."

"Two months from now, after you've been presented to society and are attending ten parties a day, you'll yearn for the quiet of the country."

Alexandra made a face. "I can't say that I'm looking forward to being a wallflower at ten different places a day."

"You're going to be a great success," Sunny said firmly. "It's remarkable what good clothing can do for one's confidence. After Worth has outfitted you, you won't recognize yourself."

Unconvinced, Alexandra returned to petting

Daisy. Though young in many ways, the girl was surprisingly mature in others. She was also well-read and eager to learn about the world. The two young women had become good friends.

Deciding that she needed some fresh air, Sunny said, "I think I'll take a walk before I bathe and change. Would you like to join me?"

"Not today, thank you. I have a book I want to finish." Alexandra grinned, for at the word "walk," Daisy jumped to the floor and began skipping hopefully around her mistress. "But someone else wants to go. I'll see you at dinner."

After Alexandra left, Sunny donned a coat—not the sables, but a practical mackintosh—and a pair of boots, then went down and out into the damp afternoon, Daisy frisking beside her. Once they were away from the house, Sunny asked, "Would you like to play fetch?" Foolish question; Daisy was already racing forward looking for a stick.

Sunny had found Daisy on a morning ride not long after her arrival at Swindon. The half-grown mongrel had been desperately trying to stay afloat in the overflowing stream where someone had probably pitched her to drown. Driven frantic by the agonized yelps, Sunny had been on the verge of plunging into the water when Justin had snapped an order for her to stay on the bank. Before she could argue, he dismounted and went in himself.

When Sunny saw her husband fighting the force of the current, she realized that he was risking his life for her whim. There had been one ghastly moment when it seemed that the water would sweep him away. As her heart stood still, Justin managed to gain his footing, then catch hold of the struggling dog. After sloshing out of the stream, he had handed her the shivering scrap of canine with the straight-faced remark that it was quite an appealing creature as long as one didn't have any snobbish preconceptions about lineage.

The sodden pup had won Sunny's heart with one lap of a rough tongue. Sunny had almost wept with gratitude, for here was a creature who loved her and whom she could love in return.

Naturally the dowager duchess had disliked having such an ill-bred beast at Swindon, but she couldn't order the dog out of the house when Justin approved. The dowager had resorted to mumbled comments that it was natural for Sunny to want a mongrel, since Americans were a mongrel race. Sunny ignored such remarks; she had gotten very good at that.

As always, Daisy's desire to play fetch exceeded Sunny's stamina. Abandoning the game, they strolled to the little Greek temple, then wandered toward the house while Sunny thought of changes she would make in the grounds. A pity that nothing could be done at this time of year, for gardening would cheer her up.

In an attempt to stave off self-pity, she said, "I'm really very fortunate, Daisy. Most of Katie

Westron's dire warnings haven't come true. Justin is the most considerate of husbands, and he is making the house very comfortable.'' She glanced toward the palace, where men were laboring on the vast roof, in spite of the weather. ''My ceiling hasn't leaked since before Christmas.''

She made a wry face. ''Of course, it might be considered a bit strange that I talk more to a dog than to my husband.''

One of Katie's warnings haunted her—the possibility that Justin might have a mistress. Could that be the real reason for his business trips? She loathed the thought that her husband might be doing those intimate, dark-of-the-night things to another woman. She tried not to think of it.

The dull afternoon had darkened to twilight, so she summoned Daisy and headed toward the house. If the best part of the day was riding with Justin, the worst was dining with the dowager duchess. Familiarity had not improved her opinion of her mother-in-law. Most of the dowager's cutting remarks were directed at Justin, but she also made edged comments about Alexandra's lack of looks and dim marital prospects. She usually spared Sunny, rightly suspecting that her daughter-in-law might strike back.

Sunny wondered how long it would be before she disgraced herself by losing her temper. Every meal brought the breaking point closer. She wished that Justin would tell his mother to hold her tongue, but he was too courteous—or too detached—to take action.

When she got to the house, she found that her husband was in the entry hall taking off his wet coat. She thought his expression lightened when he saw her, but she wasn't sure; it was always hard to tell with Justin.

"Hello." She smiled as she took off her mackintosh. "Did you have a good trip to London?"

As the butler took away the coats, Justin gave Sunny a light kiss on the cheek, then rumpled Daisy's ears. He was rather more affectionate with the dog. "Yes, but I'm glad to be home."

He fell into step beside her and they started up the main stairs. The thought of a possible mistress passed through Sunny's mind again. Though she knew that it was better not to probe, she found herself saying, "What are all these trips about, or wouldn't I be able to understand the answer?"

"The Thornborough income has traditionally come from the land, but agriculture is a chancy business," he explained as they reached the top of the stairs. "I'm making more diverse investments so that future dukes won't have to marry for money."

She stopped in mid-stride, feeling as if he had slapped her. When she caught her breath, she said icily, "God forbid that another Aubrey should have to stoop to marrying a mongrel American heiress."

He spun around, his expression startled and distressed. "I'm sorry, Sunny—I didn't mean that the way it sounded."

Her brows arched. "Oh? I can't imagine any meaning other than the obvious one."

When she turned and headed toward the door of her suite, he caught her arm and said intensely, "You would have been my choice even if you weren't an heiress."

Her mouth twisted. "Prettily said, but you needn't perjure yourself, Justin. We both know this marriage wouldn't have been made without my money and your title. If you invest my money wisely, perhaps our son, if we have one, will be able to marry where he chooses. I certainly hope so."

Justin's hand fell away and Sunny escaped into her sitting room, Daisy at her heels. When she was alone, she sank wretchedly into a chair. She had been better off not knowing what Justin really felt. Before she had wondered if he had a mistress; now, sickeningly, she wondered if he had a woman who was not only his mistress, but his beloved. There had been a raw emotion in his voice that made her think, for the first time, that he was capable of loving deeply. Had he been forced to forsake the woman he loved so that he could maintain Swindon?

Sensing distress, Daisy whimpered and pushed her cool nose into Sunny's hand. Mechanically she stroked the dog's silky ears. What a wretched world they lived in. Yet even if Justin loved another woman, he was her husband and she must make the best of this marriage. Someday, if she was a very good wife, perhaps he would love her, at least a little.

She desperately hoped so, for there was a hole in the center of her life that the frivolity of the season would never fill.

Sunny's depression was not improved by the discovery that the dowager duchess was in an unusually caustic mood. Throughout an interminable dinner, she made acid remarks about the neighbors, the government and most of all her son. As fruit and cheese were served, she said, "A pity that Justin hasn't the Aubrey height and coloring. Gavin was a much more handsome man, just as Blanche and Charlotte are far prettier than Alexandra."

Sunny retorted, "I've studied the portraits, and the first duke, John Aubrey, was dark and of medium build. Justin and Alexandra resemble him much more than your other children do."

The dowager sniffed. "The first duke was a notable general, but though it pains me to admit it, he was a very low sort of man in other ways. A pity that the peasant strain hasn't yet been bred out of the family." She gave an elaborate sigh. "Such a tragedy that Justin did not die instead of Gavin."

Sunny gasped. How *dare* that woman say she

wished Justin had died in his brother's place! Justin was worth a dozen charming, worthless wastrels like Gavin. She glanced at her husband and saw that he was carefully peeling an apple, as if his mother hadn't spoken, but there was a painful bleakness in his eyes.

If he wouldn't speak, she would. Laying her fork beside her plate, she said, "You must not speak so about Justin, Duchess."

"You forget who I am, madame." The dowager's eyes gleamed with pleasure at the prospect of a battle. "As the mother who suffered agonies to bear him, I can say what I wish."

"And you forget who *I* am," Sunny said with deadly precision. "The mistress of Swindon Palace. And I will no longer tolerate such vile, ill-natured remarks."

The dowager gasped, her jaw dropping open. "How dare you!"

Not backing down an inch, Sunny retorted, "I dare because it is a hostess's duty to maintain decorum at her table, and there has been a sad lack of that at Swindon."

The dowager swept furiously to her feet. "I will not stay here to be insulted by an impertinent American."

Deliberately misinterpreting her mother-in-law's words, Sunny said, "As you wish, Duchess. I can certainly understand why you prefer to have your own establishment. If I were to be widowed, I would feel the same way. And the Dower House is a very charming residence, isn't it?"

The dowager's jaw went slack as she realized that a simple flounce from the table had been transformed into total eviction. Closing her mouth with a snap, she turned to glare at Justin. "Are you going to allow an insolent American hussy to drive me from my own home?"

Justin looked from his mother to his wife, acute discomfort on his face. Silently Sunny pleaded with him to support her. He had said that she was the mistress of Swindon. If he didn't back her now, her position would become intolerable.

"You've been complaining that the new central heating gives you headaches, Mother," Justin said expressionlessly. "I think it an excellent idea for you to move to the Dower House so that you will be more comfortable. We shall miss you, of course, but fortunately you won't be far away."

Sunny shut her eyes for an instant, almost undone by relief. When she opened them again, the dowager's venomous gaze had gone to her daughter. "The Dower House isn't large enough for me to have Alexandra underfoot," she said waspishly. "She shall have to stay in the palace."

Before her mother-in-law could reconsider, Sunny said, "Very true—until she marries, Alexandra belongs at Swindon."

"*If* she ever marries," the dowager said viciously. Knowing that she was defeated and that

the only way to salvage her dignity was to pretend
that moving was her own idea, she added, "You
shall have to learn to run the household yourself,
Sarah, for I have been longing to travel. I believe
I shall spend the rest of the winter in southern
France. England is so dismal at this season." Ram-
rod straight, she marched from the room.

Sunny, Justin and Alexandra were left sitting in
brittle silence. Not daring to meet her husband's
eyes, Sunny said, "I'm sorry if I was disrespectful
to your mother, but...but I'm not sorry for what I
said."

"That's a contradiction in terms," he said,
sounding more weary than angry. After a long silence, he said, "By the way, I saw Lord Hopstead
in London, and he invited us for a weekend visit
and ball at Cottenham. I thought the three of us
could go, then you could take Alexandra on to
Paris for her fittings."

Relieved that he didn't refer to her confrontation
with the dowager, Sunny said, "That sounds delightful. Are you ready for your first ball, Alexandra? I have a gown that will look marvelous on
you with only minor alterations."

"That's very kind of you," a subdued Alexandra said.

For several minutes, they stiffly discussed the
proposed trip, none of them making any allusion
to the dowager's rout. It was like ignoring the fact
that an elephant was in the room.

Finally Sunny got to her feet. "I'm very tired tonight. If you two will excuse me, I'll go to bed now."

Her temples throbbed as she went to her room, but under her shakiness, she was triumphant. Without the dowager's poisonous presence, life at Swindon would improve remarkably.

She changed to her nightgown and climbed into bed, wondering if Justin would visit her. Ordinarily he did after returning from a journey, but perhaps he would stay away if he was displeased with the way she had treated his mother.

Though it shamed her to admit it, she had come to look forward to his conjugal visits. One particular night stood out in her mind. She had been drifting in the misty zone between sleep and waking when her husband came. Though aware of his presence, she had been too drowsy to move her languid limbs.

Instead of waking her, he had given a small sigh, then stretched out beside her, his warm body against hers, his quiet breath caressing her temple. After several minutes he began stroking her, his hand gliding gently over her torso. She had lain utterly still, embarrassed by the yearning sensations that tingled in her breasts and other unmentionable places. Pleasure thickened inside her until she had had to bite her lip to keep from moaning and moving against his hand.

Fortunately, before she disgraced herself, he

dozed off, his hand cupping her breast. Slowly her tension had dissipated until she also slept. Her rest was remarkably deep, considering that she had never in her life shared a bed with another person.

But when she awoke the next morning, he was gone. She might have thought she had dreamed the episode if not for the imprint of her husband's head on the pillow and a faint, lingering masculine scent. It had occurred to her that people who could not afford to have separate bedrooms might be luckier than they knew.

She had been mortified by the knowledge that she had the nature of a wanton. The next time she saw Katie Westron, she must find the boldness to ask how a woman could control her carnality, for surely Katie would know. Until then, Sunny would simply have to exercise willpower. She could almost hear her mother saying, "You are a lady. Behave like one."

Yet still she longed for her husband's company. She had almost given up hope that he would join her when the connecting door quietly opened and he padded across the deep carpet. As he slipped into the bed, she touched his arm to show that she was awake and willing. He slid his hand beneath the covers and drew up the hem of her nightgown.

Perhaps the evening's drama was affecting her, for she found it particularly difficult to keep silent while he prepared her for intercourse. Those strange feelings that were part pleasure, part pain, fluttered through her as he smoothed lotion over her sensitive female parts.

When he entered her, heat pulsed through those same parts, then expanded to other parts of her body. She caught her breath, unable to entirely suppress her reaction.

Immediately he stopped moving. "Did I hurt you?"

"N-no." She knotted her hands and pressed her limbs rigidly into the mattress. "No, you didn't hurt me."

Gently he began rocking back and forth again. The slowness of his movements caused deeply disquieting sensations. Yet curiously, instead of wanting them to stop, she wanted more. It was hard, so hard, to be still....

His breathing quickened in the way that told her that the end was near. He gave a muffled groan and made a final deep thrust. Then the tension went out of him.

She felt a corresponding easing in herself, as if her feelings were intertwined with his. She was tempted to slide her arms around him, for she had a most unladylike desire to keep his warm, hard body pressed tightly against her. Perhaps he might fall asleep with her again.

But that was not what men and women of good breeding did. Her parents had not shared a room. After Sunny's birth, they had probably not even had conjugal relations, for she was the youngest in the family. Once her father had two sons to work in the business and her mother had a daughter for companionship, there had been no need for more babies.

Justin lifted his weight from her. After pulling her gown down again, he lightly touched her hair. She wanted to catch his hand and beg him to stay, but of course she didn't.

Then he left her.

When the connecting door between their chambers closed, Sunny released her breath in a shuddering sigh, then rolled over and hugged a pillow to her chest. She felt restless impatience and a kind of itchy discomfort in her female parts. Her hand slid down her torso. Perhaps if she rubbed herself there…

Horrified, she flopped onto her back and clenched her hands into fists. Her nurse and her mother had made it clear that a woman never touched herself "down there" unless she had to.

She closed her eyes against the sting of tears. She was trying her very best to be a good wife. But from what she could see, a good wife was a lonely woman.

In a flurry of trunks and contradictory orders, the Dowager Duchess of Thornborough moved herself and a substantial number of Swindon's finest antiques to the elegant Dower House on the far side of the estate. Then she promptly decamped to the French Riviera, there to flaunt her rank and make slanderous hints about her son's inadequacies and her daughter-in-law's insolence. The one thing Justin was sure she would not say was the truth—that a slip of a girl had maneuvered the dowager out of Swindon Palace.

Life was much easier with his mother gone. He and Sunny and Alexandra dined *en famille,* with much less formality and far more enjoyment. His sister was blossoming under Sunny's kind guidance, and no longer dreaded her social debut.

What wasn't prospering was his marriage. Ever since his incredibly clumsy remark about sparing future dukes the necessity of marrying for money, there had been strain between him and Sunny. What he had meant was that he wanted financial considerations to be irrelevant.

Unfortunately, she had believed the unintended insult rather than his heartfelt declaration that he would have wanted to marry her anyhow. Because he had accidentally hurt her, she had struck back, hurting him in return when she had underlined the fact that their marriage had nothing to do with love.

Fearing that more explanations would only make matters worse, he hadn't raised the subject again. Eventually memory of the incident would fade, but in the meantime Sunny had pulled further away from him. She was courteous, compliant—and as distant as if an ocean still divided them. Sometimes she trembled during their wordless conjugal couplings, and he feared that she was recoiling from his touch. If she had verbally objected, perhaps he could have controlled his desires and stopped inflicting himself on her. But she said nothing, and he did not have the strength to stay away.

As they prepared to go to the ball at Cottenham Manor, he hoped that Sunny's return to society would cheer her. She deserved laughter and frivolity and admiration.

Yet though he wanted her to be happy, the knowledge that she would be surrounded by adoring, predatory men terrified him. If she was miserable in her marriage, how long would it be before she looked elsewhere?

If you would be troubled, take a wife.

Chapter Eight

Cottenham Manor
March

Cottenham Manor, seat of the Earl of Hopstead, was almost as grand and large as Swindon Palace. Lord and Lady Hopstead were famous for their entertainments, and Sunny had spent a long and happy weekend at Cottenham the previous summer. It was a pleasure to return, and as her maid fastened a sapphire and diamond necklace around her neck, she hummed softly to herself.

"Madame is happy tonight," Antoinette observed as she handed Sunny the matching eardrops.

Sunny put on the eardrops, then turned her head so she could see the play of light in the sapphire pendants. "I've been looking forward to this ball for weeks. What a silly custom it is for a bride to rusticate for months after the wedding."

"But think how much more you will appreciate society after wintering in the depths of the English countryside."

"That's true." Sunny rose with a rich whisper of taffeta petticoats. She was wearing a sumptuous blue brocade gown, one of Worth's finest, and she was ready to be admired.

"You must sit until I have put on your tiara," Antoinette said reprovingly.

Obediently Sunny sat again and braced herself for the weight of the Thornborough tiara. The massive, diamond-studded coronet would give her a headache, but it wouldn't be proper for a duchess to attend a ball without one, particularly since the Prince of Wales would be present.

Just as the maid was finishing, a hesitant knock sounded at the door. Antoinette crossed the room and admitted Alexandra. Dressed in a white silk gown that shimmered with every movement, the younger girl had a fairylike grace. Her dark hair had been swept up to show the delicate line of her throat, and her complexion glowed with youth and good health.

"You look marvelous," Sunny said warmly. "Turn around so I can see all of you."

Her sister-in-law colored prettily as she obeyed. "You were right about the gown. Even though this one wasn't made for me, it's so lovely that one can't help but feel beautiful."

"It looks better on you than it ever did on me. You'll be the belle of the ball."

"No, you will." Alexandra chuckled. "But at least I don't think that I'll be a wallflower."

Another knock sounded on the door. This time it was Justin, come to take his wife and sister down to the dinner that would precede the ball. Sunny had hoped that there would be so many people at Cottenham that they would be put in the same room, but such intimacy was unthinkable in the fashionable set. The previous night, she had slept alone. Perhaps tonight...

Hastily she suppressed the improper thought.

After he examined them both, Justin said gravely, "You will be the two most beautiful women at the ball. Alex, I shall have a dozen men clamoring for your hand before the evening is over."

As Alexandra beamed, he offered one arm to his wife and one to his sister, then led them into the hall. As they descended the broad stairs, Sunny asked, "Will you dance with me tonight?"

He gave her a quizzical glance. "You would dance with a mere husband?"

"Please." Afraid that she might sound pathetic, she added lightly, "I know that it's not fashionable to dance with one's spouse, but it isn't actually scandalous."

He gave her one of the rare smiles that took her

breath away. "Then it will be my very great pleasure."

As they entered the salon where the other guests
had gathered, Sunny's heart was already dancing.

The Hopsteads' ball was an excellent place to
rejoin society, and Sunny enjoyed greeting people
she had met the year before. During a break after
the fourth dance, she came across her godmother,
who was resplendent in coral-and-silver silk.
"Aunt Katie!" Sunny gave her a hug. "I hoped
you would be here. You're not staying at Cottenham, are you?"

"No, I'm at the Howards'. Every great house in
the district is full of guests who have come for this
ball." Katie affectionately tucked a tendril of
Sunny's flyaway hair in place. "You're in fine
looks. By any chance are you...?"

"Please, don't ask me if I'm expecting a blessed
event! I swear, every female at the ball has inquired. I'm beginning to feel like a dreadful failure."

"Nonsense—you've only been married a few
months." Katie chuckled. "It's just that we're all
such gossips, and like it or not, you're a subject of
great interest."

Sunny made a face. "Luckily there will soon be
other heiresses to capture society's attention." The
two women chatted for a few minutes and made
an engagement for the next morning.

Then Sunny glanced beyond Katie, and her heart froze in her breast. On the far side of the room was Paul Curzon, tall and distinguished and heart-stoppingly handsome.

As if feeling her gaze, he looked up, and for a paralyzing instant their eyes met. Shocked by the way her knees weakened, Sunny turned to Katie and stammered, "I must go now. I'll see you to-morrow."

Then she caught her train up with one hand and headed for the nearest door, scarcely noticing when she bumped into other guests. Sometimes escape was more important than manners.

One of the drawbacks of socializing was the number of people who hoped to enlist ducal support for some cause or other. This time, it was a junior government minister talking about an upcoming bill. Justin listened patiently, half of his attention on the minister, the other half anticipating the next dance, which would be with Sunny. Then, from the corner of his eye, he saw his wife leave the ballroom, her face pale. He frowned, wondering if she was feeling ill.

He was about to excuse himself when he saw Paul Curzon go out the same side door that Sunny had used. Justin's face stiffened as a horrible suspicion seized him.

Seeing his expression, the minister said earnestly, "I swear, your grace, the scheme is perfectly sound. If you wish, I'll show you the figures."

Justin realized that he couldn't even remember what the damned bill was about. Brusquely he said, "Send me the information and I'll give you my decision in a week."

Hoping desperately that he was wrong, he brushed aside the minister's thanks and made his way after his wife and the man whom she might still love.

Without conscious thought, Sunny chose the conservatory for her refuge. It was at the opposite end of the house from the ball, and as she had hoped, she had it to herself.

Cottenham was noted for its magnificent indoor garden, and scattered gaslights illuminated banks of flowers and lush tropical shrubbery. Though rain drummed on the glass panels far above her head, inside the air was balmy and richly scented.

She took a deep breath, then set out along one of the winding brick paths. It had been foolish to become upset at the sight of Paul Curzon, for she had known that inevitably they would meet. But she had not expected it to be tonight. If she had been mentally prepared, she would have been able to accept his presence with equanimity.

Yet honesty compelled her to admit that in the first instant, she had felt some of the excitement she had known in the days when she had loved him. In the days when she *thought* she loved him, before she had discovered his baseness.

As always, nature helped her regain her composure. If she hadn't been dressed in a ball gown, she would have looked for some plants to repot. Instead, she picked a gardenia blossom and inhaled the delicate perfume.

As she did, a familiar voice said huskily, "The conservatory was a perfect choice, darling. No one will see us here."

"Paul!" The shock was as great as when she had first seen him, and spasmodically she crushed the gardenia blossom in her palm. After a fierce struggle for control, she turned and said evenly, "I didn't come here to meet you, Paul, but to get away from you. We have nothing to say to each other."

Unfortunately the way out lay past him. As she tried to slip by without her broad skirts touching him, he caught her hand. "Sunny, don't go yet," he begged. "I'm sorry if I misunderstood why you came here, but I wanted so much to see you that hope warped my judgment. I made the worst mistake of my life with you. At least give me a chance to apologize."

Reluctantly she stopped, as much because of the narrow aisle as because of his words. "I'm not interested in your apologies." As she spoke, she looked into his face, which was a mistake. He didn't look base; he looked sincere, and sinfully handsome.

"If you won't let me apologize, then let me say how much I love you." A tremor sounded in his voice. "I truly didn't know how much until I lost you."

Reminding herself that he had looked equally honest before he had broken her heart, she tried to free her hand, saying tartly, "Perhaps you think that you love me *because* you lost me. Isn't that how people like you play at love?"

His grip tightened. "This is different! The fact that you were willing to marry me is the greatest honor I've ever known. But I let myself be blinded by worldly considerations, and now I'm paying for my folly. Both of us are."

"There's no point in talking like this! The past can't be changed, and I'm a married woman now."

"Perhaps the past can't be changed, but the future can be." He put his hand under her chin and turned her face to his. "Love is too precious to throw away."

His gaze holding hers, he pressed his heated lips to her gloved fingers. "You are so beautiful, Sunny. I have never loved a woman as much as I love you."

She knew that she should break away, for she didn't love him, didn't really trust his protestations of devotion. Yet her parched heart yearned for warmth, for words of love, even ones that might be false.

Her inner struggle held her paralyzed as he put his arms around her and bent his head for a kiss. In a moment, she would push him away and leave. Yet even though it was wrong, for just an instant she would let him hold her....

The conservatory seemed like the most likely spot for dalliance, but Justin had only been there once, and he lost precious time with a wrong turn. His heart was pounding with fear when he finally reached his destination and threw open the door. He paused on the threshold and scanned the shadowy garden, praying that he was wrong.

But through the dense vegetation, he saw a shimmering patch of blue the shade of Sunny's gown. Down a brick path, around a bend...and he found his wife in Paul Curzon's arms.

The pain was worse than anything Justin had ever known. For a moment he stood stock-still as nausea pulsed through him.

Then came rage. Stalking forward, he snarled, "If you expect me to be a complaisant husband, you're both fools."

The two broke apart instantly, and Sunny whirled to him, her face white. Justin grabbed her wrist and pulled her away from Curzon. Then he looked his rival in the eye and said with lethal precision, "If you ever come near my wife again, I will destroy you."

"No need to carry on so, old man," Curzon said hastily. "It was merely a friendly kiss between acquaintances."

Justin's free hand knotted into a fist. *"I will destroy you."*

As Curzon paled, Justin turned and swept his wife away, heedless of the difficulty that she had keeping up in her high-heeled kid slippers. When she stumbled, his grip tightened to keep her from falling, but he did not slow down.

Wanting to ease the rage in his face, she said desperately, "Justin, that wasn't what you think."

He gave her a piercing glance. "It looked very much like a kiss to me. Am I wrong?"

"Yes, but...but it didn't really mean anything."

"If kisses mean nothing to you, does that mean you'll give them to any man?" he asked bitterly. "Or only those with whom you have assignations?"

"You're deliberately misunderstanding me! I went to the conservatory to avoid Paul, not to meet him. I know that I shouldn't have let him kiss me, but it was just a...a temporary aberration that happened only because there were once...warmer feelings between us."

"And if I hadn't come, they would have become warmer yet. If I had been ten minutes later..." His voice broke.

Guilt rose in a choking wave. Though she had not sought the encounter with Paul, she had not left when she should, and she had allowed him to kiss her. Might the warmth of Paul's embrace have dissolved her knowledge of right and wrong? She wanted to believe that morality would have triumphed—but treacherous doubt gnawed at her. Since she had discovered her wanton nature, she could no longer trust herself.

They reached the hallway below the main staircase. Several couples were enjoying the cooler air there, and they all turned to stare at the duke and duchess. Dropping her voice, Sunny hissed, "Let go of me! What will people think?"

"I don't give a tinker's dam what anyone thinks." He began climbing the staircase, still holding tightly to her wrist to keep her at his side. "Your behavior is what concerns me."

He followed the upstairs corridor to her bedchamber, pulled her inside, then slammed the door behind them and turned the key in the lock. The room was empty, lit only by the soft glow of a gas lamp. She edged uneasily away, for this furious man was a stranger, and he was starting to frighten her.

They stared at each other across the width of the room. With the same lethal intensity he had directed at Paul, Justin growled, "In the Middle Ages, I could have locked you in a tower or a chastity belt. A century ago, I could have challenged any man who came near you to a duel. But what can a man do about a faithless wife in these modern times?''

His words triggered her secret fear. ''What about faithless husbands?'' she retorted. ''I've been told that men like you always have mistresses. Is the real reason for your trips to London another woman—one that you couldn't have because you had to marry for money?''

Renewed fury blazed in his gray eyes, and a dark hunger. ''I have not looked at—or touched— anyone else since I met you. I wish to God that you could say the same. But since you choose to act like a whore, I will treat you as one.''

Then he swept across the room and shattered her with a kiss.

Sunny had thought that her months of marriage had educated her about what happened between husband and wife, but nothing had prepared her for Justin's embrace. The quiet consideration to which she was accustomed had been replaced by blazing rage.

Trapped in the prison of his arms, she was acutely aware of his strength. Even if she wanted to resist, any effort on her part would be futile. Yet as they stood locked together, his mouth devouring hers, she sensed that his fury was changing into something that was similar, but was not anger at all. And it called to her.

Her head tilted and the heavy tiara pulled loose

and fell to the carpet, jerking sharply at her hair. When she winced, his crushing grip eased and he began stroking her head with one hand. His deft fingers found and soothed the hurt. She didn't realize that he was also removing the pins until coils of hair cascaded over her shoulders.

He buried his face in the silken mass, and she felt the beating of his heart and the soft exhalation of his breath against her cheek. "Oh, God, Sunny," he said with anguish. "You are so beautiful—so painfully beautiful."

Yet his expression was harsh when he straightened and turned her so that her back was to him. First he unhooked her sapphire necklace, throwing it aside as if it was a piece of cut-glass trumpery. Then he started to unfasten her gown.

She opened her mouth to object, but before she could, he pressed his mouth to the side of her throat. With lips and tongue, he found sensitivities she hadn't known she possessed. As he trailed tiny, nibbling kisses down her neck and along her shoulder, she released her breath in a shuddering sigh, all thoughts of protest chased from her mind. Potent awareness curled through her, pooling hotly in unmentionable places.

When the gown was undone, he pushed it off her shoulders and down her arms. The rough warmth of his fingers made an erotic contrast to the cool silk that skimmed her flesh in a feather-light caress, then slithered in a rush to the floor, leaving her in her underthings. Instinctively she raised her hands to cover her breasts, stammering, "Th-this is highly improper."

"You have forfeited the right to talk about propriety." He untied her layered crinolette petticoat and dragged it down around her ankles. Then he began unlacing her blue satin corset. Stays were a lady's armor against impropriety, and she stood rigidly still, horribly aware that every inch of her newly liberated flesh burned with life and longing.

Then, shockingly, he slid his hands under the loose corset and cupped her breasts, using his thumbs to tease her nipples through the thin fabric of her chemise. It was like the time he had caressed her when he thought she slept, but a thousand times more intense. Unable to suppress her reaction, she shuddered and rolled her hips against him.

"You like that, my lady trollop?" he murmured in her ear.

She wanted to deny it, but couldn't. Her limbs weakened and she wilted against him, mindlessly reveling in the waves of sensation that flooded through her. The firm support of his broad chest, the silken tease of his tongue on the edge of her ear, the exquisite pleasure that expanded from her breasts to encompass her entire being, coiling tighter and tighter deep inside her....

She did not come to her senses until he tossed aside her corset and turned her to face him. Horrified by her lewd response and her near-nakedness, she stumbled away from the pile of crumpled clothing and retreated until her back was to the wall. "I have never shirked my wifely duty," she said feebly, "but this...this isn't right."

"Tonight, right is what I say it is." His implacable gaze holding hers, he stripped off his own clothing with brusque, impatient movements. "And this time, I will have you naked and in the light."

She could not take her eyes away as he removed his formal garments to reveal the hard, masculine body beneath. The well-defined muscles that rippled beneath his skin...the dark hair that patterned his chest and arrowed down his belly...and the arrogant male organ, which she had felt but never seen.

She stared for an instant, both mortified and fascinated, then blushed violently and closed her eyes. No wonder decent couples had marital relations in the dark, for the sight of a man's body was profoundly disturbing.

A Vienna waltz was playing in the distance. She had trouble believing that under this same roof hundreds of people were laughing and flirting and playing society's games. Compared to the devastating reality of Justin, the outside world had no more substance than shadows.

Even with her eyes closed, she was acutely aware of his nakedness when he drew her into his arms again, surrounding her with heat and maleness. Her breath came rapid and irregular as he peeled away the last frail protection of chemise, drawers and stockings. His fingers left trails of fire as they brushed her limbs and torso.

She inhaled sharply when he swept her into his arms and laid her across the bed, his taut frame pinning her to the mattress. Though she tried to control her shameful reactions, she moaned with pleasure when his mouth claimed her breast with arrant carnality.

No matter how hard she tried, she could not lie still as he caressed and kissed and tasted her, the velvet stroke of his tongue driving her to madness. His masterful touch abraded away every layer of decorum until she no longer remembered, or cared, how a lady should act. In the shameless turmoil of intimacy, she was tinder to his flame.

She was lovely beyond his dreams, and everything about her intoxicated him—the haunting lure of wild violets, her tangled sun-struck hair, the lush eroticism of removing layer after layer of clothing until finally her flawless body was revealed. Her lithe, feminine grace wrenched his heart.

Yet side by side with tenderness, he found savage satisfaction in her choked whimpers of pleasure. His wife might be a duchess and a lady, but for tonight, at least, she was a woman, and she was *his*.

This time there would be no need of lotion to ease their joining. She was hotly ready, and she writhed against his hand as he caressed the moist, delicate folds of female flesh. Her moan gave him a deep sense of masculine pride, dissolving the aching emptiness he had known in their inhibited marriage bed.

When he could no longer bear his separateness, he entered her. The voluptuous welcome of her body was exquisite, both torment and homecoming. Trembling with strain, he forced himself to move with slow deliberation. This time he would not let their union end too quickly.

Vivid emotions rippled across her sweat-sheened face. But he wanted more; he wanted communion of the mind as well as the body. He wanted acknowledgment of the power he had over her. Hoarsely he asked, "Do you desire me?"

"You...you are my husband." She turned her head to the side, as if trying to evade his question. "It is my duty to comply with your wishes."

Mere obedience was not what he wanted from his wife. He repeated, *"Do you desire me?"* Slowly, by infinitesimal degrees, he began to withdraw. "If not, perhaps I should stop now."

"No!" she gasped, her eyes flying open for an instant and her body arching sharply upward. "Don't leave me, please. I couldn't bear it...."

It was what he had longed to hear. He responded to her admission by surrendering to the fiery need that bound them. No longer passive, she was his partner in passion, her nails slashing his back as they thrust against each other. She cried out with ecstasy as long, shuddering convulsions rocked them both, and in the culmination of desire he felt their soaring spirits blend.

In the tremulous aftermath, he gathered her pliant body into his arms and tucked the covers around them. As they dozed off together, he knew they had truly become husband and wife.

Justin was not sure how long he had slept. The ball must have ended, for he could no longer hear music and laughter, but the sky outside was still dark. He lay on his side with Sunny nestled along him, her face against his shoulder.

Not wanting to wake her, he touched the luscious tangle of her hair with a gossamer caress. He had never known such happiness, or such peace. Not only was she the loveliest and sweetest of women, but she was blessed with an ardent nature. If he hadn't been so blasted deferential, he would have discovered that much sooner. But now that they had found each other, their lives would be different.

Her eyes opened and gazed into his. For a long moment, they simply stared at each other. He stroked the elegant curve of her back and prepared to make the declaration of love that he had never made to any other woman.

But she spoke first, saying in a thin, exhausted voice, "Who are you?"

A chill touched his heart as he wondered if she was out of her senses, but she seemed lucid. Carefully he replied, "Your husband, of course."

She gave a tiny shake of her head. "You are more a stranger to me now than on the day we married."

He looked away, unable to face the dazed bleakness in her aqua eyes. He had known that she had not yet been unfaithful; not only was she not the sort of woman to engage lightly in an affair, but buried at Swindon she hadn't even had an opportunity. Yet seeing her in Curzon's arms had devastated Justin because it was a horrific preview of the possibility that he would lose her.

Despair had made him furiously determined to show her what fulfillment was. He had wanted to possess her, body and soul, to make her his own so profoundly that she would never look at another man. He realized that he had also hoped to win her love by demonstrating the depth of his passion.

But the fact that he had been able to arouse her latent ardor did not mean that she suddenly, miraculously loved him. With sickening clarity, he saw that in his anger he had ruthlessly stripped away her dignity and modesty. Instead of liberating her passion, he had ravished her spirit, turning her into a broken shadow of the happy girl who had first captured his heart.

His unspoken words of love withered and died.

Instead he said painfully, "I am no different now from what I was then."

He wanted to say more, to apologize and beg her forgiveness, but she turned away and buried her face in the pillows.

Feeling that he would shatter if he moved too suddenly, he slid from the bed and numbly dragged on enough clothing to make his way the short distance to his room.

As he left, he wondered despairingly if he would ever be able to face his wife again.

Chapter Nine

Sunny awoke the next morning churning with tangled emotions. The only thing she knew for certain was that she could not bear to face a house full of avid-eyed, curious people. With a groan, she rolled over, buried her head under a pillow and did her best not to think.

But her mind refused to cooperate. She could not stop herself from wondering where Justin was and what he thought of the events of the previous night. She was mortified by memories of her wantonness, and angry with her husband for making her behave so badly. But though she tried to cling to anger over his disrespect, other things kept seeping into her mind—memories of heartwarming closeness, and shattering excitement....

At that point in her thoughts, her throat always tightened. Justin had said he would treat her as a whore, and her response had confirmed his furious accusation.

For the first time in her life, Sunny understand why a woman might choose to go into a nunnery. A world with no men would be infinitely simpler.

Eventually Antoinette tiptoed into the dim, heavily curtained room. "Madame is not feeling well this morning?"

"Madame has a ghastly headache. I wish to be left alone." Remembering her obligations, Sunny added, "Tell Lady Alexandra not to be concerned about me. I'm sure I'll be fine by dinner."

There was a long silence. Even with her eyes closed, Sunny knew that her maid was surveying the disordered bedchamber and probably drawing accurate conclusions. But tactful Antoinette said only, "After I straighten the room, I shall leave. Perhaps later you would like tea and toast?"

"Perhaps."

As the maid quietly tidied up the evidence of debauchery, someone knocked on the door and handed in a message. After the footman left, Antoinette said, "*Monsieur le Duc* has sent a note."

Sunny came tensely awake. "Leave it on the table."

After the maid left, Sunny sat up in bed and stared at the letter as if it were a poisonous serpent. Then she swung her feet to the floor. Only then did she realize that she was stark naked. Worse, her body showed unaccustomed marks where sensitive skin had been nipped, or rasped by a whiskered masculine face. And her body would not be the only one marked this morning....

Face flushed, she darted to the armoire and grabbed the first nightgown and wrapper she saw. After she was decently covered, she brushed her wild hair into submission and pulled it into a severe knot. When she could delay no longer, she opened the waiting envelope.

She was not sure what she expected, but the scrawled words, *I'm sorry. Thornborough* were a painful letdown. What was her husband sorry about—their marriage? His wife's appallingly wanton nature? His own disproportionate rage, which had led him to humiliate her? The use of his title rather than his Christian name was blunt proof that the moments of intimacy she had imagined the night before were an illusion.

Crumpling the note in one hand, she buried her face in her hands and struggled against tears. The wretched circle of her thoughts was interrupted by another knock. Though she called out, "I do not wish for company," the door swung open anyhow.

In walked Katie Westron, immaculately dressed in a morning gown and with a tray in her hands. "It's past noon, and you and I were engaged to take a drive an hour ago." She set the tray down, then surveyed her goddaughter. "You look quite dreadful, my dear, and they say that Thornborough left Cottenham this morning at dawn, looking like death."

So he was gone. Apparently he couldn't bear being under the same roof with her any longer. Trying to mask the pain of that thought, Sunny asked, "Are people talking?"

"Some, though not as much as they were before I said that Thornborough had always intended to leave today because he had business at Swindon." Briskly Katie opened the draperies so that light flooded the room. "And as I pointed out, who wouldn't look exhausted after a late night at such a delightful ball?"

"He *was* planning to leave early, but not until tomorrow." Sunny managed a wry half smile. "You lie beautifully."

"It's a prime social skill." Katie prepared two cups of coffee and handed one to Sunny, then took the other and perched on the window seat. "There's nothing like coffee to put one's troubles in perspective. Have a ginger cake, too, they're very good." After daintily biting one, Katie continued, "Would you like to tell me why you and Thornborough both look so miserable?"

The scalding coffee did clear Sunny's mind. She was in dire need of the advice of an older and wiser woman, and she would find no kinder or more tolerant listener than her godmother.

Haltingly she described her marriage—the distance between her and her husband, her loneliness, her encounter with Paul Curzon and the shocking result. Of the last she said very little, and that with her face burning, but she suspected that her god-mother could make a shrewd guess about what went unsaid.

At the end, she asked, "What do you think?"

"Exactly why are you so upset?"

After long thought, Sunny said slowly, "I don't understand my marriage, my husband or myself. In particular, I find Justin incomprehensible. Before, I thought he was polite but basically indifferent to me. Now I think he must despise me, or he would never have treated me with such disrespect."

Katie took another cake. "Do you wish to end the marriage?"

"Of course I don't want a divorce!"

"Why 'of course'? There would be a ghastly scandal, and some social circles exclude all divorced women, but as a Vangelder, you would be able to weather that."

"It...it would be humiliating for Thornborough. If I left him, people would think that he mistreated me horribly."

Katie's brows arched. "Aren't you saying that he did exactly that?"

"In most ways, he's been very considerate." She thought of the bathroom that he had had installed for her, and almost smiled. Not the most romantic gift, perhaps, but one that gave her daily pleasure.

"You'd be a fool to live in misery simply to save Thornborough embarrassment," Katie said tartly. "A little singed pride will be good for him, and as a duke he will certainly not be ruined socially. He can find another wife with a snap of his fingers. The next one might not be able to match your dowry, but that's all right—the Swindon roof has already been replaced, and you can hardly take it back. What matters is that you'll be free to find a more congenial husband."

The thought of Justin with another wife made Sunny's hackles rise. "I don't want another husband." She bit her lip. "In fact, I can't imagine being married to anyone else. It would seem wrong. Immoral."

"Oh?" Katie said with interest. "What is so special about Thornborough? From what you say, he's a dull sort of fellow, and he's not particularly good-looking."

"He's *not* dull! He's kind, intelligent and very witty, even though he's quiet. He has a sense of responsibility, which many men in his position don't. And he's really quite attractive. Not in a sleek, fashionable way, but very…manly."

Her godmother smiled gently. "You sound like a woman who is in love with her husband."

"I do?" Sunny tried the idea on, and was shocked to realize that it was true. She was happy in Justin's presence; on some deep level that had nothing to do with their current problems, she trusted him. "But he doesn't love me—he doesn't even respect me. Last night he said that since I had behaved like a...a woman of no virtue, he would treat me like one.'' A vivid memory of his mouth on her breast caused her to blush again.

"Did he hurt you?"

"No, but he...offended my modesty." Sunny stared at her hands, unable to meet her godmother's gaze. "In fairness, I must admit that I did not behave as properly as I should. In fact...I was shocked to discover how wantonly I could behave."

"In other words, your husband made passionate love to you, you found it entrancing as well as alarming, and are now ashamed of yourself."

The color drained from Sunny's face, leaving her white. "How did you know?"

Setting aside her coffee cup, Katie said, "The time has come to speak frankly. I suppose that your mother told you that no decent woman ever enjoyed her marriage bed, and that discreet suffering was the mark of a lady."

After seeing her goddaughter nod, she continued, "There are many who agree with her, but another school of opinion says that there is nothing wrong with taking pleasure in the bodies that the good Lord gave us. What is the Song of Solomon but a hymn to the joy of physical and spiritual love?"

Weakly Sunny said, "Mother would say you're talking blasphemy."

"Augusta is one of my oldest and dearest

friends, but she and your father were ill-suited, and naturally that has affected her views on marital relations.'' Katie leaned forward earnestly. "Satisfaction in the marriage bed binds a couple together, and the better a woman pleases her husband, the less likely he is to stray. And vice versa, I might add.'' She cocked her head. "If you hadn't been raised to believe that conjugal pleasure was immodest, would you have enjoyed the passion and intimacy that you experienced last night?''

The idea of reveling in carnality was so shocking that it took Sunny's breath away—yet it was also powerfully compelling. She had come to look forward to Justin's visits and to long for more of his company. The idea that her response was natural, not wanton, was heady indeed.

More memories of the previous night's explosive passion burned across her brain. Though the episode had been upsetting, there had also been moments of stunning emotional intimacy, when she and her husband had seemed to be one flesh and one spirit. If such intensity could be woven into the fabric of a marriage, it would bind a man and woman together for as long as they lived. And if passion made a marriage stronger, surely fulfillment could not be truly wicked.

There was only one problem. "I'd like to think that you're right, but what does it matter if I love my husband and he holds me in contempt? Justin has never said a single word of love.''

Katie smiled wryly. "Englishmen are taught to conceal their emotions in the nursery, and the more deeply they care, the harder it is for them to speak. In my experience, the men who talk most easily of love are those who have had entirely too much practice. The more sparingly a man gives his heart, the more precious the gift, and the less adept he is at declarations of love. But deeds matter more than words, and an ounce of genuine caring is worth a pound of smooth, insincere compliments."

Abruptly Sunny remembered that Justin had said that he hadn't looked at another woman since meeting her. She had thought that was merely a riposte in their argument, but if true, it might be an oblique declaration of love. Hesitantly she said, "Do you think it's possible that Justin loves me?"

"You would know that better than I. But he seems the sort who would be more of a doer than a talker." Katie's brows drew together. "Men are simple creatures, and for them, love and passion often get knotted up together. If he does love you in a passionate way, the kind of restrained marriage you have described must be difficult for him."

And if he was finding the marriage difficult, he would withdraw; that much Sunny knew about her husband. She had regretted the fact that he had never reached out to her with affection—yet neither had she ever reached out to him. Perhaps she was as much responsible for the distance between them as he was. Attempting lightness, she said, "I suppose that the way to find out how he feels is to hand him my heart on a platter, then see whether he accepts it or chops it into little pieces.''

"I'm afraid so." Katie shook her head ruefully. "All marriages have ups and downs, particularly in the early years. I was once in a situation a bit like yours, where I had to risk what could have been a humiliating rejection. It wasn't easy to humble myself, but the results were worth it." She smiled. "A witty vicar once said that a good marriage is like a pair of scissors with the couple inseparably joined, often moving in opposite directions, yet always destroying anyone who comes between them. The trick is for the blades to learn to work smoothly together, so as not to cut each other."

That's what she and Justin had been doing: cutting each other. Feeling a century older than she had the day before, Sunny gave a shaky smile. "Apparently I must learn to speak with American bluntness."

"That's the spirit. But first, you might want to ask yourself what you want out of your marriage."

"Love, companionship, children. I certainly don't want to withdraw entirely from society, but the fashionable world will never be the center of my life, the way it is for my mother." Her brow wrinkled. "Perhaps if my parents had been happier together, my father would not have worked so hard, and my mother would not have cared as much about society.''

"I've often suspected that many of the world's most dazzling achievements are a result of a miserable domestic situation." Katie considered. "You might want to wait until both you and Thornborough have had time to recover from what was obviously a distressing episode. You were about to take Alexandra to Paris, weren't you? In your place, I would carry on with my original plans. That will give you time to think and decide exactly how to proceed."

"I'm going to need it." Sunny rose and hugged her godmother. "Thank you, Aunt Katie. What can I do to repay you?"

"When you're old and wise like me, you can give worldly advice to other confused young ladies." Katie smiled reminiscently. "Which is exactly what I was told by an eccentric, sharptongued Westron aunt who sent me back to my husband when I was a bewildered bride."

Sunny nodded gravely. "I promise to pass on whatever womanly wisdom I acquire."

But before she was in a position to give good advice, she must fix her own frayed marriage. And that, she knew, would be easier said than done.

Chapter Ten

Alexandra looked eagerly from the carriage window. "Almost home! It's hard to believe that it's been only a month since we left Swindon. I feel *years* older."

Sunny smiled, trying to conceal her frayed nerves. "Paris has that effect on people. You really have changed, too. You left as a girl and are returning as a young woman."

"I hope so." Alexandra grinned. "But I'm going to go right up to my room and take off my wonderful Worth travel ensemble. Then I'll curl up in my window seat and read that new Rider Haggard novel I bought in London. Though Paris was wonderful, there's nothing quite like a good book."

"You've earned the right to a little self-indulgence." Sunny gave her sister-in-law a fond smile. Petite and pretty, Alexandra would never be called the Gargoylette again, and the difference was more than mere clothing. Now that Alexandra was free of her mother's crushing influence, she was developing poise, confidence and a quiet charm that would surely win her whatever man she eventually honored with her heart.

The carriage pulled up in front of the palace and a footman stepped forward to open the door and let down the steps. Even though Sunny had lived at Swindon for only a few months, and that interval had been far from happy, she felt a surprising sense of homecoming. It helped that the full glory of an English spring had arrived. All nature was in bloom, and the sun was almost as warm as high summer.

As they entered the main hall, Sunny asked the butler, "Is my husband in the house or out on the estate?"

She assumed the latter, for Justin was not expecting them to return until the next day. But the butler replied, "I believe that the duke is taking advantage of the fine weather by working in the Greek gazebo. Shall I inform him of your arrival?"

Sunny's heart lurched. She had thought she would have several hours more before confronting her husband about the state of their marriage, but perhaps it would be better this way. "No, I shall freshen up and then surprise him."

As she walked toward the stairs, a black-and-tan whirlwind darted across the hall and leapt against her, barking joyfully. "Daisy! Oh, darling, I missed you, too.'' Sunny knelt and hugged the slender little dog, feeling that such a warm welcome was a good omen.

A moment later, the wolfhounds thundered up and greeted Alexandra eagerly, then escorted her upstairs. Canine snobs of the highest order, they could tell aristocratic British blood from that of an upstart American, and they reserved their raptures for Justin and his sisters.

Sunny didn't mind. Her charming mongrel at her heels, she went to her room and changed from her traveling suit to her most flattering tea gown, a loose, flowing confection of figured green silk that brought out the green in her eyes.

She chose the costume with care, and not just because it was comfortable. The free and easy design of a tea gown was considered rather daring because it hinted at free and easy morals. She hoped that Justin would see her garb as the subtle advance that it was.

Because he always seemed to like her hair, she let it down and tied it back with a scarf. She needed all the help she could get, for she was terrified by the prospect of baring her heart to the man who could so easily break it. Apart from a brief note that she had written to inform Justin of their safe arrival in Paris, there had been no communication between them. For all she knew, he was still furious over Paul Curzon's kiss.

Fortunately, she had news that should mollify

any lingering anger. God willing, it would also bring them together.

Chin high, she sailed out of the house and down the path toward the gardens.

A breeze wafted through the miniature Greek temple, carrying exuberant scents of trees and spring flowers. Justin scarcely noticed. He was hardly more aware of the pile of correspondence that lay on the cushioned bench beside him, for thoughts of his wife dominated his mind. All of his grief, guilt and anguished love had been intensified by that night of heartbreaking passion, when he had briefly thought that their spirits and bodies were in total harmony.

Sunny had sent him a single impersonal note from Paris. Though it gave no hint of her feelings, its civility implied that she was willing to go on as if nothing had happened.

Yet he feared her return almost as much as he longed to see her. Having once found passion in her arms, it was going to be almost impossible for him not to try to invoke it again, whether she was willing or not.

Absently he slit an envelope with the Italian dagger that he used as a letter opener. Before he could pull out the folded sheet inside, a soft voice said, "Good day, Justin."

He looked up to see Sunny poised on the edge of the folly, her right hand resting on one of the

Ionic columns that framed the entrance. She wore a flowing green tea gown that made her look like an exquisite tree nymph. The garment was distractingly similar to a nightgown, and the breeze molded the fluttering, translucent layers of fabric to her slim figure.

For an instant all his tormented desire must have showed in his face. He wanted to cross the marble floor and draw her into his arms and never let her go. But he didn't. She looked ready to run if he made a move toward her, and it was unbearable to think that she might fear him.

He set the pile of letters on the bench beside him and courteously got to his feet. ''I hope you had a good journey. I wasn't expecting you and Alex until tomorrow.''

''Rather than spend another night in London, we decided to come home early.''

''I'm glad. The house has seemed empty without the two of you.'' Afraid to look at her because of what his expression would reveal, he turned the dagger over and over in his hands. The impact of her presence had driven away all of the eloquent, romantic speeches he had been rehearsing in his mind.

After a strained silence, she said, ''I have good news. I'm almost certain that...that I am with child.''

His first reaction was delight, but that was instantly shadowed by the implications. Augusta

Vangelder had told him that once her daughter conceived, she was not to be troubled by husbandly lust. The fact that Sunny was brandishing the possibility of her pregnancy like a shield was clear proof that she welcomed the excuse to ban him from her bed.

His fingers whitened around the handle of the dagger. If she bore a son, her obligation to the Aubrey name would be fulfilled, and their marriage would effectively be over. Driving the dagger into his belly would have hurt less than that thought.

During the last lonely month, he had resolved to take advantage of the quiet intimacy of the marital bed to speak more openly to his wife. If she was willing, perhaps they could build a closer, warmer relationship. Now that hope was gone; any discussions between them must endure the harsh light of day.

Knowing that the silence had been too long, he said, "Excellent. I hope you are feeling well?"

She nodded.

After another awkward pause, he said, "Good. We shall have to get a London physician here to make sure that your health is all it should be." He laid the dagger precisely on top of his correspondence so that the letters would not blow away in the wind. "You need not worry that I will continue to…force my attentions on you."

"Very well." She bent her head, and a slight shiver passed through her. Relief, perhaps. "I'm a bit tired. I think that I'll skip dinner and have a tray in my room.''

Thinking that she looked pale, he said, ''Of course. You must take good care of yourself.''

Back straight and head high, she turned and started down the grassy path. Every inch a lady, and as unapproachable as Queen Victoria herself.

He watched her leave, very aware of what an effort it was to breathe. Inhale, exhale. Inhale, exhale. He had been breathing all his life, yet never noticed before how difficult it was.

There was a tearing sensation deep inside, as if his heart was literally breaking, and he knew that he could not let the deadly silence continue. He called out, ''Sunny!''

She halted, then turned slowly to face him. In the shadows cast by the tall boxwoods that lined the path, he could not see her face clearly.

He stepped from the folly and moved toward her, then stopped when she tensed. ''Sunny, I want to apologize for what I did at Cottenham. I am profoundly sorry for distressing you.''

''You were within your rights, and your anger was justified,'' she said expressionlessly.

''Perhaps, but that doesn't make it right to mistreat you. It won't happen again.''

''Should I be grateful for that?'' she said with sudden, chilling bitterness. ''That night was upsetting, but it was also the one time in our marriage that you have shown any feelings about me. I have begun to think that even anger is better than indifference.''

The gay ribbons on her gown shivered as she bowed her head and pressed her fingertips to her brow. When she looked up, her eyes were bleak. ''We can't continue to live together as strangers, Justin. I can't endure it any longer.''

Her words struck with the force of a blow, nearly destroying his fragile control. It seemed impossible that their marriage could be ending like this, on a day full of sunlight and promise. Yet he could not hold her against her will; somehow he must find the strength to let her go. ''If you wish to be free of me,'' he said tightly, ''I will set no barriers in your way.''

Her mouth twisted. ''Is that what you want—to end our marriage now that you have your damned roof?''

''I want you to be happy, Sunny.'' Hearing the anguish in his voice, he stopped until he could continue more steadily. ''And I will do anything in my power that might make you so.''

The air between them seemed to thicken, charged with indefinable emotions. Then she said passionately, ''What I want is to be a real wife! To be part of your life, not just another expensive bauble in Swindon Palace.'' Her hands clenched at her sides. ''Or perhaps I should wish to be your mistress, since English lords seem to save their hearts for women who are not their wives.''

Stunned, he stammered, "I don't understand."

"It's a simple matter, Justin. I want you to love me," she said softly. "Do you think that you ever could? Because I'm horribly afraid that I love you."

He felt as if his heart had stopped. Her declaration was so unexpected that it seemed she must be mocking him. Yet it was impossible to doubt the transparent honesty in her eyes.

Before he could find the words to answer, her face crumpled and she spun away from him. "Dear God, I'm making a fool of myself, aren't I? Like the brash, vulgar American that I am. Please—forget that I ever spoke."

Justin's paralysis dissolved and he caught her arm and swung her around before she could dart down the path. To his horror, tears were coursing down her face. The sight delivered a final, shattering blow to his reserve. Crushing her in his arms, he said urgently, "Don't cry, Sunny. If you want my love, you already have it. You always have."

Though her tears intensified, she did not pull away. Instead, she wrapped her arms around him and hid her face in the angle between his throat and shoulder. She was all pliant warmth, honeyed hair and the promise of wild violets.

He groped for the best way to tell her how much he loved her until he realized that words had always failed and divided them. Action would better demonstrate the depth of his caring. He raised her head and brushed back her silky hair, then kissed her with all of the hunger of his yearning spirit.

Salty with tears, her lips clung to his, open and seeking.

Subtle currents flowed between them—despair and comfort, wonder and promise, trust and surrender. In the stark honesty of desperation, there was no place for shame or doubt or misunderstanding. One by one, the barriers that had divided them crumbled away to reveal the shy grandeur of love.

At first the sweetness of discovery was enough, but as the kiss deepened and lengthened, sweetness slowly blossomed into fire. Murmuring her name like a prayer, he kneaded the soft curves that lay unconstrained beneath her flowing gown. She pressed against him, breathless and eager, and he drew her down to the sun-warmed grass.

They had had dutiful conjugal relations, and once they had come together with chaotic, disquieting passion. This time, they made love. She yielded herself utterly, for the awesome needs of her body no longer frightened her now that she knew she was loved.

Rippling layers of green silk were easily brushed aside, buttons undone, ribbons untied. Then, too impatient to wait until they were fully disrobed, they joined in the dance of desire. Swift and fierce, their union was a potent act of mutual possession that bound them into one spirit and one flesh.

Only afterward, as she lay languidly in the haven

of his arms, did she realize the scandalousness of her behavior. The Duchess of Thornborough was lying half-naked in the garden, as bold as any dairymaid in a haystack. How strange. How shocking. How right.

His head lay pillowed on her shoulder, and she slid her fingers into his tousled dark hair. "How is it possible for us to say so much to each other in ten minutes when we didn't speak a single word?" she asked dreamily.

"Words are limiting. They can only hint at an emotion as powerful as love. Passion comes closer because it is itself all feeling." Justin rolled to his side and propped himself up on one elbow, his other arm draped over her waist to hold her close. Smiling into her eyes, he said, "For someone who seemed to hate being touched, you have developed a remarkable talent for physical intimacy."

She blushed. "At first I was afraid of the unknown. It wasn't long until I began to look forward to your visits, but I was ashamed of my desire. And…and my mother said that a man would never respect an immodest woman who reveled in her lower nature."

"In this area, your mother's understanding is sadly limited. There may be men like that, but for me, the knowledge that we can share our bodies with mutual pleasure is the greatest of all gifts." He leaned over and dropped a light kiss on the end of her nose. "Let us make a pact, my love—to pay no attention to what the world might say, and care only about what the two of us feel.''

With one hand, she unbuttoned the top of his shirt and slipped her fingers inside so she could caress his warm, bare skin. ''I think that is a wonderful idea. I only wish that we had started sooner. I was so sure that you married me only because you needed my fortune.''

Expression serious, he said, ''Don't ever doubt that I love you, Sunny. I have since the first time we met, when you were the Gilded Girl and I was an insignificant younger son who could never dare aspire to your hand.''

Her eyes widened. ''We hardly even spoke that day.''

''On the contrary—we walked through the gardens for the better part of an hour. I could take you along the exact route, and repeat everything you said. It was the most enchanting experience of my life.'' His mouth quirked up wryly. ''And you don't remember it at all, do you?''

''I do remember that I enjoyed your company, but I was meeting so many people then. You were simply a quiet, attractive man who didn't seem interested in me.'' She looked searchingly into his eyes. ''If you loved me, why didn't you say so sooner?''

''I tried, but you never wanted to hear.'' He began lazily stroking her bare arm. ''Since it never occurred to me that you could love me, there was no reason to burden you with my foolish emotions, even if I had known how to do it.''

A vivid memory of his proposal flashed through her mind. He had said then that she had had his heart from the moment they met. There had been other occasions when he had haltingly tried to declare himself, plus a thousand small signs of caring, from his wedding orchids to the way he had risked his life to rescue a puppy for her. Yet because of her pain over Paul's betrayal and her conviction that Justin had married her only for money, she had spurned his hesitant words and gestures, convinced that they were polite lies. Dear heaven, no wonder he had preferred to conceal his feelings.

''I'm the one who must apologize. Because I was hurting, I ended up hurting you as well.'' She laid her hand along his firm jaw, thinking how handsome he looked with that tender light in his eyes. ''Yet you were always kind to me.''

He turned his head and pressed a kiss into her palm. ''We gargoyles are known for kindness.''

''I *hate* that nickname,'' she said vehemently. ''How can people be so cruel? You are intelligent, amusing, considerate, and a gentleman in the best sense of the word.''

''I'm very glad you think so, but society loves cleverness, and a good quip counts for more than a good heart,'' he said with dry amusement. ''The fact that you love me is clear proof that much of love comes from simple proximity.''

"Nonsense," she said tartly. "Proximity can just as easily breed dislike. But it's true that I would never have learned to love you if we hadn't married. You are not an easy man to know."

"I'm sorry, my dear." He sighed. "As you know, my mother can be...difficult. I learned early that to show emotions was to risk having them used against me, so I became first-rate at concealing what I felt. Unfortunately, that made me at a flat loss at saying what matters most. I promise that from now on, I will say that I love you at least once a day."

"I'd rather have that than the Thornborough tiara." Shyly she touched her abdomen, which as yet showed no sign of the new life within. "Are you happy about the baby? You didn't seem very interested."

"I'm awed and delighted." A shadow crossed his face. "If my reaction seemed unenthusiastic, it was because I feared that if it was a boy, you would go off to Paris or New York and never want to see me again."

"What a dreadful thought." She shivered. "May I ask a favor?"

"Anything, Sunny. Always." He laced his fingers through hers, then drew their joined hands to his heart.

"I would very much like it if we slept together every night, like people who can't afford two bedrooms do." Her mouth curved playfully. "Even with central heating, it's often chilly here."

He laughed. "I would like nothing better. I've always hated leaving you to go back to my own cold and lonely bed."

"We can start a new fashion for togetherness." She lifted their clasped hands and lovingly kissed his fingertips.

He leaned over and claimed her mouth, and the embers of passion began glowing with renewed life. As he slid his hand into the loose neckline of her gown, he murmured, "We're both wearing entirely too many clothes, especially for such a fine day."

Remembering their surroundings, she said breathlessly, "Justin, don't you dare! We have already behaved disgracefully enough for one day."

"Mmm?" He pulled her gown from her shoulder so that he could kiss her breasts, a process that rendered her quite unable to talk. She had not known that there was such pleasure in the whole world.

She made one last plea for sanity as he began stripping off his coat. "If someone comes along this path and sees us, what will they say?"

"They'll say that the Duke of Thornborough loves his wife very much." He smiled into her eyes with delicious wickedness. "And they'll be right."

* * * * *

Dear Reader,

These days, we tend to think that marrying for love is the only acceptable grounds for committing matrimony, but historically marriages have usually been contracted for more practical reasons such as money, or social gain or to build political bridges between opposing interests. Or simply because the families involved thought it a good idea.

But after the wedding is over and family and duty have been satisfied, there are two people left warily eyeing each other across a bed and wondering about this stranger whom they have married. Whatever the reason for the marriage, these people are now stuck with each other, and it's in their best interests to work together to make their relationship as rewarding as possible. This is why the marriage-of-convenience plot is endlessly interesting. Even someone we've known for years is a stranger in many ways. How much more exciting—and alarming—it is to have the wedding first, and hope to fall in love later!

Marriages between rich or famous people intrigue me in particular, because to the outside world such people seem larger than life, beyond the needs and insecurities of average folk. Yet often the appearance of being above mundane problems is an illusion. *The Wedding of the Century* was inspired by the real-life marriage of Consuelo Vanderbilt and the ninth Duke of Marlborough, which was a huge media sensation in its day.

Though that marriage ended in divorce after two sons were born, the facts stimulated my imagination to create a version of my own. Justin may be Duke of Thornborough, but at heart he is a quiet, honorable man with the cynical knowledge that it is his title women covet, not himself. Though Sunny is a great heiress, the subject of endless gossip and speculation, she is also a very nice girl who likes gardens and mongrel dogs, and is intimidated by her mother-in-law.

The challenge in *Wedding of the Century* is for the Duke and the Heiress to find the real person hidden behind the glittering image. Naturally they do—this is a romance after all!—but happiness can't be bought. It must be earned, even for the rich and famous. I hope you enjoy watching Sunny and Justin work their way through the maze of publicity and expectations to find each other.

Mary Jo Putney

To my husband, Al, who once trudged twenty blocks in a torrential downpour to the London bookstore that had the *one* Georgette Heyer novel I hadn't yet read. Is that true love, or what?

MISMATCHED HEARTS
by Merline Lovelace

Chapter One

"Good morning, Trevor."

Trevor Alcott lifted his head from the stack of papers he'd been sorting through. He rose politely as his employer strolled into the well-appointed library on the second floor of the St. Germaine London town house a little before noon on a balmy April morning.

"Good morning, Sir."

Sunlight streamed through the library windows and illuminated the features and figure of Giles Moore, fourth Baron St. Germaine. While the more romantic of the young debutantes who'd tried in vain to capture the baron's affection these past several years tended to rhapsodize about raven locks styled à la Brutus and blue eyes that smiled at one in the *most* devastating way, Trevor, a serious young man hoping to make his mark in the political world at some later point in his career, knew his employer rather better than most.

He'd seen those seemingly lazy blue eyes cut like a rapier into anyone so unwise as to rouse his ire. This rarely happened, however. The baron was possessed of the even, some said controlling, temperament that had allowed him to take the reins of a large, rambunctious family at a very young age upon the untimely death of his father. Shrewd investments on St. Germaine's part had vastly increased the modest fortune left him and his younger siblings. Exhibiting a maturity well beyond his years, he'd managed his affairs and restored the ramshackle family estate to something approaching its original magnificence.

With the ease of manner that made Trevor feel far more like a welcome member of St. Germaine's large household than the third son of a country curate, the baron invited his secretary to resume his seat.

"Sharpen your quill, Trevor. We must compose a notice to *The Times*."

"*The Times*, Sir?"

"Yes. To announce my betrothal."

The secretary's jaw dropped ludicrously. "Your be-betrothal?"

A smile lurked at the back of St. Germaine's eyes. "Yes, I'm quite astonished myself that any woman would accept my suit, but there's no accounting for tastes, is there?"

Just in time, Trevor caught back the very improper suggestion that his employer cut line! Both

men were well aware that the baron constituted a
matrimonial prize of the first order. His quite substantial wealth aside, he carried himself with just
the sort of style and elegance that must please any
woman, as his fond mama so often pointed out to
anyone who cared to listen.

Trevor agreed with the doting and justifiably
prejudiced Lady St. Germaine. There was nothing
of the dandy about the baron. He affected no ex-
travagance of style, sported no startling waistcoats.
Nor did he pad his coats or indulge in exaggerated
shirt points so starched and high as to render the
wearer unable to turn his head.

Indeed, St. Germaine required no padding to emphasize his wide shoulders and tall, muscled frame.
He allowed Weston's subtle handiwork, apparent
in the exquisite tailoring of the coat of green Bath
superfine, to speak for itself. He disdained such
absurdities as gold tassels on his polished Hes-
sians, and wore no jewelry other than a signet ring
and a modest gold pin securing the folds of his
snowy linen neckcloth.

"I beg your pardon, Sir," Trevor said, recovering his wits. "Since you stated just last week that
Sir Harry's deplorable habit of pledging his heart
to the most, er, ineligible women was enough to
put you off the idea of matrimony for the rest of
your natural life, you must forgive my surprise."

The smile in St. Germaine's eyes deepened, but
he shrugged aside this reminder of how he'd been

obliged to extricate his brother from yet another folly—an opera dancer of glorious proportions and an extremely grasping nature.

"Harry's but feeling his oats a bit since he recovered from his wounds," he said mildly.

Privately, Trevor thought the former lieutenant had been feeling more than just oats since recovering from the fever that had nearly carried him off. He'd sustained a gunshot wound to the shoulder in an attack by Bedouins in the distant deserts of Arabia. The wound had gone putrid during the long sea voyage home and had come close to costing Sir Harry his life.

Lady St. Germaine had almost fainted when her second son was carried through the front door, so pale and feverish. She'd vowed to wear herself to the bone nursing the poor boy back to health. Everyone belowstairs was well aware, however, that it was the baron who'd gone without sleep night after night, forcing noxious draughts down his brother's throat and holding him fast when he thrashed about in delirium.

After that harrowing experience, it was only to be expected that the lieutenant would decide to sell out of the army. He described regimental life as a dead bore in peacetime, anyway, except for the occasional jolly encounter with rascals like those wily Bedouins. Shedding his uniform, he embarked on a course of lively dissipation natural to young men of independent means and healthy appetites.

Curate's son that he was, Trevor couldn't quite approve of opera dancers and Covent Garden flower girls, but would certainly never venture to say so. Instead, he dipped his quill in the inkwell, drew forward a fresh sheet of foolscap, and applied himself to the task the baron had charged him with.

"I'd be most happy to compose a notice to *The Times,* Sir, if you'd care to share with me the name of your betrothed."

Extracting an exquisitely enameled snuff box, St. Germaine flipped it open with his thumb. "The Lady Chrysanthe Ayers has graciously accepted my suit."

"Lady Chrysanthe!"

Giles took a pinch of his private blend, put up for him by Masters Dawes and Dun, and hid his amusement at the reverential awe in his secretary's voice. Chrysanthe had that effect on men of all ages.

The daughter of his father's oldest friend, whose lands marched with those of St. Germaine, Lady Chrysanthe had arrived in town only a month ago to make her debut under the auspices of her god-mama. Kindhearted Lady St. Germaine had long ago promised the girl's dear, dear departed mama that she would launch her little Chrysanthe in style. And so she had, with a rout party attended, much to her delight and fluttery consternation, by the Prince Regent himself.

Prinny, like every other man in the room, had

fallen instantly under the spell of the slender goddess with shining, silver-blond hair, rosebud mouth and eyes the color of winter violets. The aging prince's stays had creaked alarmingly when he'd bent to ogle the furiously blushing Chrysanthe through his quizzing glass.

Even Giles had felt his stomach clench at the sight of the girl he'd known all her life rigged out for her first season. He'd certainly entertained no thought of marrying her, however. He was in no hurry to set up his nursery, and truth be told he'd always considered Chrysanthe a lovely widget, with more sensibility than sense behind that incomparable face. Four weeks with her residing under his roof had *not* altered his opinion.

Then Lord Ayers, Chrysanthe's father and the third Baron St. Germaine's closest friend, had made the fatal mistake of traveling up to the city to see how his little puss was taking. Unused to late town hours and the deep play at Waiters and Whites, the bluff Ayers had recklessly wagered far more than he could afford on the roll of the dice. In a desperate attempt to come about, he'd signed chit after chit, sinking deeper in his cups and into debt with each flourish of his pen.

Luck had not been with him that night.

Or the nights that followed.

Which was why Giles had received an urgent missive from his father's old friend two days ago. And why, just last night, the Lady Chrysanthe, her cheeks pale and her magnificent eyes awash with maidenly tears, had stammered that yes, indeed, her father had told her of Giles's extremely flattering offer and...and...she was most honored to accept.

Giles had dropped a kiss on the perfect bow of her mouth, felt it tremble beneath his, and told himself they'd contrive as well as any other couple in a marriage of convenience. It wasn't as if he'd formed a lasting passion for another woman, nor even imagined himself in love. So he'd offered, and Chrysanthe had accepted, and now he had to set about retrieving his prospective father-in-law from the River Tick.

"When you finish the notice to *The Times*," he instructed Trevor, "would you be so good as to send a note to my man of business? Tell him I wish to draw up the settlements as soon as possible for Lord Ayers to review."

"Yes, my lord. And I'll..."

The sound of the library door opening turned their heads. John Nethersby, who'd begun his career as a third footman to the second Baron St. Germaine some forty-five years ago and worked his way up to the exalted position of butler, entered with a measured tread.

"Excuse me for interrupting, my lord. There's a young woman downstairs, accompanied by a companion." His tone dismissed the companion as being of no consequence. "She asked to see Sir Harry."

"Did she?"

"I told her he wasn't to home," Nethersby continued, his countenance wooden, "not wanting to let her know he maintains separate lodgings."

"For which Harry will profoundly thank you," Giles drawled. Particularly since the little opera dancer had made several unannounced and embarrassingly unexpected visits to his apartments.

"The young woman then asked to see Lady St. Germaine."

Giles stiffened. He might look with tolerant amusement on his brother's excess of inamoratas, but in no way would he allow those excesses to impinge upon his mother.

"Is there some reason you didn't show this young woman and her companion the door?"

For the first time, Nethersby lost some of his stately composure. "She's not quite..." Frowning, he cast about for words. "Not quite in Sir Harry's usual style."

Like any butler worth his salt, Nethersby could depress the pretensions of mushrooming cits or an importuning tradesman with a single loft of a gray eyebrow. That he hadn't done so with this particular visitor told Giles he'd best deal with her himself.

"Very well. Show her up."

While Nethersby trod back downstairs, the ever-discreet Trevor gathered up his papers and departed the library. Idly wondering just what sort of female Harry had become entangled with this time, Giles leaned a hip against the desk and twirled the massive globe in its mahogany stand. His eye fell on the pins his fifteen-year-old sister Amelia had stuck in the globe. The pins tracked Harry's route when he'd shipped out last December as part of the military escort for a scientific expedition.

The Royal Geographical Society and a private firm of cartographers had mounted a survey effort, spurred by the defeated Napoleon's grandiose scheme to reopen the canal originally dug by the pharaohs to connect the Mediterranean and Red seas. The expedition had been ill-starred, its distinguished surveyor succumbing to fever some months into the project and its military escort forced to fight off attacks by fierce Bedouins. Yet Harry, when he'd recovered from his brush with death, had termed it a jolly escapade.

What extraordinary events his brother had participated in during the past few years, Giles thought. First with the 13th Hussars at Waterloo, then this excursion to Egypt.

As he stared down at the gold-embossed borders of the distant land, a feeling of suffocation rose in his throat. He fought an almost overpowering urge to abandon all responsibilities, throw off his many burdens, and, like Harry, plunge into danger and excitement. Just for a day. Perhaps two.

His palm slapped the globe, halting its slow spin. He was two and thirty, for pity's sake. The head of his household since his seventeenth birthday. How ridiculous to feel so trapped just because he'd pledged to marry a teary-eyed slip of a girl who...

"Miss Isabella Chessington, Sir."

The name struck a chord in Giles's memory, but the female who nodded her thanks to Nethersby and swept into the library was a complete stranger. Had he met her before, he wouldn't have forgotten her tall, slender frame and unfashionably tanned complexion. Nor that pair of speaking gray eyes and rich auburn hair tucked neatly into a bonnet.

With a socially gregarious mother, three lively sisters, and a series of discreet liaisons to his credit, Giles was no stranger to feminine fashion. He saw at once that his visitor's poke bonnet with its slightly bedraggled ostrich plume was sadly out of date, as was her braided and frogged pelisse, which covered a gown of twilled muslin, rather dusty at its hem. Yet, Giles noted, she carried herself with an assurance quite at odds with her outmoded attire.

"How good of you to receive me, my lord. I'm sorry to have forced myself upon you at such an early hour, but Mrs. Walsh and I only just posted up to London from Dover, you see, and since Harry swears you're such a..." dimples appeared in her cheeks, "...such a *right one,* I thought not to stand on ceremony with you."

Nethersby was right, Giles decided, swiftly reordering his thoughts. She was *not* in Harry's usual style. Despite her unfashionable appearance, she had a touch of quality about her.

Damn Harry! he thought on a spear of anger. With all the willing opera dancers and Covent Garden misses available, he had to play fast and loose with the shabby-genteel. Giles suspected it would cost him far more to extricate his brother from this imbroglio than the last.

"No, there's no need for us to stand on ceremony, Miss...Chessington, is it?"

He salted his voice with a polite disinterest that halted her in her tracks. A look of dismay crossed her face. She stared at him for a long moment, then burst into musical laughter. The rippling sound took Giles aback, and caused the most extraordinary reaction within his chest.

He was no green youth. Although more discreet and far more discriminating than Harry, he'd never lacked for female companionship. Yet not one of his very talented, very expensive mistresses had ever generated such an intense and immediate desire to kiss her ripe, laughing mouth.

No little annoyed by this unexpected lust for his brother's bit of muslin, Giles stood impassive as she tilted her head and surveyed him with merry eyes.

"You haven't the least idea who I am, do you?"

"No."

Instead of casting her down, the blunt reply elicited another choke of laughter.

"How like Harry!" she exclaimed in mingled amusement and exasperation. "I *told* him it wasn't quite the thing. Yet nothing would do but that I should come to London as soon as I might and let him take me under his protection. Of course, he was a bit out of his head at the time he extracted that promise..."

"Foxed, was he?"

"No, at least I don't *think* so. Although he did guzzle the better part of a bottle of brandy before the surgeon cut into his shoulder."

"The surgeon?"

Giles felt a frown snap into place. Had Harry injured his shoulder again? What the devil kind of scrape was he in now?

"Did he not tell you about his skirmish in the desert?" The visitor's smile took on a whimsical tilt. "That, too, is just like him. He's so foolishly brave and handsomely foolish, is he not?"

At this point Giles began to suspect he'd seriously misjudged the situation. Not only had this unusual young woman pegged his brother's character with unerring accuracy, but the connection between them appeared to be more long-standing than Giles had supposed.

His suspicion was confirmed a moment later

when her gaze alighted on an object beside the desk. Delight suffused her expressive face.

"You have one of Papa's globes!"

Brushing past him, she laid a hand on the massive orb and tenderly traced the outlines of the distant land Giles had been staring at just moments ago. When she turned her face up to his once again, her mouth trembled just a bit at the corners.

"I'm afraid these borders are somewhat inaccurate...or will be when I have delivered Papa's last surveys to the globe-makers."

Of course! Giles berated himself for being so slow to place her name. Sir Arthur Chessington had headed the survey team Harry's troop had escorted into the deserts along the Nile. She must have read his dawning comprehension in his face. Her enchanting dimples made another appearance.

"I see I have confused you completely." Smiling, she held out a hand gloved in worn lavender kid. "Shall we begin again?"

Slowly, Giles took her hand in his. A small shock jolted through him when his fingers folded around the warm, supple kidskin.

Damn Harry! he thought again, just before he looked down and lost his heart to a pair of dancing gray eyes.

"How do you do, Baron St. Germaine?" she said in her lilting way. "I'm Isabella Chessington, daughter of Sir Arthur Chessington and your brother's affianced wife."

Chapter Two

Sir Harry, summoned from his bachelor apartments by a somewhat terse note from his older brother, received the news that Isabella Chessington had arrived in London this very morning with goggle-eyed astonishment.

"Never say it! Belle's here?"

"She is," Giles corroborated with a touch of acid. "She's upstairs with Mama. Who, I might add, professes herself as surprised as I that you somehow forgot to inform your family of the attachment between you and Miss Chessington."

"Attachment? Well, I suppose you might call it that." Harry's careless shrug tightened his brother's jaw. "We did become quite close on the march."

"So I would gather," Giles drawled.

A tall, handsome young man, Harry thrust a hand through his brown locks. His blue eyes, a shade paler than his brother's, kindled with memories.

"Belle's a regular trooper. She's been racketing about to the most outlandish places with her father from the time she was in short skirts, you know."

"No, how should I?"

Ignoring the sardonic reply, Harry warmed to his topic. "I tell you, that girl is pluck to the backbone. You should have seen her in the desert, Giles. She scribbled notes for Sir Arthur in the fiercest heat and scrambled into the saddle of her camel with hardly a boost. She's a crack shot, too. Always insisted on loading her own pistol. Damned if she didn't trim the wick on an oil lamp from thirty paces when we got up a shooting match for fun one night."

Somehow, Harry's revelations didn't surprise Giles. His short acquaintance with Miss Chessington had given him the impression she was a rather remarkable young woman. He said nothing, however, as Harry's reminisces gave way to less pleasant memories.

"She nursed Sir Arthur all through that devilish bout of fever. Near broke her heart when he died, but she stood solid as a wheelbarrow when we buried him, then finished his notes on the march back to Cairo. She was riding beside me when those plaguey Bedouins attacked."

Giles watched him intently. To this point, his account of the ill-fated expedition dovetailed with that of Miss Chessington's, although she hadn't reflected on her own accomplishments, only on her father's...and Harry's. She'd recounted in glowing terms the dashing young lieutenant's bravery during the attack, and how he'd rallied his men for a daring counteroffensive.

"When I took that hit, damned if she didn't stuff her handkerchief in the hole in my shoulder and snatch up my rifle," Harry related, beaming in remembered admiration. "Gave a good account of herself, too."

"A most redoubtable female."

"Indeed, she is! I don't remember much after that little skirmish. Dashed nuisance, losing all that blood. Got back to Cairo the next day, that much I recall. Then the colonel insisted on shipping me home. I think—" his forehead creased "—yes, I'm sure I tried to get Belle to take ship with me. Egypt's no place for a female alone. Not sure how she managed after that," Harry confessed with a frown. "Damned fever grabbed me."

"She hired the widow of one of the troopers to act as her chaperone while she tended to her father's affairs," Giles informed him. "That done, she sailed for England to join her betrothed."

"She went and got herself engaged?" Harry's face lit up with unalloyed delight. "Good for her! Sir Arthur was all the family she had. Hate to think of her without someone to protect her. Not that Isabella needs protection, mind you. But she's lived in the most outlandish places all her life and I daresay even she would find London a bit overwhelming without someone to show her the ropes. Besides, I've no doubt her father left her without a feather to fly with. Brilliant, you know, but a bit potty."

If this artless disclosure hadn't confirmed the suspicion that had been forming in Giles's mind for some time, Harry's next question would have done the trick.

"Who's she getting leg-shackled to?"

"You, it appears."

His brother's jaw sagged. Eyes popping, he stared at Giles with much the same expression as a carp startled from a muddy river bed. Sighing, St. Germaine mentally assembled the various pieces of the puzzle and laid them before his stunned sibling.

"It seems you suffered an excess of chivalry along with that hit to your shoulder. Miss Chessington informs me you offered her your heart as well as the protection of your name during the trek back to Cairo."

Actually, Miss Chessington had dimpled in that delightful way of hers and said that Harry had labeled her a great gun and swore he could never, ever, admire any female as much as he did her.

"She refused you, she tells me. Several times. But you became so agitated just before they carried you aboard ship that she relented and promised to join you here in London as soon as she could.''

''But...but....''

''Yes?''

The cool rejoinder cut through Harry's stammering incoherence. Swallowing, he drew himself up.

''If Isabella says I offered for her, I'm sure I did. Must have been the fever that put it out of my head. She's a great girl,'' he reiterated, squaring his shoulders. ''Be most fortunate man alive to have her as my wife.''

The brothers' eyes met. Understanding passed between them. The sense of honor that had been bred into their bones couldn't allow Harry to act differently, any more than it had Giles.

Seeing the resolution in his eyes, Giles abandoned his half-formed intent of extricating his brother from yet another entanglement. His brief acquaintance with Miss Chessington had stirred something deep within him. Harry could do worse than wed such an extraordinary woman.

Far worse.

Thrusting aside the thought of his own lachrymose fiancée, he strode forward and clasped his brother's arm.

''If you really intend to marry her, I will wish you happy. And you must do the same for me. Chrysanthe graciously accepted my offer last night.''

"The devil you say!"

Giles lifted a brow at this unflattering reaction to his own piece of news.

"The silly twit will bore you to flinders within a week of your wedding!" Harry expostulated, surprised into brutal candor. He, like his brother, had known the beauteous Chrysanthe since she was in leading strings.

The baron leveled a warning look. "I shall excuse you this time."

"Dash it, Giles, you can't want to tie yourself to such a watering pot!"

"But *only* this time, Harry."

The message was unmistakable. His brother bit his lip. After a moment, he was forced to accept that, for whatever reasons of his own, Giles had indeed bound himself to Chrysanthe.

"Very well," he conceded gruffly. "If that's the way the land lies, I wish you joy."

"Thank you."

In a mood far more somber than one would expect of two men about to enter the happy state of matrimony, the brothers climbed the stairs to join their mother, Miss Chessington and the dour widow who'd accompanied the explorer's daughter back to England.

The ladies seated in the upstairs sitting room greeted their arrival with varying degrees of relief and impatience.

Lady St. Germaine because she was feeling more than a little overwhelmed by the astonishing fact that she'd acquired not one but two prospective daughters-in-law in a space of mere hours.

Mrs. Walsh, because she wished to discharge her duties as chaperone and travel straight on to Kent, where she planned to take up residence with her elderly sister.

And Isabella because she'd discovered the dashing young lieutenant who'd pressed such ardent offers of marriage on her not four months ago appeared to have forgotten her existence.

Since she'd inherited a lively sense of the ridiculous from Sir Arthur along with his adventuresome spirit, Belle was more amused than dismayed. Really, it was too bad of Harry to have placed them all in such an awkward position, but his mama had explained that he'd been out of his head with delirium for weeks after his return to England. After such a debilitating experience, Belle could certainly understand how he might have forgotten such a trifling matter as an offer of marriage.

She was, if nothing else, a very practical girl. One had to be, when junketing about with a father more concerned with plotting latitudes and shooting azimuths than such mundane concerns as whether dried camel dung would burn hot enough to boil sufficient water for drinking and washing one's stockings.

It was in this spirit of practicality that she'd accepted Harry's last, almost feverish offer. Although she'd been reared with extraordinary freedoms unknown to most females of her station, Belle understood the way of the world. With her father's death, she'd faced a choice between the life of a somewhat eccentric spinster or the more conventional role of married woman. Since she possessed what she recognized as very natural urgings for marital intimacy and sincerely hoped to hold a babe of her own in her arms one day, she'd sensibly decided on marriage.

If she didn't love Harry with anything approaching the passion symbolized by the Taj Mahal built by Shah Jehan, for his beloved consort, which an awed Isabella had toured some years ago, she had certainly enjoyed the lieutenant's company during the expedition. What's more, she was female enough to admit he had cut a very dashing figure in his regimentals.

The Harry who smiled warmly and strode forward to greet her looked far different from the handsome lieutenant of her memories, however. In fact, Belle's first startled thought was that he looked rather silly. She'd been out of touch with current fashions for some time now, but *surely* skin-tight pantaloons in a delicate shade of primrose, garishly embroidered waistcoats hung with half a dozen fobs and starched shirt points reaching clear up a fellow's cheeks couldn't have become the latest in masculine attire?

Involuntarily, her glance shifted to the man who entered the room just behind Harry. St. Germaine's smooth-fitting buckskins and exquisitely tailored coat of Bath superfine were far more to Isabella's taste, but she banished the disloyal thought and dimpled prettily when Harry lifted her hands to kiss them.

"I say, Belle, you could have knocked me over with a feather when Giles told me you'd arrived in London."

Imps of mischief danced in her gray eyes. "I understand you weren't expecting me."

"No, I dashed well wa—" He caught himself, flushing. "Thing is, didn't know precisely when you would arrive. Glad you're finally here. And just at the right time, too. Giles is about to announce his engagement. We can puff ours off at the same time, do it all up right and tight with suppers and balls and such."

Belle searched his face. Behind those determinedly cheerful blue eyes she was sure she detected something akin to the desperation of a trapped hare.

With only a small inner wrench, she put aside any thought of marriage to Harry. She could live very happily without great passion, or so she believed. And she would not hold a man to a promise he hadn't even remembered making. Casting about

for a way to bring them both out of this bumble-
bath without embarrassing him further in front of
his family, she gave his hands a gentle squeeze and
tugged hers free.

"Let's not plan any announcements for the present. I've only just arrived, and we didn't have time
to really discuss our future before you left Cairo,
did we?"

"Nothing to discuss. We'll announce our betrothal with a splash and I'll introduce you to all
my friends. You'll like 'em," he promised with
engaging charm.

"You couldn't wish to introduce me to *anyone*
looking as I do," she countered, laughing. "I'm
sadly out of fashion and must refurbish my wardrobe as soon as may be. If I can prevail on my
dear Mrs. Walsh to put off her departure for Kent
and lend me countenance for another few days,
we'll settle at a hotel. You may come visit me there
and we'll talk."

At this point, Harry's surmise that Sir Arthur
had left Miss Chessington in straitened circumstances played heavily on Giles's mind. Smoothly,
he intervened.

"There's no need for Mrs. Walsh to delay her
departure or for you to take up residence at a hotel.
You'll stay with us, of course, and let Mama take
you about to all the shops. No doubt she'll wish to
include my betrothed in these expeditions as well,
for Lady Chrysanthe, like you, has no mother to

share with her the delights of selecting her bride clothes.''

With a mental note to make sure his mama directed all bills for both Miss Chessington and Chrysanthe be forwarded to him, Giles sent Lady St. Germaine an inquiring glance. She blinked at this arbitrary ordering of her time, but agreed with the good-natured complaisance for which her children adored her.

''Yes, I would enjoy showing you about above all things! And we shall hold a ball to announce your betrothal,'' she decided, throwing herself into the spirit of things. ''Yours, too, Giles, if you and Chrysanthe should care to wait a week or two to make a formal announcement.''

Giles buried the instant and most traitorous thought that he would gladly wait a year or more. ''I've no objection,'' he said politely, ''if Chrysanthe doesn't.''

''I'm sure she won't,'' Lady St. Germaine replied. ''There, it's settled. Do say you'll stay with us, Miss Chessington. Or may I call you Isabella?''

''Please, call me Belle, as my own dear papa did. But I can't impose upon you like this.''

Rising, she pulled on her gloves. Lady St. Germaine cast an imploring look at her oldest son, seeking his guidance in this as she did in most matters.

Giles strolled forward, smiling. ''It's hardly an imposition for Harry's family to welcome the woman he's asked to be his wife. We shall feel quite slighted if you choose to rack up at an inn instead of with us.''

She hesitated, chewing on her lower lip in a way that drew his gaze to that smooth, ripe flesh.

Cursing inwardly, Giles wrenched his thoughts back in line. She was Harry's betrothed, for pity's sake, and had been thrust into a damnably awkward situation! If she hadn't recognized the shallowness of his brother's affection at the time he offered for her, she couldn't doubt now. She'd arrived in London to find herself not only unexpected by, but completely unknown to, his family. Silently, Giles castigated Harry yet again, and swore to do what he could to smooth over any doubts Miss Chessington might harbor about her future.

Isabella had, indeed, recognized the transitory nature of Harry's devotion, and now found herself somewhat at point non plus. Until she delivered Papa's surveys and notes to the distinguished firm of cartographers who'd financed his last expedition, and visited his solicitor, she didn't know the exact amount of her inheritance. She rather thought it would be enough to set her up comfortably with another companion for the rest of her life if she didn't marry at some future date. It would *certainly* cover the cost of a new wardrobe, which she so badly needed after her years abroad.

She hated to ask Mrs. Walsh to delay her departure for the week or so it would take to sort out these affairs. The widow was most anxious to finish her long journey. On the other hand, she much disliked continuing the farce of her engagement to Harry...particularly when Giles smiled down at her in a way that set her eminently practical heart to fluttering.

"No more argumentation," he said, once more taking charge. "You'll stay here and allow us all get to know you better. If it makes you feel more comfortable, we shan't announce your betrothal until you've had time to buy such fripperies as you desire and feel ready to meet Harry's friends."

"Yes, that would certainly make me more comfortable."

Harry, too, if the grateful look he cast his brother was any indication. Belle didn't blame him. She knew she looked the veriest dowd. Still, his almost palpable relief stung her pride. Lifting her chin, she met Giles's steady gaze. Her traitorous heart fluttered once again when he bent to drop a brotherly kiss on her cheek.

"Welcome to the family, Belle."

Until that moment Miss Chessington had thought herself immune to such passion as had inspired the Shah Jehan to construct the Taj Mahal for his beloved. To her astonishment, she felt the featherlight brush of Giles's lips all the way to her sensible walking boots.

Chapter Three

Within ten minutes of making Lady Chrysanthe's acquaintance, Belle had taken her measure. The girl was stunningly beautiful and as kind as a sunbeam, but two thoughts could *not* rub together inside her head at the same time.

After three days in her company, Belle had reached the inescapable conclusion that Chrysanthe and St. Germaine wouldn't suit, any more than she and Harry.

They were a busy three days. Lady St. Germaine had fallen wholeheartedly into her son's suggestion that she take charge of outfitting her prospective daughters-in-law. With great zest, she orchestrated such a flurry of visits to modistes, milliners, and bootmakers that even the redoubtable Belle could scarce catch her breath, much less snatch a half hour alone with Harry to inform him she had no intention of holding him to his promise.

Even more disconcerting to sensible, level-headed Belle, every chance meeting with Giles during those busy three days raised him in her esteem. For reasons she'd yet to admit, even to herself, she found herself watching him with the keen powers of observation that had made her such an invaluable assistant to Sir Arthur. St. Germaine was courteous to his household staff, lovingly attentive to his mother and a hero to his younger brothers and sisters, all of whom turned to him with every problem, great or small.

With his fiancée, he was gentle. Patient. Unfailingly polite, even when she stammered and blushed and groped for her handkerchief to dab at her eyes...which she did quite often.

For all St. Germaine's gentleness with the overly sensitive Chrysanthe, however, Belle could detect no note of ardent devotion in his voice when he addressed his betrothed.

Still, she had to banish a tiny pang on the third day of her visit when Giles, leaving the house on an errand of his own, bowed gracefully over Chrysanthe's hand and helped her into the St. Germaine town carriage for yet another shopping excursion. Nor could Belle halt the silly squeeze of her lungs when he turned to perform the same courtesy for her.

"You've been so busy these past days," he said, "I haven't had the opportunity to tell you how much that style of cut becomes you."

A sensible girl, Belle knew her new, feathery

auburn curls framed her face in a very flattering manner, but in no way brought her up to Chrysanthe's level of elegance. Laughing, she gathered her skirts in one hand and placed her other in St. Germaine's strong palm.

"I'll admit I don't miss my heavy braids. I shouldn't like to think what I would look like after two days in the desert, though, without Lady St. Germaine's dresser to wield her hot tongs and Chrysanthe to weave ribbons through all these ringlets."

His blue eyes smiled down at her from under the brim of his fawn-colored beaver hat, set at a jaunty angle on his brow. "I've no doubt you would look as enchanting as you do at this moment."

The rattle of carriage wheels on cobblestones faded. A slightly foggy April afternoon suddenly glowed golden. Belle curled her fingers in his and forgot how to breathe.

Giles, too, appeared to suffer a sudden affliction. He stiffened, and the smile in his eyes died, to be replaced by a slicing frown.

"Come, come, Giles," Lady St. Germaine called from the barouche, breaking the spell that held them both. "Do hand Belle up. We need to be on our way. We're off to choose ballgowns for Lady Cowper's fête, you know."

"No, I didn't." Recovering both his equanimity and his smile, he helped Belle into the carriage.

"No doubt Harry and his friends from the 13th

will fill your dance card as soon as you arrive at Lady Cowper's, but you must promise to save me one waltz, at least.''

With that, he bowed and headed for his own vehicle, a very sporty curricle drawn by rather restive matched grays, presently being held in check by his groom.

As she settled beside Chrysanthe and arranged her skirts, Belle made an instant change in her plans. She'd resolved to leave St. Germaine's house long before Lady Cowper's fête. In fact, she'd intended to visit not Lady St. Germaine's favorite modiste this afternoon, but the cartographers who'd financed her father's last expedition.

Tomorrow, she told herself firmly. She'd visit the cartographers tomorrow. And her talk with Harry could wait another week. They'd kept all knowledge of their betrothal within the family and put out only that Miss Chessington had come for a visit with Lady St. Germaine, a one-time friend of her late mother. It harmed no one if Belle continued her *tiny* deception for another week.

Just long enough to dance one waltz.

Only one.

She couldn't know, of course, that her *tiny* deception would lead to the most dire consequences, and on the very night of Lady Cowper's extravagant ball.

Belle took the first step along the path to disaster that same evening.

Harry and Giles were to escort their mama and their promised wives to the opera. Chrysanthe finished her toilette early and knocked on Belle's bedroom door with a gracious offer to help with hers. Dressed in a high-waisted gown of Imperial muslin in palest lilac, with a scarf of spangled gauze draped over her elbows and a lustrous string of pearls adorning her neck, she quite took the shine from Belle, who nevertheless considered herself passable in her new, puff-sleeved gown of figured ivory crepe.

The rich cream color was, perhaps, a shade too mature for an unmarried young woman, or so Lady St. Germaine had informed her protégée. But it set off her deep auburn curls to perfection and, she confided with a consoling pat on Belle's knee, would diminish just a bit the hue of her sunwarmed complexion.

With a shy smile at Lady St. Germaine's dresser, Chrysanthe laid the reticule that dangled from her wrist aside and begged to be allowed to arrange a set of gold and ivory combs in Belle's hair. Not even Buxton could deny the beauty's deft touch. Packing up her brushes and curling tongs, the stout dresser left the girls and went to attend her mistress.

While Chrysanthe carefully placed the combs, Belle smiled at her in the mirror. "You look especially lovely tonight. Those pearls are beautiful."

The hand positioning a comb faltered. "St. Germaine gave them to me," the younger woman replied in a small voice.

Belle battled a mortifying dart of envy, not for the pearls themselves, but for the fact that Giles had given them to her. "What a handsome gift."

"Yes, St. Germaine is—" the beauty's lower lip trembled "—is most...kind and...generous."

Observing the unmistakable signs in the mirror, Belle said quickly, "Oh, no! Whatever did I say to make you weepish? Please don't, Chrysanthe! We shall be late going down to dinner."

Her admonition did no good. A shimmering teardrop spilled down a porcelain cheek. Another followed. That the girl could cry without the least reddening of her eyes or nose caused another, most ignoble, dart of envy in Belle's breast. Sighing, she waited while Chrysanthe reached for her reticule and fumbled for her handkerchief, then Belle wrapped an arm around her shaking shoulders.

"I'm so sorry for whatever I said that set you off," she began.

"You didn't.... You couldn't.... I'm just..." After this spate of half sentences, Chrysanthe sobbed, "I'm so unhappy."

"Unhappy? When you've just become engaged to Giles?"

"I...I..." The blonde shredded her linen handkerchief in nervous hands.

"Out with it, Chrysanthe. You must tell me the whole now."

"I don't wish to marry Giles." Amethyst eyes awash with tears lifted to Belle's face. She gathered her courage with a visible effort and announced in tragic accents, "I love another!"

"Well, for pity's sake! Why in the world would you be such a goose as to say you'd marry Giles if you love someone else?"

This bracing retort caused the beauty to blink. "My father..." she replied vaguely. "It was his greatest wish...."

"Come now, Chrysanthe," the ever-practical Miss Chessington admonished briskly. "Don't try to tell me Lord Ayers is forcing you to marry Giles against your wishes. Why, not even the Prince Regent could force *his* daughter to marry William of Orange, although poor Princess Charlotte did have to climb out a third-story window and run away to her mama before she was allowed to marry her beloved Prince Leopold."

Instead of taking heart from the royal romance that had thrilled a nation quite disgusted by the Prince Regent's shabby treatment of both his mistress, Mrs. Fitzherbert, and his wife, the Princess Caroline, Chrysanthe looked thoroughly alarmed.

"Belle! Surely you don't think I should climb out a window! Why, I should...I should...be quite terrified!"

"Yes, I suppose you would," replied the woman

who'd calmly stanched the blood gushing from Harry's wound and then shouldered his rifle. After a moment she asked curiously, "Who is it you love?"

"A poet."

"Ah, a poet."

"He's of respectable birth," Chrysanthe rushed to add, "but quite…quite…"

Breaking down once more, she buried her face in her hands. Belle waited for the latest storm to pass before hazarding a guess.

"Quite penniless, perhaps?"

A low moan and a nod signified she'd hit the mark.

"Well, I can understand why Lord Ayers would not wish you to tie yourself to a man unable to support you."

At this, Chrysanthe's head lifted. "Oh, no! Papa doesn't know about Adolphus! I could never bring myself to tell him. Then…then there are the settlements Giles offered. Papa says they're quite generous, more than enough to cover his debts, and I must…I must be grateful."

Belle observed her drooping shoulders with something less than sympathy. "I don't know about your poet, but any woman would be fortunate to take the Baron St. Germaine to husband."

"But Adolphus has my heart! And I his." Dashing the tears from her cheeks, the beauty dug in her reticule once again and pulled out a folded slip of paper. "Just look at the poem he sent to me wrapped around a posy of violets."

Belle scanned the sonnet, fully prepared for gushing verse and a revolting excess of emotion. To her surprise, the sentiments expressed in the spare lines soared as pure and high as the voices of a boys' choir.

"I know more about maps and charts than poetry," she said slowly, impressed despite herself, "but this is quite...beautiful."

"Do you think so? He's sent me many such poems, and each is better than the last."

The pathetic eagerness in Chrysanthe's voice tugged at Belle's conscience. She had no business meddling in affairs that weren't her own.

Or were they?

Giles's face floated before her eyes, smiling in that way that caused her pulse to trip so absurdly. He didn't love Chrysanthe, any more than Harry loved Belle. Yet both brothers had pledged themselves to marry women whose hearts belonged to another.

There! Belle couldn't deny it any longer! In little more than three days, the practical young woman who'd accepted Harry's offer with the idea he'd do as well as any other had fallen ridiculously, passionately in love with his brother. No, it hadn't even taken three days. The moment she'd walked into the library and held out her hand to Giles, she'd felt something arc between, some frisson of awareness that had set her blood to pounding. She, like the Shah Jehan, had found her one true love.

Now what in the world was she to do about it?

Belle had not the vaguest notion at this point, but, having set her mind to a problem, her nature was such that she'd keep at it until she found a solution.

"You said yourself Giles is a most kind and generous man, Chrysanthe. He won't hold you to a betrothal that gives you such grief. You should go to him and explain your feelings."

"Oh, no! I couldn't!" Tears welled once more. "The settlements, you know...."

"Yes, yes, don't go off again," Belle said hastily. "I daresay I shall think of something."

She stared down at the poem, a thought forming in the back of her mind. "May I keep this? Just for a day or two?"

Sniffling, Chrysanthe assented.

Some moments later, two rather subdued young women went down the stairs to join their fiancés. If Belle hadn't admitted to herself not five minutes earlier that she'd completely and irrevocably lost her heart, a single glimpse of Giles in formal evening dress would have banished all doubts.

Tall, broad-shouldered and impossibly elegant in black breeches and swallow-tailed coat, with a snowy cravat tied around the strong column of his throat, he quite literally took her breath away.

Yet it wasn't his handsome face or tall, lean

frame that started her stomach quivering like the jellied crocodile eggs she'd so enjoyed in Egypt. It was the fond smile he bestowed on his mama when he seated her at the table. His gentle manner with Chrysanthe. And, most of all, the teasing light in his eyes when he turned to Belle and said he must be *sure* to pay his compliments to his mother's dresser for the way she wielded her hot tongs.

Chapter Four

Since Lady Germaine had so generously offered Belle the use of the town carriage if she had any errands to run, the younger woman set out from Brook Street just after lunch the following day. She arrived at the offices of Simon and Simon a little more than a half hour later. Mr. Simon the Elder tottered out to greet her personally and express his deepest condolences on her father's death. His gray-haired and equally stooped son did the same, then carried in the bulging canvas bag Belle had brought with her.

Having served as her father's assistant since she had declared herself done with nurses and nannies, Belle regarded both men as kindly mentors, as indeed they regarded themselves. Their long association with the somewhat eccentric Sir Arthur had brought them a great deal of profit, after all, and no little acclaim for the quality of the maps and globes they produced as a result of his many explorations.

After the condolences and a fortifying glass of wine, the map-makers pored over the notes and surveys Belle had brought back with her. Relief swept through her when it became clear she'd considerably underestimated the income that would derive from her father's last efforts.

"You may mark my words!" Simon the Elder stated gleefully. "We shall see another canal dug through the deserts of the Suez. If not along the route the pharaohs followed, then close to it. For all that Bonaparte's Egyptian campaign came to naught in '98, he lit the spark. And these surveys shall fan the flames! We shall keep our bookbinder busy for years to come printing copies of these maps!"

"Indeed, I hope so," Belle said, her throat tight as she smoothed a gloved hand along the edge of a chart. It was her father's last, and finest, work. The measurements so exact. The details so precise.

But Sir Arthur had had no patience with mawkish sentiment, and would have owned himself astonished if his cheerful, stalwart daughter had given in to a missish bout of tears. The bracing thought eased the ache in Belle's throat and reminded her of a secondary purpose of her visit.

"I know the publisher who sees to the binding and distribution of your maps also produces literary works." Tugging on the strings of her reticule, she drew out a sheet of folded paper. "I wonder if you might show him this, and see if he thinks it worthy of publication."

Simon the Elder pushed his spectacles higher on his nose and peered at the scribbled lines. His scraggy white brows rose. "A poem, my dear Miss Chessington? Did you compose it?"

"No, it was done by an acquaintance of a friend. I understand he's composed many more. I've written his name and direction on the back of that paper. If your publisher is interested, he may contact him personally."

"I will pass it on," Mr. Simon promised, tucking the paper into his pocket. "Now perhaps you'll allow us to show you the design for the base of the new globe we shall produce incorporating your father's last works."

After another half hour with the Simons, Belle left with assurances that a draft in her name would be sent to the bank immediately to cover her present expenses. The rest of the sums owed to Sir Arthur would be worked through the solicitor handling his and Belle's affairs. Her immediate financial worries disposed of, and Chrysanthe's problem temporarily pushed to the back of her mind, Belle now turned her attention to the urgent task of learning to waltz.

This dance, in which each couple wrapped their arms around each other in a way many still con-

sidered *most* immodest, had displaced the minuet
in France during the ascendancy of Bonaparte and
rather more slowly made its way across the Chan-
nel. It was still not quite the thing at some remote
country assemblies, but, Belle discovered, was now
accepted in London.

She enlisted Chrysanthe's help in this effort, as
well as that of Giles's lively young sister, Amelia.
The girls appropriated the second-floor music room
one sunny afternoon two days before Lady Cowper's fête. Chrysanthe spun out tunes on the pi-
anoforte with delightful skill. A giggling Amelia
trod on Belle's toes while attempting to direct her
around the room. Their merriment as much as the
lilting music soon attracted Lady St. Germaine, followed shortly by her second son. After watching
Amelia's inexpert tutelage for some moments,
Harry offered to replace her as instructor.

"It's a simple pattern," he told Belle as he
strolled forward. "Six evenly executed steps, making a full turn in two bars of the music."

"It may seem simple to you," Belle retorted,
laughing, "but I'm more used to climbing on and
off camels than whirling about a ballroom."

Harry grinned. "Since I've seen how adept you
are climbing onto camels, I've no doubt you'll
master the waltz quickly enough."

He held out his hand, and Belle went into his
arms. He moved slowly at first, giving her time to
pick up the pattern. Only after she was sure of the

steps did he tighten his hold about her waist, lengthen his stride, and introduce a series of dips and swirls.

Chrysanthe moved from one tune to another without missing a beat. Amelia clapped her hands and swore Harry beat all other dance partners to flinders. Lady St. Germaine smiled indulgently from her chair. Belle...

Belle could only wonder why being held so intimately in Harry's arms left her completely unmoved, when just the press of Giles's fingers as he handed her into a carriage should steal her breath.

It was time to end the charade, she decided after several turns about the room. Past time.

She waited until Harry had declared her a first-rate waltzer and Lady St. Germaine had suggested the ladies repair upstairs to rest before dressing for dinner to beg a few moments private conversation with her betrothed. To her surprise, Harry proved reluctant to end their arrangement.

"I won't say I didn't feel a touch of panic when you first arrived," he admitted with a grin, "but I've since grown quite comfortable with the idea of marriage."

"Have you, indeed?"

"You're just the kind of sensible wife every man should have," he assured her. "You wouldn't make a fuss if a fellow wants to fire up a cheroot after dinner or nabble off to see a sparring match when you'd planned some bothersome party."

Much moved by this tribute, Belle exclaimed, "I hope I would not! And it's true I've always considered myself a most sensible sort of person. But…"

She glanced away for a moment, then turned an apologetic smile on Harry. "Of late I've discovered I'm quite as silly as the most romantical miss. I wish my husband to be desperately in love with me, you see."

"No! Do you?"

The astonishment in his voice had her biting back a laugh. "Yes, I'm afraid I do."

Rather belatedly it occurred to her betrothed that he should have pressed some signs of affection on his promised wife. "Quite fond of you," he said manfully, sliding an arm around her waist once more. He tipped her chin up with a knuckle. "Daresay I should enjoy kissing you, too."

Whether or not Harry would have enjoyed the kiss was to remain moot, because at that moment Giles strolled into the music room. He stopped short at the sight of Belle wrapped in his brother's arms. Apologizing coolly for disturbing the lovers, he turned on his heel and strode out again.

Belle's eyes followed his tall, broad-shouldered figure until it disappeared. With a small sigh, she brought her attention back to the man who held her.

Harry was staring down at her with an arrested

expression in his blue eyes. He whistled softly, long and low. "So that's the way of it, is it?"

Incurably honest, Belle could only bite her lip and nod.

"That's why we must end our betrothal, Harry. I can't trespass on your mama's hospitality any longer or pretend to an engagement that doesn't hold my heart."

Harry prided himself more on his horsemanship than his intellect, but at this point several very salient facts crowded into his brainbox. First, Giles was the best sort of brother. He'd pulled Harry from more scrapes than he cared to remember, with never a lecture or long face. Second, Giles *couldn't* wish to marry Chrysanthe, any more than Belle apparently wished to marry Harry. The beauty would drive his brother to distraction with her vapors.

No, Giles needed a wife like Belle. One who'd tease him to laughter and keep his many responsibilities from weighing him down. In fact, now that he thought about it, it struck Harry rather forcibly that Giles smiled more frequently when in Belle's company. And damned if his brother's gaze hadn't held a certain warmth when it lighted on Belle the night of the opera!

Struggling with the thoughts swirling through his head, Harry came to the conclusion that he owed it to his brother to relieve him of one bride and present him with another. He didn't have the foggiest notion at the moment *how* he was to accomplish that Herculean task. Something would occur to him, he decided with characteristic optimism. With that thought in mind, he grinned down at Belle in his engaging way.

"There's no need to break off our betrothal just yet, is there? I mean, Lady Cowper's ball is coming up and you've only just learned to waltz. Be a shame if I can't puff off my pupil's skill."

"But..."

"Now, now don't fret. Just leave everything to me. We'll come about right and tight, see if we don't."

Much against her better judgment, Belle allowed herself to be persuaded.

As she dressed for the long-awaited ball, Belle's thoughts whirled. She prided herself on being such a level-headed girl, yet Giles had but to look her way, or share a smile at some silliness that tickled them both, and her knees turned watery as gruel. Only the utter conviction that Giles and Chrysanthe would no more suit than she and Harry lessened her mortification at having fallen topside over bottom in love with another woman's betrothed...and that while engaged to his brother!

If she didn't hear something from Mr. Simon on the morrow, Belle decided as she submitted to Buxton's curling tongs, she'd have to come up with another scheme to aid Chrysanthe's poet. And tomorrow, she *must* end the charade with Harry, before Lady St. Germaine started penning invitations to the ball at which Giles and Harry would both make public their engagements.

Tonight, however...

Tonight she planned to enjoy the purely selfish delights of her sinfully expensive new ballgown and the promised waltz with Giles.

With that firm resolve in mind, she was admiring Buxton's artistic arrangement of her dark red locks when a rapid knock fell on her bedroom door. A moment later, an agitated Lady St. Germaine entered, a piece of notepaper in her hand.

"Belle dearest, Chrysanthe's not in her room. When I inquired for her, her maid brought me this note. I can make neither head nor tail of her wretched handwriting, except for your name. Do tell me you can decipher it!"

Surprised but not unduly alarmed, Belle took the note and held it up to the last of the late April sunlight slanting through the window.

The lines, obviously written in great haste and perturbation, were so closely scribbled and the ink so blotched by what could only be tears that it took some time for Belle to make sense of them. She recognized her name, and, after much effort, made out an obscure reference to vipers nursed at one's breast.

Suddenly, the splotch she'd thought was "Precious Chocolate" became, in fact, the "Princess

Charlotte.'' Frowning, Belle applied herself to the note once more. She interpreted several distraught-sounding adjectives, but when she discerned a phrase that very much looked like ''Gretna Green,'' her heart began to hammer.

Oh, no! Surely, Chrysanthe hadn't climbed out the window and eloped to Scotland to marry her poet across an anvil! What might be dismissed as romantic and dashing behavior in a Princess Royal—or even the daughter of an eccentric explorer—would put the Lady Chrysanthe beyond the pale.

Yet another perusal of the hastily scribbled lines left her with no other conclusion. Stricken, Belle nevertheless managed to infuse her voice with careless nonchalance. She didn't doubt that word of Chrysanthe's disappearance would circulate among the household staff within hours, if not minutes, but she did her best to kill the wide-eyed interest of Buxton and the maid delegated to help her heat the tongs.

''She's not in her room, you say? From the tone of her note, I would guess she had the headache. Perhaps she went for a ride, hoping the air would clear her head before Lady Cowper's ball. Shall we go downstairs and inquire of Giles? He might know how she does.''

It was a weak tale, but the best she could come up with at the moment. Lady St. Germaine grasped at it gratefully.

"Yes, indeed! We must find Giles. He will know just what is about."

"You surprise me, Miss Chessington." Eyes as frigid as blue ice fixed on Belle. "I had not thought you so meddlesome."

Never before having felt the whip of St. Germaine's anger, the recipient of that withering remark found it disagreeable in the extreme. Belle had endured far worse discomforts than a tonguelashing in her adventuresome life, however. Lifting her chin, she took full responsibility for the beauty's disappearance.

"Yes, I see now it was quite wrong of me to put such a chuckleheaded idea in Chrysanthe's mind. I never dreamt she'd have the gumption to...that is, I didn't think she'd..."

Giles advanced on her, his jaw tight. "You didn't think she'd what, Miss Chessington?"

Really, the man could assume the *most* intimidating mien when he chose! Belle stood her ground, but it required far more resolution than she would have imagined a mere half-hour ago.

"Quite obviously, I didn't think she'd climb out a window and make a bolt for the border in such a havey-cavey fashion."

"She didn't climb out a window," he replied in arctic accents. "Nethersby has already informed me that a footman opened the front door for her less than an hour ago, and that a carriage was waiting for her outside.''

"Why didn't you say so when we began this conversation?" Belle exclaimed.

"Perhaps because I thought it none of your business, Miss Chessing...."

"Oh, *do* stop calling me 'Miss Chessington' in that odious way! I've admitted I'm at fault. Can't we put aside blame for now and decide what must be done to bring Chrysanthe out of the suds?"

"I've already ordered my curricle brought around," he informed Belle stiffly. "I'll bring her back and..."

His listener spun on one heel and headed for the door before he finished. "Only give me ten minutes to change my dress and put on a pelisse and bonnet!"

A strong hand caught her arm and swung her back around. "You've interfered enough in matters that don't concern you. Your further involvement is neither required nor desired."

"Fustian!"

Obviously, St. Germaine wasn't used to such blunt retorts. His eyes narrowed dangerously, and the grip on her arm tightened.

"It's already past seven," Belle reminded him tartly. "You'll be lucky to overtake Chrysanthe by nine, and she will no doubt break down when she sees you. Indeed, she probably wept all the way out of town and is sobbing still. She'll need another female to support her, as well as lend her countenance. I'll be ready within ten minutes.''

With that, she shook off his hold and swept out of the room.

Giles was in a savage mood by the time Belle was handed up into the sporty, two-seat curricle. Waiting only until she had settled her skirts, he told the groom to stand away and set his grays off at as fast a pace as the traffic rattling over the cobblestones would allow.

To be obliged to chase after a runaway betrothed was mortifying enough. Not to have recognized that his promised wife was, apparently, in love with a poet grated even deal more. Yet, in the space of little over a week, Belle had managed to extract information which neither Giles, Lady St. Germaine, nor Lord Ayers had even suspicioned.

Instead of feeling the least gratitude to the woman beside him for opening his eyes, Giles battled a fierce urge to pull the grays to a halt, drop the reins, and throttle her. Her meddling had changed nothing. Lord Ayers desperately needed the generous marriage settlements Giles had offered to pay off his debts. Chrysanthe would sob and weep and be brought to understand how inappropriate her poet was as a husband. And Giles himself was still bound by honor to a woman he didn't love and who, he now knew, believed herself in love with someone else. The comfortable if somewhat empty marriage of convenience he'd envisioned when he'd offered for Chrysanthe now loomed bleak indeed.

Much of that dismal prospect was due to the woman seated beside him. She'd come into his life at exactly the wrong moment. Her ready smile, rippling laughter, and zest for life had enchanted him from the instant she'd swept into the library. Even worse, the sight of her slender body wrapped in Harry's arms had engendered in Giles a primitive urge to put out his brother's lights.

In short, she'd turned his world upside down. He recognized he'd have to find a way to right it, but at the moment his first concern was to save Chrysanthe from a folly that would make her a social outcast and considerably embarrass his mama and her father.

Silence prevailed between him and his passenger as they cleared the outskirts of town. Once on the North Pike, Giles gave the grays their head. They sprang forward, eating up the roadway at a clipping pace. Thankfully, no clouds marred the April twilight. Sufficient light still lingered to allow Giles to feather around a lumbering mailcoach with ease.

Belle observed this maneuver with silent approbation, and couldn't help but admire the skill with which he controlled the prime bits of blood between the shafts.

"Would it help you to recover from your black

mood if I said you did that very nicely?'' she inquired politely.

''No.''

''I thought not.''

She twitched her pelisse over her knees and sat quietly for another mile or so. They were just swinging around a bend in the road when she decided enough was enough.

''Really, Giles, we must talk about what we shall do when we overtake Chrysanthe and her poet. Do come down from the boughs and tell me.... Oh! Oh, look out!''

Belle barely had time to catch at her seat. Horrified, she watched Giles pull on the reins in a grim attempt to avoid a traveling carriage broken down in the middle of the road. The grays danced to the far side of the pike. The curricle swung after them.

If an afternoon rain hadn't softened the bank beside the roadway...

If the occupants of the disabled coach had moved it even a yard or two to the side...

But it had, and they hadn't.

The curricle's right wheel went off the edge of the road. The vehicle tipped, then tilted violently. Belle clung to her precarious perch until it was ripped from her hold and she tumbled off. She heard the ominous crack of wood splintering just before she landed in the ditch.

Her head hit a stone, and the hazy April twilight went black.

Chapter Five

Belle awoke to find herself being carried through the deepening night. Blinking at the sharp pain that lanced through her temple, she tried to lift her head.

"Giles?"

"Lie still," his gruff voice commanded just above her ear. "We're but a few hundred yards from a posting inn. I'll set you down in a comfortable bed and send for a doctor."

It took a few moments for her spinning senses to right themselves enough to make out the little troop who marched alongside Giles. She rather thought one was a matron wearing a purple silk turban. And was that a maid carrying her mistress's jewel case? There were several other persons, all of whose faces seemed to swim in the dusk.

How absurd, Belle thought woozily. She'd sustained many a bruise and lump in her various travels. One little bump on the head shouldn't roll her up like this. Then her cheek drifted back down to its pillow of hard muscle, her lids fluttered shut, and the twilight dimmed once more.

Giles had spent some anxious moments watching those he loved endure great suffering. Once as a mere stripling, when his father had moaned and frothed blood for days after the hunting accident that finally took his life. Again when Harry had been carried in the door, out of his mind with feverish delirium.

Yet never had he experienced such gutwrenching terror as when he'd dragged the plunging grays to a halt, jumped clear of the overturned curricle, and spun around to find Belle sprawled lifeless in the ditch. Even after tucking her up in the Red Boar's best bedchamber and receiving assurances from the local physician that she'd sustained nothing worse than a mild concussion, he refused to leave her to the care of the innkeeper's wife.

For the same reason, he declined the services of the turbaned matron's maid, somewhat grudgingly offered by her mistress, who identified herself as Lady Litchfield. Instead, he took upon himself the duty of waking Belle every hour to make sure her pupils hadn't dilated or her mind become confused. He spent the long stretches in between sprawled in a chair set under the eaves.

Only now, with soft April dawn painting the

wavery glass of the inn's windows and Belle's breathing light and steady, did he rise to stretch his cramped limbs. He was reaching for the flagon of ale the innkeeper had thoughtfully provided when the rattle of wheels rose above the sounds of a busy inn greeting a new day. Fortified by the rich, dark home brew, Giles glanced idly out the window and caught sight of his brother alighting from a carriage.

He cast a quick eye over Belle, saw that she was sleeping peacefully, and shrugged into his coat. Stopping only to request the innkeeper's wife to attend the patient, he descended the stairs and met Harry just coming up.

"I say," his brother expostulated, no little aggrieved. "You and Belle have run me a merry chase."

Giles's brows lifted. "Have we?"

"I couldn't believe it when I got back to town and Mama told me you'd gone racketing off to the border in pursuit of Chrysanthe."

Seeing that Harry's impetuous remarks had attracted the attention of several of the inn's other patrons, who'd come down for their breakfasts prior to resuming their various journeys, Giles steered his brother into a private parlor and firmly closed the door.

"Perhaps you don't think Chrysanthe's reputation worth saving," he began coldly. "I, however, have some responsibility toward her and…"

"But she didn't go to Gretna Green!" Harry protested. "She went to *Grayling* Green with this poet of hers. I particularly instructed her to inform you of her direction, only the silly twit would cry all over her note. Even I could make no sense of the thing when Mama showed it to me, and I knew what it was intended to say."

Giles stared at his brother for long moments. "Perhaps we should start at the beginning," he said slowly. "You will tell me why Chrysanthe decided to go to Grayling Green…"

"Her papa's there," Harry interjected. "Visiting one of his hunting cronies."

"…and what you know of my betrothed's penniless poet."

"Well, he's a dashed peculiar chap, if you ask me," Harry pronounced. "Spouts the most nauseating stuff about lilacs and pansies and Chrysanthe's eyes at the drop of a hat. But he's not penniless. At least, not any longer. Seems some bookmaker offered him five thousand pounds for his scribbles. Chrysanthe seemed to think that would solve her papa's embarrassments, and begged me to escort them both to Grayling so the chap could tell Lord Ayers so."

"Five thousand will barely scratch the surface of her father's losses," Giles informed his brother dryly.

"Well, you know that and Ayers knows that, but when Chrysanthe sobbed all over her papa's waistcoat, he decided he'd rather sell his estate and pay off the most pressing of his debts than force his little puss into a marriage she don't wish for. I assured him there was no need to go to such drastic measures."

"Did you?"

"Yes. I, er, also offered to loan him another twenty thousand to keep his head above water."

Giles, who'd laid out at least as much over the years to extricate his brother from various entanglements, knew what a dent that sum would put in Harry's income.

"Why didn't you come to me before pledging such an amount?" Giles demanded.

"You've pulled me out of the suds often enough," his brother said gruffly. "Figured it was time I did the same for you."

Much moved, Giles said quietly, "You have my thanks, but even that generous offer won't save Lord Ayers's estate."

"Well, the thing is," Harry admitted with a sheepish grin, "I told him you'd make up the rest. Old friend of our father's and all that."

After a stark silence, Giles gave a crack of laughter. Only after he'd recovered his poise did he remark dryly, "You appear to feel quite as much license to meddle in my affairs as your betrothed."

"Speaking of Belle...."

Recalled to the reason he'd returned from Grayling only to turn right around to set off again, Harry shook his head.

"Can't imagine why she...or you, for that matter!...would think Chrysanthe had it in her to throw her heart over her sleeve and make a bolt for the border. Something Belle herself might do, but Chrysanthe? No!"

He shook his head again, then frowned.

"I say, Giles, I was never more shocked than when I came upon your curricle in a ditch beside a traveling coach someone had pushed off the pike. Don't try to tell me you were so ham-handed as to run off the road, 'cause I won't believe it!"

"I'm afraid you must."

Succinctly, Giles apprised him of the circumstances that led to his arrival at the Red Boar last night with Belle in his arms.

"Glad to hear she's all right and tight," Harry said cheerfully when he finished. "Take more than a knock on the noggin to do our Belle in, you know. Once saw her thrown off a horse who shied from a nest of cobras. Got right up, dusted herself off, and climbed back on without so much as a squeak."

This decidedly cavalier attitude toward his betrothed's injury wiped out much of the credit the younger brother had just gained with the elder, who'd spent the night in a sweat of worry.

Tucking his hands behind him, Harry rocked

back on his boot heels. "Belle's a great gun, but, well, the truth is, we just don't suit."

"The devil you say!"

Rather than afford Giles any sort of gratification, Harry's pronouncement narrowed his brother's eyes in a decidedly dangerous way.

"You said Sir Arthur left her in straitened circumstances," he got out through tight jaws. "Now you want to cry off and..."

"Lord, Giles, I ain't the one who wants to cry off. Fond of her. Told her so, too! The thing is, she don't want to marry me. Told *me* so, just the other day."

"Did she?" Giles said slowly.

"She did." Harry appeared to consider the matter for a moment before assuming a stern tone. "Now that I think on it, seems to me that if anyone should do the right thing by Belle, it should be you, Giles. You're the one who spent the night with her at an inn, after all, without so much as an abigail to observe the proprieties. Not at all the thing, old man."

As it had on the very first day the redoubtable Miss Chessington had appeared in London, a look of understanding passed between the two brothers. After a moment, a slow grin tugged at Giles's mouth.

"If you think I should do the right thing by her..."

"I do," Harry said severely.

"...I suppose I shall have to."

Waiting only until he'd instructed the innkeeper to supply his brother with a hearty breakfast of beef and ale, Giles once more climbed the stairs. He might not have approached the task of explaining how he'd been shorn of one betrothed before offering his hand and his heart to another with such a light step if he'd been privy to the conversation at that moment taking place in the Red Boar's best bedchamber.

"I declare," Lady Litchfield sniffed with a bob of her turbaned head, "I own myself quite surprised that Lord St. Germaine would refuse the services of my maid and tend to you himself."

She looked about the spacious chamber, which, she thought on a disgruntled note, should have been given to her use. To be sure, her lumbago affected her far more than the little bump on the head appeared to have affected Miss Chessington. A night spent in a bed in all ways inferior to the one that had awaited her in London had made her naturally peevish disposition even more sharp-set.

That grievance, added to the fact that St. Germaine had quite callously ordered *her* coachman to push *her* carriage into the ditch to avoid further accidents before striding off with this slip of a girl in his arms, had quite irritated Lady Litchfield.

Having perceived it her Christian duty to check on the invalid's condition, she found her up and dressed in a sadly crumpled gown and somewhat wan of face. She now gave outlet to her irritation of the nerves by probing quite shamelessly into Miss Chessington's circumstances.

"I'm only slightly acquainted with Lady St. Germaine, but I daresay she'll be as surprised as I to hear that her son provided what can only be described as such *intimate* care. Unless, of course," she added pointedly, "you tell me the innkeeper's wife was in error when she told me St. Germaine spent the whole night in this room with you."

Belle, whose head had ached only a bit when she awoke a little while ago, was now feeling decidedly peevish herself.

"I can't tell you where he spent the night," she retorted. "Nor do I consider it in any way your business."

"Well!"

Affronted, Lady Litchfield swelled her massive bosom. The feather on her turban bobbed as she made a terse farewell.

"I've rented a conveyance and must resume my journey. Despite your impertinence, I shall call upon Lady St. Germaine to let her know how you contrive. I tell you quite frankly, I hope she will lay my own misgivings as to your relationship with her son to rest."

"Wait!"

Despite her aching temple, Belle couldn't repay

Lady St. Germaine's many kindnesses by letting this hatchet-faced busybody descend upon her unannounced, much less spread outrageous tales about her son.

"The truth is, I'm betrothed to…"

"To St. Germaine?" Lady Litchfield's penciled brows shot up to the edge of her purple turban. "When did this come about? I'm sure I haven't seen an announcement in *The Times*."

"No, no, not to…"

Her agitated reply was cut off by the sudden appearance of the gentleman under discussion. His keen eyes traveled from Belle's flushed face to that of her obviously disapproving visitor.

"My dear girl, I could hear you halfway down the stairs," he said in mild reproof. "Is your head hurting you?"

"No! Yes! Oh, Giles, do tell Lady Litchfield she's being *most* nonsensical. She means to spread about the farradiddle that you spent the night in my chamber."

His gaze cut once more to the matron, who puffed up her bosom with righteous indignation.

"Farradiddle! Indeed!"

"Lady Litchfield may spread about what she wishes," Giles drawled in a bored way, ushering the sputtering visitor to the door. "If she wishes to appear ridiculous by implying I should not attend my promised wife when it was, in fact, *her* carriage that caused your injuries, it's not of the slightest interest to me.''

With that masterly set down, he closed the door in the woman's face. Belle essayed a weak laugh at her adversary's openmouthed astonishment, but couldn't help remonstrating.

''Now you've done it! The odious creature will hold her tongue for now, but only think what a hue and cry she'll make when she learns you're not betrothed to me, but to Chrysanthe.''

The drawl came back, even more pronounced than before. ''Since I'm not betrothed to Chrysanthe, that particular problem won't arise.''

''Whatever do you mean? Unless that little knock to my head disordered my memory, I was sure we set out last night to retrieve your bride.''

''I mean, my dear Belle, that Harry has relieved me of both my bride and a good portion of my ready funds.''

''I...I seem to be a bit dense this morning.'' Her hand lifted to her temple. ''I don't quite understand what you're telling me.''

At once concerned and infinitely tender, St. Germaine took her in his arms. Stunned, Belle could only stare up at him.

''It's quite simple,'' he told her with a smile. ''Chrysanthe shall marry her poet. Harry and I shall help Lord Ayers keep his head above water. And you, since you've told my brother you won't have him, I sincerely hope will marry me, if for no other reason than to spike Lady Litchfield's guns."

A tide of heat stole in Belle's cheeks. "Don't be absurd, sir. I don't expect you to sacrifice yourself to save my reputation."

He laughed down at her. "I rather think it's the other way around. You don't wish that windbag to spread it about that I played nurse to a miss who refused to have me, do you?"

"Oh, hang Lady Litchfield," Belle said roundly. "Let's be done with talking about her!"

"If your head doesn't hurt too badly, I think it's time we were done with talking altogether."

Her heart thumped at the expression in his eyes. No schoolroom miss, she couldn't mistake his intent.

"It doesn't hurt *too* badly," she said on a cautious note. "In fact, the ache seems to have quite disappeared."

"Good."

With that, he bent his head and kissed her. Gently, at first. Then, when Belle rose up on her toes and wrapped her arms about his neck, with a thoroughness that set her head to spinning even more than it had the night before.

She was breathless when at last he lifted his head. The warmth rushing through her veins heated to liquid fire when he smiled down at her.

"Say you'll marry me, my darling, and soon! I

don't think either of us needs to endure another
round of betrothals.''

"Oh, Giles, if you're sure?''

"Quite...''

He dropped a kiss on her nose.

"...quite...''

Another on her mouth.

"...sure.''

In a state of blissful ignorance, Belle accepted
his offer.

Not until her wedding night did she understand
that Giles had married her out of a sense of obligation that went deeper than affection, and well
beyond love.

Chapter Six

Despite the fact that Giles insisted on a wedding within the month, he made sure it was done with all the pomp and elegance due the bride of the Baron St. Germaine.

Harry escorted a blushing Belle down the aisle. Awash in tears of happiness, Chrysanthe attended the bride. Lady St. Germaine sighed and told every second guest at the lavish feast following the ceremony that she was sure she'd never seen her dear, dear Giles so well content.

It was Harry, imbibing his fourth glass of champagne, who all unknowingly burst the bubble of Belle's shimmering happiness. In preparation for her wedding journey, she'd changed into a traveling dress of green-and-white striped silk flounced with an embroidered border, white ruchings, and sleeves decorated with knots of green ribbon. A matching pelisse of forest green and a poke bonnet with curling ostrich plumes completed the fashionable ensemble.

Her various new relatives came up to wish her well, Harry among them. Grinning, he planted a kiss on her cheek and declared she looked shiny as a new guinea.

"Dashed if you don't come close to making me regret I told Giles you gave me my marching orders."

"Come close?" she echoed, laughing. "How unhandsome of you, Harry."

"Don't hand me that gammon," he retorted. "Admit you're happy Giles snabbled you up before you could change your mind yet again about marrying one of us."

"Very happy."

Together, they sought out the figure of the groom. Tall and strikingly handsome in glossy black topboots, neat buckskins, and the coat of blue superfine he'd changed into for traveling, Giles took Belle's breath away.

"He's a good man," Harry said on a note of brotherly affection. "He'll take care of you, and not just when you're so silly as to fall out of a carriage."

Belle, who until recently had disdained the whole idea of being coddled and cosseted and taken care of, merely smiled.

"I daresay Sir Arthur would be pleased to know

you're now set,'' Harry murmured casually into his champagne.

"Sir Arthur?'' She turned to him in surprise. "What do you mean, 'now' set? Did you think he hadn't provided for me?''

She saw the answer in his face.

"Good gracious, Harry, never say you told Giles my father left me without any means of support!''

"No, how should I? Don't know what Sir Arthur left you, after all. Guessed it couldn't be much, though. Not that it mattered a whit to Giles,'' he added hastily when Belle's eyes widened in dismay.

No, she thought with a sinking sensation. It wouldn't matter a whit to Giles...if Harry hadn't just informed him that he and Belle had ended their betrothal!

Was that why Giles, newly freed of his obligation to Chrysanthe, had offered for Belle? Because he thought she needed the protection of his name and wealth, just as Harry had back in Egypt?

Or because of the rumors that horrid Lady Litchfield might spread about her?

Or because he'd made up his mind to take a wife, and one would do as well as another?

No! She knew better than that. Giles could not have kissed her so deliciously these past weeks if he didn't feel...feel *something!*...for her.

But was it, could it be, the quite ridiculous passion she now nursed in her bosom for him? Doubt, uncertainty, dismay at Harry's revelations, all warred within her as Giles strode across the room and advised her it was time to take leave of their guests and begin their wedding journey.

Giles needed only one glimpse at Belle's expressive face to recognize that his wife was in the grip of an emotion she tried very hard to disguise.

He had a good idea what that emotion was. He'd spent some years on the town, after all, and although he looked forward to reaching the elegant hostelry where they'd spend their wedding night with a heat in his blood bordering on fever, he schooled himself to patience. He'd hold Belle in his arms soon enough. And barring any unforeseen carriage accidents, he thought wryly, she'd be in possession of her senses this time.

But not, he hoped, for long.

Thankfully, they arrived at the Rose and Crown before his impatience led him to the impropriety of pulling his wife into his lap, tossing her bonnet out the window, and kissing away her doubts, as he very much desired to do.

As it was, he barely waited until they'd finished the light supper he'd ordered to knock lightly on the door separating the well-appointed sitting room from that of the bedroom. Belle called to him to come in, then blushed and stammered that the maid Lady St. Germaine had so kindly insisted accompany her dear, dear daughter-in-law was having some difficulty unraveling the pesky knot in her stays.

"I'll do it," he told the maid, dismissing her with a nod.

Really, Belle thought as his fingers went to work at the knot, this was absurd! She was no schoolroom miss. She'd traveled to the world's exotic spots. Observed sights that would cause most wellbred women to cover their eyes or turn away in agonies of embarrassment. Yet the mere brush of her husband's fingers against the stiffened corset sent the most ridiculous tremors through her.

The feel of his lips when he did away with the constricting garment and bent to brush a kiss across her bare shoulder sent even more.

"You have the most tantalizing skin," he murmured. "Soft and creamy where the sun doesn't touch it..."

"And brown as a berry where it does," she finished on a shaky laugh. Turning, she gave him a rueful look.

"I'm afraid your mama wasted the better part of two dozen lemons mixing potions to lighten my complexion these past weeks. She's still becoming resigned to the fact that she's acquired the harumscarum offspring of a surveyor as a daughter-inlaw."

"I see I should have made it more clear to Mama that I'm particularly partial to harumscarum offspring of surveyors."

"Are you, Giles?" She searched his eyes. "Indeed?"

"Indeed."

She wanted to believe him, wanted to believe in the joy that had infused her these past weeks as she prepared for her wedding. Yet the subject that had occupied her mind to the exclusion of all else since her talk with Harry still weighed heavily on her heart.

"I'm sure I don't know why you wished to marry me," she said, searching for a way to introduce the matter of money. "I tend to be a bit, well, managing at times."

"That hasn't failed to escape my attention," he admitted with a smile.

"And I must confess, I'm notably lacking in sensibility." She toyed with the ribbons at the neck of her lace-trimmed chemise. "At times, Chrysanthe's tears come near to putting me out of patience."

"We can only hope they don't have the same effect on her poet."

She chewed on her lower lip, then plunged to the heart of the matter. "I still won't know until my father's will goes through the courts how much I bring to this marriage."

"Harry's ready disposal of my income didn't break me, you goose. I shall contrive to keep you in pin money."

She started to protest that she rather thought her

inheritance would provide more than mere pin money, but at that moment Giles slid an arm around her waist. The other caught her beneath the knees. Swinging her up in his arms, he carried her to the bed.

Then the moment for conversation of a serious nature was lost. His hands reached for the ribbons on her chemise, and Belle discovered that all her travels and the exotic sights she'd encountered over the years in no way prepared her for the shock that jolted through her body at her husband's touch. Or for the heat that speared through her when he bent to plant a kiss on the bared slope of her breast.

Even those novel experiences paled beside the feelings engendered by her first sight of Giles unclothed. He was, she thought with the critical powers of observation that had made her so indispensable to Sir Arthur, quite magnificent. Broad of shoulder, narrow of hip, leanly muscled. Like the marble statues she'd admired during a long-ago sojourn in Greece, only warmer to the touch and far more daunting in masculine endowment.

A corner of her mind told her she should turn away in maidenly confusion. At the very least, blush and stammer when he slid up her chemise to untie her silk garters and remove the white lisle stockings embroidered with delicate rosebuds that a giggling Amelia had given her for a bride gift. She did turn her head when he tugged off the delicate linen chemise and bared her flesh to his view, but his fingers on her chin soon brought her head back around.

"I want to see your eyes," he told her, easing between her thighs. His hand stroked her waist, the smooth curve of her hip. "They're quite remarkable, you know."

"No," she gasped when his fingers teased the tip of her breast. "I didn't know."

"They were the first thing I noticed about you. Your eyes, and the dimples when you laugh in that enchanting way you have."

Belle wasn't laughing now. She could scarcely breathe, much less order her dimples to appear. When he bent his head to take her mouth with his, she stopped trying to do either.

Slowly, Giles told himself. Gently. He took his time, soothing, whispering, stroking her to a heat that soon melted her reserve. His jaw locked with the effort of holding back until she was ready, then he pierced her maiden's shield with a smooth thrust. When she'd recovered from the shock he began to move. Slowly. Gently.

It was only later, while Belle was lying in his arms still bemused and breathless from the passions he'd released in her, that she remembered she'd yet to resolve the matter that had exercised her mind all the way to the Rose and Crown.

"Giles."

He nuzzled her hair. "Mmm?"

"About the matter of pin money…"

"Mmm?"

"The cartographers who financed my father's expeditions think his last maps are quite remarkable."

"I'm sure they are," he murmured, draping an arm over her waist to pull her closer into the curve of his body. Her hand went to his chest, still damp from their exertions. A delicious tingle ran from her fingertips right up her arm.

"They…they should bring in more than mere pocket money," she told him, her sated senses quickening at his musky, male scent.

Evidently Giles experienced the same tingle, the same quickening. His eyes opened, and he smiled down at her in a way that Belle, newly awakened to passion but learning fast, had no difficulty interpreting.

"Don't worry, my darling. I said I'd take care of you and I shall."

He leaned over her, intent on proving just how well he intended to take care of her. He'd forgotten Belle's stubbornly independent streak.

"I do wish you would listen for just a moment," she begged. Rolling to one side of the bed, she tucked the sheets up around her breasts.

"All right." He folded his arms across his naked chest and leaned against the carved headboard. "I'll listen, but not, I warn you, for very long."

"You must understand I can't be wholly dependent on you," she began in what she felt was a reasonable way.

A frown formed on her husband's forehead. "I don't understand anything of the sort."

"Sir Arthur wouldn't approve. He always insisted I pull my own weight."

"For pity's sake, Belle, we're speaking of marriage, not a march through the desert."

"Well, forgive me if I fail to see any great distinction between the two. Each takes teamwork and great fortitude to succeed."

It was apparent that that aspect of their joint venture hadn't occurred to Giles. His frown deepened.

"Do you think me unable to support a wife?"

"No, of course not. But neither must you think me unable to be a partner in this enterprise."

"Dammit, we didn't enter into a business arrangement."

"You worked out marriage settlements with Lord Ayers," she pointed out. "What was that, if not a business arrangement?"

Giles thrust his hand through his hair, not at all pleased at the sudden turn his wedding night had taken. In the past hour, Belle had proved all he wished for in a wife...passionate, spontaneous, joyful in her exploration of marital intimacies. He couldn't believe she could tuck the sheets up around her breasts and talk of settlements and dependencies with the sheen of their lovemaking still on her golden skin. He stared at her, thoroughly disgruntled, as she pressed on.

"You needn't frown at me in that way. In marriages such as ours, it's best to speak openly about matters of...."

"What do you mean, in marriages such as ours?"

She plucked at the sheets, not quite meeting his gaze. "Harry told me that the two of you talked about my...my straitened circumstances at the Red Boar."

"The devil he did!"

"Yes, well, I do see where that might have led you to...to do what you did."

"I'm glad you do," he drawled. "I'm damned if I can make head nor tail of this nonsensical conversation. What *are* you talking about, Belle?"

She drew in a breath and answered with great resolution, if not coherence.

"I'm talking about marrying me. It was kind and generous of you to want to protect me, Giles, and I quite like what we just...that is, I'm sure we shall contrive to..."

"To what?" he demanded, thunderstruck.

"To rub along," she finished lamely.

The eyes that had pierced Giles to the heart when they'd lifted, brimming with merriment, that day in the library held not a trace of laughter now. In all seriousness, she met his incredulous gaze.

"I know you can't love me with the passion of

Shah Jehan, but I vowed to make you a good wife and I shall, I promise.''

Her careful speech spurred him to action. Hard hands reached out and yanked her across the bed. Startled, Belle stared up into a pair of blue eyes flashing with a mix of exasperation and amusement.

''I don't know who the devil this shah fellow is, but however you came about the notion that I don't love you to distraction, you may rid yourself of it right now!''

''But…''

''If you want more proof than I have just given you, perhaps this will convince you.''

With that, he bent his head and kissed her with the savage hunger he'd so nobly restrained earlier. Crushed in his embrace, Belle submitted to this rough handling with every evidence of astonishment and delight.

When he raised his head again, the dimples he'd come to adore had made their appearance.

''That certainly alters my thinking,'' she conceded breathlessly. ''But I think I might need just a *bit* more convincing.''

Laughter sprang into his eyes. ''We have the rest of our lives. Are you sure you wish me to present all my arguments tonight?''

''Oh, yes,'' she said, wrapping her arms around his neck. ''Please.''

"Very well," he replied, grinning. "I'll endeavor to oblige you."

With that, he tumbled her to the bed.

Belle's last thought, while she could still think at all, was that she needed no marble monuments, no soaring edifices to mark their passion. The hunger with which Giles devoured her would do very nicely.

Very nicely indeed!

* * * * *

Dear Reader,

As you can probably guess from the dedication, I'm addicted to the Regency period. Besides making my sweetie walk through that London rainstorm, I also dragged him to Bath, where we wandered the elegant squares, strolled along the Royal Crescent, and even—gulp!—tasted the waters at the Pump Room.

So I was thrilled to re-create one of my favorite time periods in *Mismatched Hearts*. I hope you enjoy watching Isabella and Giles trying to sort out their obligations and their engagements as much as I did.

And if you're looking for some sizzling romances to help you through the winter doldrums, I've got a few more coming out:

> —In December 2000 watch for a 3-in-1 anthology of hijacked hearts and terror in the skies, coming from Silhouette Intimate Moments.

> —In January 2001 there's *The Spy Who Loved Him*, part of the exciting YEAR OF LOVING DANGEROUSLY series by Silhouette Intimate Moments.

> —In January 2001 MIRA Books will release the first in my sweeping new WYOMING WINDS series. Set on the turbulent American frontier, *The Horse Soldier* tells the tale of cavalry Major Andrew Garrett and the woman who once betrayed him.

Happy reading!

Merline Lovelace

For Tracy Farrell, with my admiration, love
and deep gratitude.

MY DARLING ECHO
by Gayle Wilson

Chapter One

London 1823

He would rather be facing the advance of a line of French cavalry, the Earl of Huntingdon thought, as the strained silence deepened. At least during his service on the Peninsula, he had been able to tell something about what was happening. Now, however—

"Marriage, my lord?" Arabella Simmons said faintly.

Yesterday he would have claimed that he knew every subtle nuance of her remarkable voice, but there was something in that breathless inquiry he had never heard before. Shock, certainly. And after all, he had expected that. Was there disgust there as well?

Damn you, Ingalls, Hunt thought. *Damn you for talking me into this. And damn me for being fool enough to let you.*

"Purely as a matter of convenience, Mrs. Simmons," he said aloud, his voice betraying none of that mental self-castigation. "If the idea is distasteful to you, however, we need never mention it again. I assure you I meant you no disrespect."

"And I took none, my lord," Arabella said.

There was now a hint of amusement underlying the pleasantly husky timbre of her reply. And hearing it, the sickening sense that he had made an irretrievable blunder began to ease.

"An offer of marriage can seldom be considered insulting," she continued. "And certainly in our case..."

The words trailed. There were, however, so many aspects of their case that were unlike other couples who might be contemplating matrimony that a dozen interpretations could be put on the unfinished phrase.

The most obvious was the difference in their stations, of course. Mrs. Simmons was in his employ, and he was Alexander Coltrain, the seventh Earl of Huntingdon, the last of his immediate family who would bear that old and distinguished title. A match between them would be, therefore, a misalliance by almost every standard the ton might apply.

Since he had determined more than ten years ago that he would never marry, Huntingdon was unconcerned about any opinion society might venture about the proposal he had just made. A proposal that was as unexpected to him, he acknowledged, as it would be to those who knew him.

To the few remaining members of his family, whom he had informed long ago about his intention not to marry. To his friends, who had chided him often enough about that decision. To his servants, who were more familiar than anyone with the relationship he and Mrs. Bertrand Simmons had enjoyed for more than two years.

A relationship which had never, at least until today, strayed anywhere near the personal. Unless, he amended, one could consider as personal the undeniable pleasure he had felt from the first day Arabella had read for him.

At that time, Hunt had endured his blindness for eight years without giving voice to any sentiment that could possibly be interpreted as a complaint, so he felt he had earned the right to Mrs. Simmons's voice. He had known the first day that, having once heard it, he could never go back to the dry recitations he had suffered before she had arrived on the doorstep of his London town house, the advertisement he had had placed in *The Times* clutched in her hand.

Employing a female reader was highly irregular, even in these modern times. However, Bertrand Simmons had been a schoolmate. And during the course of the interview he had granted Arabella, strictly on the basis of that long-ago friendship

with her deceased husband, the earl had learned of
her straitened circumstances.

That and her voice had guaranteed his decision
to employ her, despite what anyone might think.
He considered Mrs. Simmons his one self-
indulgence—and had decided that day that surely
one was allowed. Now, however, he was suggesting something which would cause far more comment among his set.

"In our case?" he repeated when she didn't go
on.

Had his pride prompted that query? he wondered. Or a simple tendency to masochism?

"I doubt your family would be pleased should
I accept your offer, my lord," she said.

He was relieved to find that the trace of amusement he had heard before had not disappeared.

"I think we are both of an age to make our own
decisions. Your birth is perfectly acceptable, Mrs.
Simmons. And whatever objections my family
might pose will be of no concern to me, I assure
you."

There was little enough family left. His mother
had died when he was only ten; his father while
he was at Cambridge. His older brother, to whom
the title had belonged, had been killed in a riding
accident while Hunt was still in Iberia. Rather than
sell out, the new earl had decided to stay at least
until the army had successfully pushed across the
frontier into Spain. That had proven to be a fateful

decision and had led, of course, to his decision not to marry.

The occasional guilt he felt about letting the direct line of descent die with himself had a great deal more to do with the unsuitable cousin who would ultimately inherit both the title and the estates than with the opinions of the other members of that small familial band. Of course, neither of those considerations was what had prompted his offer today.

"Past our primes, are we, my lord?" Bella suggested, the hint of laughter he had heard before still running through the words. He wondered if her eyes were smiling as well, and if they were, he wished that he might—if only once—see them.

"My apologies, Mrs. Simmons," he said easily. "My social skills, as you of all people must be aware, are sadly lacking. I should have said *I* am of an age when I no longer need seek my family's approval."

"And what age is that, my lord?"

Hunt found he had to think about it, and when he had, he was surprised by the answer. "I am thirty-eight years old."

There was another small silence, but apparently they had both recovered from the initial shock. This one was almost contemplative.

"I am twenty-six, my lord," she said.

He tried to remember what he had been doing

when he was that age. It seemed a hundred years ago, but in actuality...

Deliberately destroying the sudden mental images from those days, because he was unwilling to dwell on the years of camaraderie and adventure he had spent with his regiment, he concentrated instead on trying to read her voice.

"Then certainly too young to consider a marriage of convenience," he suggested, his own tone carefully avuncular. He forced his lips into a smile. *Damn you, Ingalls,* he thought again, fighting embarrassment and an incredible—and incredibly surprising—sense of disappointment.

"I didn't mean that," she said quickly. "A man of your age is indeed in the prime of life. There must be a hundred highly suitable young ladies in London right now who would welcome your suit, my lord."

"I take it then, you are not one of them."

"You may take it that I am *not* considered to be in my prime. Nor could I be considered a suitable candidate to be your wife. Not by anyone's standards. Not even my own," she added, her tone verging on laughter.

"I believe it is *my* prerogative to decide who is suitable for me to take to wife."

"Forgive me, my lord, but my understanding was that it was your long-held intention never to wed. Or was I mistaken in that belief?"

Trust Bella to go straight to the heart, Hunt

thought. He couldn't even remember when he had come to think of her as Bella. He didn't know if anyone else had ever called her that, but at some time in the course of a dark winter's afternoon, the only sounds in his study the pleasant crackle and hiss of the fire and the far more pleasant tenor of her voice, reading to him from some deadly dull parliamentary bill, she had become Bella. His Bella.

It was a fantasy, of course. And a harmless one. Or so he had believed. He had never had any intention of stepping beyond the carefully prescribed boundaries of their relationship. He had fallen in love with a woman's voice, and that he had was a secret he would take to his grave. Because, of course, the alternative was unthinkable.

"I long ago determined never to marry. Not in the conventional sense," he said truthfully.

"So what you have proposed between us is...*not* to be a conventional marriage?"

"You may think of it as a business proposition."

Pompous ass, he mocked himself, as soon as the words left his mouth.

"I see," she said.

The tone he had been unable to place at the beginning of the conversation was back, and he still couldn't identify it.

"However—" he began, prepared to cut his losses and sound retreat. It was obvious, no matter

what Ingalls had suggested, that she found his proposal to be repugnant.

Why wouldn't she? he asked himself bitterly.
And then, because that corrosive bitterness was
something he had long ago recognized as skirting
too near self-pity, he blocked the thought, arranging his features in the same bland expression with
which he pretended to listen to debates in the
House of Lords.

"Why would you suddenly offer to marry me,
my lord?" she asked.

"I believe I have explained my thinking."

"To have me at your beck and call, available to
read to you at any hour of the night and day," she
said.

"I don't believe I was so gauche in my phras-
ing." Again, he allowed the small, controlled
smile, inclining his head toward her in an assenting
salute.

"You are never gauche," she said. "You are
careful. And considerate. Thoughtful. Occasionally
impatient," she added after a moment. "More frequently of yourself than of others. But you are
never gauche," she said again.

"There seems no sense in your braving the elements each day," he said, ignoring her commen-
tary on his character. "I was merely offering you
room and board here in my home in addition to
your salary. And I am offering those in the only

way that would be acceptable to society. I assure you, I have no ulterior motives."

"The salary you give me is more than generous, my lord, providing amply for my room and board."

"You need not look for excuses, Mrs. Simmons. A simple no will suffice," he said, wondering why she was drawing this painful interview out. "Nothing in our situation will change as a result of your refusal."

"I have...dependents," she said.

"Dependents?" he repeated blankly, having no idea what she meant.

"My son and my aunt, who serves as his governess. They are my responsibilities. I could not leave them."

My son. Huntingdon's brain echoed the words as if they had been spoken in some exotic language in which he was only vaguely conversant. Bella had worked in his home, had worked closely beside him day after day for two years, and he had never known she had a child.

"Indeed," he said. "I did not know."

"His name is Christopher. After Bertrand's father. He is four years old."

"You've never mentioned him," he said.

The earl had seen little enough of his own mother during his early years. A succession of nannies and later a rather strict governess had raised him. Obviously, Bella's arrangements were similar.

After all, she spent every day except Sunday in this very room, reading to him. When he realized that, Hunt felt another twinge of guilt at the length of the hours he required of her. Ingalls was right: he was a brute.

"There has been no occasion for us to speak of him," Bella said.

Which was true enough. They did not engage in social chitchat. He realized with a sense of surprise he had no idea where she lived. He supposed Ingalls had her address, or perhaps his man of business, but he couldn't remember having ever heard it.

"Surely—" he began, only to be interrupted.

"A child might disrupt your household's routine," Bella warned.

A child. A little boy. There was always the possibility that his presence would be disruptive. The house was huge, however, and as far as he was aware the nursery wing was much as it had been in his childhood—far enough removed from the rest of the living quarters to preclude any such problems.

"Surely one small boy couldn't accomplish so much," he said, smiling at her again.

Another silence. He wished he could see her face. That was the thing he had found hardest to deal with through the years. Not being able to read expressions. Of course, voices could be equally revealing, but not in a situation like this.

"Then…may I have time to think about your very kind offer, my lord?"

Again, she had taken him off guard. He'd thought she had already indicated her intent to refuse, and instead… Despite his avowals, a sense of anticipation, almost a physical reaction, stirred within him at the possibility that she might accept.

"Of course," he said. "Take as much time as you need."

"Thank you," she said.

He listened as she began to gather up the papers they had gone over this afternoon. He knew that the twilight shadows outside would be lengthening as people hurried home in the early-falling winter darkness. He tried to imagine Bella being greeted by her "dependents." He wondered if they would be as glad to hear the sound of her voice as he was each morning.

That was another part of the fantasy he had no right to indulge in, he admonished himself. They had a right to delight in her arrivals. He did not. And even if she accepted his proposal, he would still not have that right. At least not to do so openly.

"Good night, my lord," she said softly.

He could tell she was standing, probably looking down at him as he sat at his desk. He lifted his eyes, wondering what she saw when she looked at his face. He had long ago forbidden himself to think about that because it was something else he could not change.

"Good night, Mrs. Simmons."

It seemed there must be other words they should say to one another. Apparently she felt that as well, for she stood before his desk a long heartbeat before she turned and walked across the room. He didn't move until he heard the door close behind her.

Then the Earl of Huntingdon slowly lifted his hands and with trembling fingers touched the scarred skin around his unseeing eyes.

"Did you know she has a son?" the earl asked his valet that night as Ingalls helped him remove his waistcoat.

"She mentioned once that the boy had been unwell. A fever or a cough. I can't remember, but some childhood ill. That was some time before Christmas, I believe. She was fair anxious about him, I can tell you."

"And it never crossed your mind to inform me of the child's existence?" Hunt asked, his tone coldly demanding.

"Before you proposed to her, do you mean?" John Ingalls asked. He considered his master's dark, handsome face, and his thin lips twitched at the corners as he suppressed a smile.

"You know exactly what I mean," the earl said. "You suggested that Mrs. Simmons was in danger of suffering a nervous exhaustion from the demands I have made on her time and her patience. You painted a vividly heart-wrenching portrait of a woman worked far beyond her strength by a brute of an employer. A woman who was also forced to travel to and from her place of employment every day in the bitter cold."

"An accurate portrait, my lord," Ingalls said calmly, as he folded the waistcoat. "Nothing about it has changed."

"What has changed, John, is that I have offered marriage to a woman who has, I now discover, a small child."

"You don't like children, my lord?" The subtle movement at the corners of the valet's mouth flickered again.

"You know damn well what I'm talking about," the earl said.

"You're talking about installing a small boy in a household that's large enough for an army of brats to rattle about in without your ever running into one of them. I can't see what all the fuss is about."

"The fuss, as you term it, is about deception."

The earl's voice was carefully controlled, but it was a tone Ingalls had certainly heard on more than one occasion. This was an officer's voice, demanding an explanation from his subordinate. And that had been their roles when they had met.

Through the last ten years, John Ingalls's position in the Earl of Huntingdon's life had evolved into something very different. Despite the outward appearance they maintained, their relationship was a friendship. The mantle of authority that Alexander Coltrain had worn since birth, however, had not diminished. Not even with his blindness. It was in full force tonight.

"You're making a mountain out of a molehill, my lord," Ingalls said soothingly. "This marriage proposal is nothing but a business proposition. The fact that the woman has a boy changes nothing."

"What if—"

When the sentence was abruptly cut off, Ingalls glanced again at his master's face. The finely shaped lips were flattened, as if determined to keep the rest of that question from emerging between them. A muscle jumped in the hard line of the earl's jaw and the blue eyes seemed focused at a spot beyond the valet's shoulder. So intent was the focus that in spite of himself, Ingalls turned, briefly contemplating the empty corner behind him.

"What if?" he repeated cautiously, turning back to consider the classic features of a man he had known and loved for more than a decade. A man he admired more than any other of his acquaintance. A man who in battle knew no fear. Ingalls couldn't imagine, therefore, why the thought of adding a little boy to his bachelor household had so disturbed the ex-soldier.

"Nothing," the earl said.

Then his fingers, long and aristocratic and always sure in their movements, despite his blindness, began to tug impatiently at the intricate arrangement of his neckcloth. Ingalls understood him well enough not to interfere. The earl had said everything he intended to say on the subject, and questioning him would elicit no more information. It might even poison the delicate negotiations the valet had worked so hard to bring about.

However, as John Ingalls tossed and turned that night on his narrow mattress, a rare situation for a man who had never in his life suffered from self-doubt, the earl's words repeated over and over in his head. *What if...* And no matter how much he pondered on what could be worrying his master about the existence of that little boy, he had found no answer before he fell asleep.

"Marriage?" Fanny Hargreaves repeated disbelievingly.

"Marriage," Bella said, savoring the freedom finally to speak aloud the word which had haunted her thoughts all evening. She had said nothing about the earl's offer until Kit had been fed his supper, properly cuddled and then tucked into his bed.

"But why?" her aunt asked, honest bewilderment in her voice.

"I have no idea," Bella said truthfully. "He *said* it was for his convenience, but somehow..."

Still puzzling over what might be behind the sudden offer, Bella shook her head.

"Perhaps he has fallen in love with you, my dear," the older woman suggested.

Despite her advancing years, Fanny had never lost her belief in romance. Which must be a comfort, Bella thought. She herself was of a far more practical nature. As enticing as it might be to believe that the Earl of Huntingdon was in love with her, she knew better.

Never once in the two years she had worked for him had she allowed herself to think about him in those terms. It was all well and good for Fanny to entertain romantic notions, of course, but Bella was the one who was responsible for seeing that there was a roof over their heads and food on the table. She had known from the first that she could not afford to put a foot wrong with her self-contained employer.

She could not now. Desperately in need of advice, she had turned to the one person in all the world she could trust to have her best interests at heart, even if that heart were cloyingly sentimental.

"I think I should have known if the earl had suddenly developed a *tendre* for me," Bella said, smiling at her aunt.

"But he has asked you to *marry* him, my dear," Fanny said.

"Strictly as a matter of business."

"Business?" the old woman repeated. "In my

day, marriage was not a business. Not for the likes of us.''

Bella understood what Fanny meant, of course. For someone in the earl's position, marriages were often decided on the basis of how much wealth, land or distinction they would bring to the families involved. Only those who had none of those things to consider might marry for love.

Bella did not believe that Huntingdon had suddenly fallen in love with his penniless reader. If he had, he might have asked her to become his mistress, but certainly not his wife.

And even if he *had* fallen head over heels for a woman he'd never seen, he was, just as she had told him this afternoon, far too controlled to do something as impetuous as proposing marriage to her. However, try as she might, Bella had been unable to come up with any logical reason for his offer, especially since his determination never to marry was well known to his household.

"He said he wants me to live in the house because it would be more convenient. Apparently, he thinks of things he would like for me to do for him after I've gone home. Perhaps there is something he would like to hear read again for clarification. Or some letter that needs to be written. A speech. And since it's impossible for him to jot down those instructions..."

"Poor man," Fanny said. Her kind heart had always been touched by the earl's plight, since the first night Bella had come home, incredulous, despite Bertrand's connection, that she had been given the position.

"If we *did* move into his household," Bella began to warn, couching the possibility in terms her mind could deal with and not in those the earl had used this afternoon, "you must never let him hear you voice anything of that nature."

"A proud man, is he?" Fanny suggested.

"A man who does not recognize he has limitations," Bella said. Unconsciously, her voice had softened.

In the beginning she had been nervous about working so closely with a man who was blind, but she had very quickly been made aware that the earl made no allowances for his disability—at least none he could possibly avoid.

"He would not appreciate your concern for his 'plight,'" she added, smiling.

"Are you sure, Bella, my dear, that you have not developed a *tendre* for *him?*"

Shocked, Bella glanced up from the piece of needlework she had been toying with. Fanny's eyes were on her face, and in response, she blushed.

"Of course not," she said, recognizing that her denial was too abrupt.

"Is he…disfigured?" Fanny asked, the question holding the slightest edge of trepidation, perhaps even a fascinated horror.

"No," Bella said quickly, and then, knowing that she had not been completely honest, she added, "There *is* some scarring, but it is very faded. Not at all noticeable."

"You must be sure to caution Kit not to mention that. Little boys are apt to be curious."

"Of course," Bella said, but she wasn't really thinking about Kit's reaction to the earl. Or that Fanny's words seemed to imply the two of them would eventually meet.

She was picturing instead that beautifully stern visage. Of course, she admitted, it wasn't the earl's features she had come to admire, as fine as they admittedly were. It was, rather, the man himself. His character. And his courage.

A man who had asked her to marry him, she thought with a sense of wonder that had only grown stronger in the hours since he had spoken those shocking words this afternoon. A business proposition, she admonished herself, fighting against the romanticism that was Fanny's great failing. What Huntingdon was proposing was a true marriage of convenience. An arrangement simply intended to make both their lives easier.

"Are you going to accept, my dear?" Fanny asked.

"He'll probably have come to his senses tomorrow and tell me it was all a mistake."

"A gentleman would never do that."

"An employer might," Bella said, smiling.

"And if he doesn't? Oh, my dear, you would be a fool not to accept. It would put an end to all our problems. Never again to have to wonder how we shall pay the coal merchant or the greengrocer. Kit's education would be assured, as would his place in society. Why, of course it would," Fanny said, her voice suddenly full of awe. "After all, you would be a countess, Bella. The Countess of Huntingdon. Just think of it, my love."

And although she shook her head at Fanny's list of enticements, Bella was thinking of it, of course, as her eyes stared unseeingly into the fire. Finally, her lips curved into a small, secret smile.

Whatever happened tomorrow, she thought, she would always have this night to remember. The Earl of Huntingdon had asked her to be his countess, and she would treasure that offer, no matter what justification he might wish to give for having made it.

Chapter Two

"Come in by the fire," John Ingalls said as he opened the door to the earl's study the next morning. "Did they bundle you up right and tight in the carriage, Mrs. Simmons? It's cold enough out to freeze the Thames."

"Then we'll have another frost fair," Bella said, smiling.

She was accustomed to Ingalls's presence in the study, at least early in the morning. He was frequently the one who ushered her in, the earl already seated behind the huge rosewood desk that dominated the room. Automatically, her eyes sought his familiar figure, a peculiar feeling in the pit of her stomach as she did. Today, the chair behind the desk was empty. Her gaze quickly scanned the room before it returned to meet that of the earl's valet. He smiled at her.

"Lord Huntingdon will be down shortly," he said.

Not once in the two years she had worked for him had the earl broken his own rigid schedule. Despite what she had told herself during the journey to the town house this morning, she felt the strongest disappointment that he had done so today.

Not disappointment that he had thought better of his proposal, of course. She had expected him to do that, just as soon as he realized how ridiculous it was. Indeed, she herself had pointed out the impropriety of the match to him, so there was no need to be embarrassed by his apparent, if belated, recognition of that fact.

In any case, she had come this morning prepared to give him her refusal. Even if he had, during the intervening hours, failed to realize how impossible a marriage between them would be, she had not. But still...

She took a calming breath. She had thought the earl would have the courage to tell her himself instead of asking Mr. Ingalls to act on his behalf. Perhaps he had felt it would be less humiliating for her to do it in this way. After all, Bella knew that nothing went on in the earl's household that his valet wasn't aware of. Not even, it seemed, a patently ridiculous offer of matrimony.

She met John Ingalls's eyes, holding onto her smile and attempting not to let her expression reveal anything of what she was feeling. "I hope his lordship isn't indisposed."

"His lordship suffers from an incompetent staff who cannot seem to tie a cravat properly," a deep voice behind her said. "*Not* from an indisposition."

Bella turned and found the earl standing in the doorway, his shoulders almost filling the opening. He was dressed in a coat of navy superfine and a pair of fawn trousers that fitted without a wrinkle over his flat belly and strong thighs. And despite the twenty-six years through which her heart had beat quite normally within her breast, it fluttered.

There was no denying Huntingdon cut a handsome figure, but she had never before allowed herself to openly admire it. She wondered with a touch of unease if things would ever be the same in their relationship. If they ever *could* be.

"You have my sympathies, my lord," she said, controlling her smile, as her eyes found Ingalls's again.

"And mine," the valet said, his voice almost unctuous.

"Indeed." The earl's eyes seemed to consider his man.

That was something Bella had noticed before. An uncanny knack Huntingdon had of appearing to focus on the speaker. On more than one occasion she had felt as if he were really looking at her. More fanciful than poor Fanny, she thought, remembering, in spite of her intentions, her aunt's excitement last night over the earl's offer.

"Shall we begin?" Huntingdon asked.

"As you wish, my lord," she said.

"Have you had your tea, Mrs. Simmons?" John Ingalls asked.

"Of course," Bella said, surprised by the question. It was not her custom to take tea in the earl's study, not even on a morning as cold as this. She was not a guest, after all.

"Bring Mrs. Simmons tea when you bring my coffee," the earl ordered as he crossed the room, his long stride unhesitating.

He touched the corner of the rosewood desk as he approached it, his fingers finding the edge unerringly. When he slipped into the chair behind it, Bella relaxed a little, feeling as if things might be returning to normal.

The morning light from the windows beside the earl illuminated the strong planes and angles of his face, accenting the high cheekbones and playing over the slight hollows in the lean cheeks and delineating the strength of his jaw. It touched the curling raven hair with blue-black highlights.

When she heard the valet's steps on the hardwood floor of the hall and realized they were finally alone, Bella still didn't move. Instead, she stood watching the man who had yesterday asked her to be his wife, trying to fathom any possible reason for that request.

"And have you reached a decision about my suit, Mrs. Simmons?" Huntingdon asked, as if he had just read her mind. His eyes were focused almost on her face. Heartbreakingly almost.

And that, my girl, will not do, Bella admonished herself. *Not if you wish to keep this position.*

There was no doubt in her mind that the earl would dismiss her in a heartbeat if he suspected she had felt that quick surge of pity. From the beginning, that was the one thing she had known instinctively this man would never tolerate, not from her. Not from anyone.

"My lord," she began and was amazed to find that her voice trembled over the words.

She was not a woman prone to vapors or a quivering voice. Of course, she had never before been invited to become a countess, she thought. The idea of trying to assume that position was so ridiculous that, despite her nervousness, despite her tangled emotions, her sense of humor came to the rescue.

"Mrs. Simmons," he said politely, mocking her tone.

The earl's voice didn't tremble, of course. She couldn't imagine that it ever had during his entire life.

"Do you really intend that *I* should become the Countess of Huntingdon?" she asked him. The quiver was gone, replaced by her own mockery. Not of him, but of the image of her attempting to play that role.

"It is incumbent upon my wife to assume the

position. You have my apologies for any inconveniences the title may cause.''

One corner of his mouth had tilted, and that small sensation in the very bottom of her stomach happened again. This time, however, she was able to identify its cause.

After all, she was not an eighteen-year-old virgin, the sort of wife this man should be angling for. She was a widow, who had been married to a normal, healthy man for more than five years. And who had, in that time, enjoyed a normal, healthy relationship with her husband.

"And so, despite the drawbacks we both acknowledge as inherent in my offer, may I have your answer, Mrs. Simmons?" the earl said, his tone deliberately as light as hers had been.

Fanny was right, she realized. No matter how much he might now regret having made that outrageous offer, as a gentleman he wouldn't renege on it. So it was up to her, she supposed, ~~to put~~ them back on some sort of footing that would hopefully enable her to continue to work for him.

Never again to have to wonder how we shall pay the coal merchant or the greengrocer. Kit's education would be assured, as would his place in society.

Fanny's words echoed suddenly in Bella's head, momentarily closing her throat with their promise. All she had to do was say yes, and everything her aunt had predicted would become a reality. And besides that...

Her eyes again traced over the features of the man awaiting her answer. Despite the fact that no one would ever have known, she had fought against studying him like this through almost every day she had worked here.

Perhaps she had understood the temptation he represented. Because it was *so* tempting to dream, to fantasize that one day a man like this, a good and strong man, might step in and make all the hardships of her situation disappear. All she had to do was say yes, and just as Fanny had promised, they really would.

"I am very aware of the honor you do me, my lord," she began, choosing her words carefully.

"Don't let me interrupt," Mr. Ingalls said briskly, coming through the open door with a laden tray.

He carried his burden across to the earl's desk, the aroma of freshly brewed coffee and hot scones permeating the room. He set it down, and then took his master's coffee off the tray and placed it on the desk.

"Your coffee, my lord," he said. "Two inches above your right hand."

The earl's hands, clasped together on the surface of his desk, didn't move. His mouth tightened minutely, but Bella wasn't sure if that were in response to his valet's interruption or to his annoyance with those quite unnecessary instructions.

Ingalls had never before done anything like that in her presence. A little shocked, she looked at the valet's face. His eyes were on her, rather than on his master.

As she watched, they fell, and hers followed to see the earl's fingers move to locate the handle of the cup, a task which they accomplished without the slightest fumbling. Then Ingalls's gaze lifted once more to her face. One dark brow cocked, as if in question.

"Cream and sugar?" he asked after a few seconds.

She understood, however, that that was not the inquiry he had been making with that suggestively arched brow. "Cream," she said.

He fixed her tea, the spoon tinkling annoyingly in the silence. He brought it over to where she was still standing, like a visitor, in the center of the huge room. As he placed the cup in her hand, he held her eyes. And his mouth moved. The words his lips formed were perfectly clear, if soundless.

"Say yes," the Earl of Huntingdon's trusted valet mouthed. And then he turned back to face his master, as if that extraordinary exchange had not occurred.

"Will that be all, my lord?"

"Thank you, Ingalls. I believe it will be," the earl said.

There was some element in the tone of Huntingdon's response that Bella couldn't identify, but then, considering all the things that had happened yesterday and today that she didn't understand, she supposed that hardly mattered.

She held the cup of tea she had been given, her eyes on her employer's handsome face, as his valet turned toward the door behind her. As he passed, his eyes focused again on hers, and feeling the intensity of his gaze, she looked directly at him. He nodded encouragingly, and then he winked at her before he walked by her and through the door. The silence he left behind lasted a long time, and it was the earl who finally broke it.

"I believe you were about to give me your answer," he said.

So simple a thing, her heart whispered. One word, and everything about her life would change for the better. One word, and this man, who had for two years been her employer, would become something very different.

A marriage of convenience, she reminded herself. A business proposition. An arrangement suggested for his benefit. As it would be for hers, she admitted honestly. And perhaps...

Her eyes again traced his features. He was no longer looking at her. He had turned his face toward the windows on his left, lifting it to the warmth of the sun. The thin morning light outlined his profile, emphasizing its strength. Her eyes fell once more to his hands, which were lying on the top of his desk, so tightly entwined that his knuckles had whitened from the pressure.

Say yes, John Ingalls had urged her. And no one knew the Earl of Huntingdon better that he. No one, she thought.

Suddenly, as if he had realized how revealing his hands might be, the earl's fingers disengaged and he reached for the coffee the valet had brought. For the first time since she had known him, his fingers faltered, searching futilely for the cup and saucer he himself had put down only minutes before. And by the time they had been located, her decision had been made.

"Yes, my lord," Arabella Simmons heard herself say. "If you are sure this…arrangement is really what you wish, then I shall be honored to be your wife."

Wife, she thought, looking down on the thick gold band she wore on her left hand. Becoming someone's wife should surely effect more of a change in one's life. Since she had married the Earl of Huntingdon more than four weeks ago, however, there was very little difference in the even tenor of her days.

It was true that rather than being conveyed home every evening in his well-sprung coach, she simply retreated to the rooms she had been assigned upstairs to be greeted by Fanny and Kit. But other than that...

And what did you expect? she chided herself. *He gave you fair warning that to him this was simply a business arrangement. It was your own imagination that tried to believe it would become something else.*

Her imagination, spurred on by Fanny's romanticism, she supposed, and John Ingalls's mysterious behavior. She had even screwed up enough courage to ask the valet what he had meant by what he'd told her that day, and his answer, made with eyes widened in surprise, had simply echoed the earl's stated intentions. *Easier for everyone all around,* Ingalls had said, leaving her as bewildered by his motives as she had been by her husband's.

Her husband, she thought. There was so much that word should mean, which in this case it did not. Their relationship had not changed, and she had finally been forced by her own sense of disappointment to admit that she had secretly hoped it would.

As fanciful as Fanny, she thought in disgust, putting her hairbrush down on the dressing table.

Kit was standing beside her, his small body pressed against her side. There had been a low, distant rumble of thunder all evening, and she knew that was why her son was delaying the journey to the nursery upstairs. Bella had sent poor Fanny, who was suffering from the headache, to her room with the promise that she herself would see the little boy safely tucked into the narrow bed his stepfather had once occupied.

And that was another fanciful notion she should disabuse herself of, she decided, putting her arm around Kit's small yet sturdy shoulders. The idea that the earl would assume any sort of fatherly role in her son's life. That hadn't been part of the bargain they had made, and she had been very foolish to suppose that someone as self-contained—as rigid—she amended with a spurt of anger, might suddenly become paternal.

Self-contained and rigid for very good reasons, she admitted with a remorse as sudden as her anger. It would be very difficult for a blind man to attempt to interact with a lively four-year-old, however much that might please her. Not part of the bargain, she thought again, trying to be fair.

"I could sleep with you tonight," Kit said. "If you're lonely." The last was added almost hopefully.

"And what makes you think I'm lonely?" she asked, hugging him close and putting her lips against the soft fragrance of his curls that were the same dark copper as her own.

"You seem lonely. Since we moved here. Sad and lonely. Are you sad, Mama?"

"Of course not," she said, turning and putting her hands on his shoulders. She held him away from her so that she could look into his face. "I'm very happy here. Aren't you?"

Solemnly, he nodded, his eyes on hers. He should be happy, she thought. The nursery upstairs was full of toys, and he and Fanny had the whole floor to themselves during the day. There were always fires burning on the hearths, so that the rooms were warm and cheerful. Fanny had assured her that their meals were not only on time, but hot and the food plentiful. Which had certainly not always been the case when they had lived in the small house they rented in Wattington Lane, Bella admitted.

"Are you afraid of the storm?" she asked, knowing this was at the heart of Kit's reluctance to leave her.

He was usually as adventurous as the next boy, full of curiosity, but thunder and lightning, for some reason, terrified him. For the most part he had learned to mask his terror, but night and a storm and a new and rather strange house were proving to be beyond his ability.

"There's nothing to be afraid of," he said, repeating a lesson she and Fanny had reiterated often enough.

"Of course there's not," Bella said, soothing the tumbled curls off his forehead. "There really isn't, you know," she added softly, smiling at him.

She had worked very hard not to turn Kit into a mama's boy, a timid child afraid of his own shadow and clinging to her skirts. She wanted him to grow up to be the same kind of brave man... The kind of brave man he should be, she corrected, wondering as she did why the earl's face had come into her mind.

Perhaps because he had been so honored for his bravery. An acknowledged war hero, he had also handled the blow fate had dealt him with an undeniable courage. She could certainly do worse than to hold Huntingdon up as a model for Kit to follow.

That had been a part of what she had hoped for when she had agreed to this marriage. It didn't appear, however, that that would come to pass. Any more than any other of the foolish dreams she had cherished.

"I know," Kit said, his voice very low.

"Then...it's past time for bed," she suggested.

She could feel the depth of his sigh, but he made no complaint as they climbed the narrow stairs and he allowed her to tuck him in. It seemed that the storm might have moved on, content to threaten with the occasional low rumbling.

When all the rituals of bedtime had been completed, she found that she hated to leave Kit alone up here in the dark. She knew, however, that this was exactly what she must do if she didn't want him to grow up frightened of everything. If she wanted him to be the kind of brave Englishman who had defeated the Corsican monster on the battlefields of Europe.

Her mind seemed focused on military heroism tonight, she admitted, and of course, she was well aware of the reason for that near-obsession, she thought, as she hurried back to her own chamber. She pulled her dressing gown more closely about her against the chill. Not even the well-maintained fires in the bedchambers could heat the wide, drafty halls.

Bedchambers. Her mind seized on that word out of the tumbling thoughts. There had been no pretense, not even before the servants, that the arrangement between her and the earl was anything other than what it really was. She honestly couldn't decide if she were pleased by that or not.

But she had become adapt at meeting the sometimes speculative eyes of the earl's staff. Which, she admitted, always fell. After all, whatever the narrow bounds of her marriage, she was still the Countess of Huntingdon, and, overtly at least, she was treated with the respect that title demanded.

Of course, they might not treat her so if they could see her now, running shivering in her nightclothes through the near maze of hallways. She was certainly not behaving with the decorum due her position.

You have my apologies for any inconveniences the title may cause. At the remembrance of her husband's comment her lips tilted again. Hunt, at least, would see the humor in this.

And then, at that unthinking choice of words, her smile faded and her steps slowed. He might very well be the only person in this household who would find the spectacle she was making of herself amusing rather than shocking, but he would never "see" her like this.

She was the Earl of Huntingdon's wife, but he would never see whether she carried out her role with dignity or like the hoyden she appeared to be right now. He would never see her at all, and for some reason, that realization was extremely painful.

Wife, the Earl of Huntingdon thought. Surely there must be something more, some change that should have occurred in their relationship when Bella had become his wife. And yet, by design, *his* design, there hadn't been.

Her son was installed in the nursery, watched over by his governess, who was also his great-aunt. And other than that...

And what did you believe would change? he asked himself angrily, pacing back and forth across the thick Turkish carpet of his bedroom. *Did you believe that she would suddenly fall in love with you?* The short laugh that answered his mocking question held no trace of amusement.

Maudlin and self-pitying, he told himself. And

those were two things he had determined never to be. He had been satisfied with his life until she had come into it. Even as he thought it, he knew how unfair that accusation was.

It wasn't that he had been satisfied. It was that he had been numb, deliberately cutting himself off from emotions that he had thought he no longer had the right to feel. Or to expect a woman to feel for him.

Of course, he had had a mistress, at least for a while. He had hoped she would satisfy the physical cravings that had not been destroyed when he had lost his sight. He had found, however, that he could not endure her solicitousness and annoying helpfulness. After visiting her less and less frequently through the years, he had finally given her the house he'd furnished for her and the freedom to use it as she saw fit since he had no intention of ever darkening its door again.

Perhaps that had been a mistake, brought on by his pride, no doubt, as most of them were. Surely a mistake, because right now...

He took a deep breath, fighting the aching response of his body. Fighting for the control which had stood him in good stead for the last ten years. And why should he have to fight those very natural urges? he asked himself. He was a married man. A man with a wife.

Wife. The word reverberated again in his brain, echoing there as if he had shouted it into a cave.

His wife. Who lay sleeping in a chamber only a short distance from here. A room to which he could find his way without a moment's hesitation.

And when he had? That, of course, was the question that kept him pacing the floor of his chamber night after night, unable to sleep. Unable to escape into a far more forgiving darkness.

Maudlin bastard, he thought in disgust.

He walked over to one of the windows, and working by feel, pushed the draperies aside, throwing open the sash. The cold night air rushed in, carrying with it the scent of rain. The electric vigor of the storm.

He had always loved storms. The beauty of the lightning, splitting the dark sky with threads of fire. The crash of thunder that followed. Storms made him feel more alive. And they still did, perhaps even more so now than before. He could feel them. Smell them. Hear them rage and threaten.

He lifted his face into the moisture blown in by the wind, his nostrils distended to catch every subtle nuance of the forces that had been unleashed outside. He wondered if she were also awake, listening to the thunder, wincing with each brilliant flash of lightning which he could no longer see. He wondered if she were frightened, lying alone and trembling in that vast, canopied bed.

And if you knew she were? In response to that unanswerable question, he slammed the window closed and turned back to the room, which was now chilled and uncomfortable, the banked fire unable to conquer the sudden influx of cold air.

Which left him with a choice of alternatives. He could go to bed, which any sensible man would do, or he could find somewhere warmer. More comfortable. Comforting.

The progression of thought was as irritating as the question about Bella had been. Comforting? He hardly needed comforting. What he needed...

He took a deep breath, knowing very well what he needed. And knowing that was one thing he wasn't going to seek out.

There was brandy downstairs in his study. If it didn't help him sleep, it would warm him. Not as well as some other remedies perhaps, but at least it represented no risk. And there were damn few other elements in the current situation about which that could be said.

Chapter Three

The brandy was smooth, burning a passage all the way down to his stomach. Hunt closed his eyes, trying to will the tension away. Trying to let the liquor relax him.

The crack of thunder made him jump, probably because he hadn't been aware of the lightning that preceded it. He was aware, however, of the gasp that followed on its heels.

He turned, instinctively seeking the source of the sound, his senses more attuned to his surroundings than they had been when he had entered the room. His mind had been on something quite different from the possibility of an intruder then.

He realized as he listened that he was not alone. He could always tell, whether from the subliminal sound of the other person's breathing or from some primitive warning system that had grown stronger in the years since he'd been blinded.

He was not alone. And yet, whoever was in the

room had not spoken when he'd entered. Deliberately hiding?

"Who's there?" he demanded. He waited, hardly daring to breathe, but the silence stretched unbroken. Unbearable. "Answer me, damn it," the Earl of Huntingdon said, his voice rising as his fury grew. "Who are you, and what the hell are you doing in my study?"

"It's only me, sir," a small voice said.

It had come from the direction of his desk, Huntingdon realized. And his mind, although expecting a very different voice, quickly arrived at its proper identification. "Kit?"

He had never spoken the child's name, since they had not yet been formally introduced. It seemed strange to him now that they hadn't been. Of course, for reasons of his own, he had not questioned that strangeness. He wondered briefly if Bella could possibly have understood his reluctance to meet her son.

"Yes, sir," the boy said.

"Where are you?" Hunt asked.

"Under the desk."

"Under it?"

"Yes, sir," Kit reiterated, the note of unease clear in the quavering voice.

"Are you hiding from me?"

The child had probably been told he wasn't to enter this room, which would explain his original refusal to answer.

"No, sir," the boy said.

"Then why the hell—"

The earl cut off the profanity, wondering if he should apologize, perhaps more appropriately to Bella. Just at that moment, however, a clap of thunder rocked the house, eliciting a scrambling noise and another soft gasp from under the desk.

"You're afraid of the storm," Hunt realized, speaking the words aloud as soon as he thought them.

"Please don't tell Mama," Kit begged. "There's really nothing to be afraid of." It was obvious that was something the boy had been told, and just as obvious that at the moment he didn't believe it.

"There really isn't, you know," Hunt said, some of the tension that had driven him here draining away in the face of the child's desperate attempt to be brave.

Whistling in the dark, the earl guessed. Something with which he himself had a long and intimate acquaintance. *You have my sympathies, lad,* Hunt thought, but he didn't say that, of course. He could almost hear Bella's voice assuring the child there was nothing to be afraid of. Sometimes, however, even when one knew the truth of that, the demons refused to listen.

"It's only that it's so very loud," Kit said plaintively.

"It is that," Hunt agreed, moving across the

room, nearer the desk under which the child was cowering. "But I confess, there's something about the roar and grumble that I like."

"You *like* storms?" the small voice asked, disbelief writ large in the question, along with the merest hint of awe.

"I'm afraid so," Hunt said humbly. "I find them exciting."

"I expect that's because you can't see them."

"Perhaps," Hunt agreed, fighting a smile at the boy's honesty, "but I think I have always liked them."

"Even when you were little?"

"Even then," the earl acknowledged.

The gasp he heard was warning. It had obviously been elicited by another lightning bolt, which was rapidly followed by the noise of more thunder. Almost before it had faded, the Earl of Huntingdon felt a small, trembling hand slip into his. His fingers automatically closed over those of the child, who grasped them like a lifeline.

"It's all right," Hunt said. "Nothing can happen to you here."

"You won't let anything happen to me?" the child whispered.

It required a simple enough reassurance, but the request produced an unaccustomed thickness in his lordship's throat. After all, it had been a long time since anyone had expected him to offer protection.

"Nothing can happen to you here," he said

again, unable to rephrase his answer to accord with the real question the child had asked.

The hand holding his eased its grip somewhat. After a moment, Hunt walked over to his desk, leading the child with him. He touched the edge and then eased down into his chair. The little boy followed him as willingly as a puppy on a string.

As soon as the earl was seated, a small warm body pressed against his leg. He resisted the urge to run his hands over the boy's frame. With Kit's obvious relief at having company in the midst of the terror of the storm, he doubted the child would object to his examination. For some reason, however, Hunt found himself reluctant to make it, despite his curiosity about his new stepson.

"This is your study," Kit said. It was not a question.

"Yes, it is. Your mother and I work here."

"Doing important things for England," Kit said, a hint of pride in his voice.

Hunt's lips moved into a smile, which he hoped the darkness would hide. There was a time when he had been as convinced of that as Kit seemed now.

"I'm trying to," he said.

"And my mama helps you."

"Yes, she does."

"That's why we came to live with you. So she could help you even more."

Hunt couldn't imagine why he found that explanation disappointing. After all, it was the same one he had given Bella when he asked her to marry him. It hadn't been his reason, of course, which had had far more to do with the picture Ingalls had painted of Bella's supposed suffering than with any concern for his work.

In the weeks she had lived in his house, however, he had gradually been forced into an admission of why he had really gone along with Ingalls's suggestion. And it was not because he had decided he had no more interest in women and might as well marry for the sake of convenience. It was, rather, because he had a great deal of interest in *one* woman. An interest that had only grown since that woman had become his wife.

"And because I thought it would be nice if you all lived here," Hunt said aloud. "Do you like living in my house, Kit?"

"Most of the time."

"When it isn't storming?" the earl guessed.

"I like the nursery. And all the toys. Mama says some of them were yours."

"Your mama's right. Which do you like best?"

"The soldiers," Kit said promptly. "I play with them every day."

"So did I," Hunt said, his voice softened by remembrance, and not only of days spent in that room upstairs.

"And the fire," Kit said. "Mama says Aunt

Fanny and I may have a fire at any time we wish. Is that true?''

''At any time,'' the earl agreed, wondering at what deprivations in the child's past would prompt that question.

He felt the boy's physical shrinking, and it prepared him this time for the following roll of thunder. It did not prepare him for the small, solid body that suddenly came clambering onto his lap. Or for the childish arms which wrapped themselves fiercely around his neck.

Unthinkingly, Hunt pulled the boy closer, sheltering the trembling body against his own. Even when the thunder had faded into an indistinct and distant rumble, neither of them seemed eager to move. After a long time, the small, curly head that rested against the earl's shoulder turned. The child's breath sighed out, warm against Hunt's cheek.

In relief? the earl wondered. And then the breathing settled down into a regular rhythm. Far too regular to indicate anything other than sleep.

Again, that unfamiliar thickness settled in the Earl of Huntingdon's throat. It seemed that whatever the terms he and Bella might come to in regards to this ''arrangement,'' his stepson had his own idea about what the boundaries of their relationship should be. And although Hunt could never have envisioned what his first meeting with this child might be like, he had to admit he was not disappointed in the outcome.

Perhaps he had the darkness to thank for the child's ready acceptance of him, but still... Not disappointed at all, he thought again, moving his hand up to soothe over the softly tumbled curls at the back of the little boy's head.

The crash was loud enough that Bella paused in her reading, her voice cut off abruptly midsentence. Together they listened a moment, the sound of the rain outside, beating against the room's tall Palladian windows, drowning out the low noises of the fire.

Hunt waited for her to go on, but the silence lengthened. There were voices raised in the distance, and then Bella said, "Would you excuse me a moment, my lord?"

He heard her put down the newspaper she had been reading aloud to him. He heard the rustle of her skirts as she crossed the room, and then, when the door was opened, the voices from the hall, much louder now.

The words were still indistinguishable, but he could identify the speakers: Mrs. Crutchen, his housekeeper; Ingalls; and occasionally the deeper, more sonorous tones of Blair, his majordomo. And then finally Bella's voice, her dismay quite clear.

"Oh, no," she said.

Curious, the earl rose and walked across the

room, still listening to the hubbub. It was evident Mrs. Crutchen was extremely upset. Ingalls's tones, however, were soothing.

And Bella? he wondered. *What the hell had become of Bella?*

He touched the frame of the study door, and then he walked forward, counting his steps without being conscious of what he was doing. The habit was ingrained now, requiring no thought.

"What's going on?" he asked into the din.

The resulting silence was instantaneous. He had the feeling that every eye had focused on him. It wasn't a particularly comfortable experience.

"Nothing, my lord," Ingalls said. "At least nothing that need concern you."

"It's your great-grandmother's Vincennes vase," Mrs. Crutchen said indignantly. "Smashed to smithereens," she added with a sniff. "I should think *that* would be of concern to your lordship."

"Indeed it is," he said, wishing he hadn't interfered.

Whichever of the servants had been careless enough to break such a valuable piece of porcelain would have to be punished, of course, but that was Blair's domain. Hunt supposed all sorts of things would go into the decision of how to handle that punishment. Blair and Mrs. Crutchen were privy to information about each member of the staff he himself couldn't possibly know. He would be told if the servant were to be dismissed as a result of this, but he would bow to their judgment.

"Mrs. Simmons?" he said, and realized his mistake. Bella was no longer Mrs. Bertrand Simmons. She was his wife.

Perhaps that was why she had come out here, he realized. He hoped she would be wise enough not to intervene in whatever punishment Blair meted out, but if she did, he would have to stand behind her. Even if it meant going against his butler's decision.

"I didn't mean to."

It was the same plaintive voice Hunt had heard last night at the height of the storm and hearing it now, everything fell into place. Including Bella's dismayed exclamation.

"You shouldn't have been downstairs," she said to her son. "If you had only done what you were told, Kit, this would never have happened."

"Have someone clean it up, Blair," the earl ordered, deciding that since his great-grandmother had been dead more than three decades, far too much fuss was being made over the loss of her vase.

The decision might have had something to do with his sudden suspicion as to why Kit was in this hall this morning, a place he had obviously been told to avoid. Last night he had come downstairs to find not only welcome, but solace. The possibility that the boy had been seeking him created a warmth in the center of Hunt's chest that meant far more than a broken pot, no matter its age or value.

"Yes, my lord," Blair said obediently, but Hunt could hear the displeasure in his tone.

"And nothing further is to be said about the accident," he added, the order edged with the same politely iced tone his father had used with such effect.

"Come on, lad," John Ingalls said cheerfully. "I'll take you back upstairs. We'll have another look at those soldiers you are so fond of. I'll show you how Boney set up his forces at Waterloo, if you want me to."

His voice faded as he directed the boy toward the massive staircase. The child said something in response, but they were far enough away by then that the words were indecipherable. The earl had the urge to ask them to wait for him, but of course, no invitation to join them had been issued.

"That will be all, I should think," he suggested, raising one brow, as if to question any objection to that pronouncement.

"Very good, my lord," his butler said.

Mrs. Crutchen sniffed again, but he could hear her bustling away, perhaps to round up the maids to take care of the mess.

"Bella?" he said softly.

"I'm here, my lord," she answered.

The note of dismay, or perhaps even of something more profound, was still in her voice. And she was nearer than he had anticipated. Near enough that he could reach out and squeeze her arm reassuringly. Except he couldn't be certain she would welcome his comfort.

"Shall we," he asked, indicating the direction to his study with one outstretched hand.

"Of course," she said, her voice too subdued. Definitely not Bella's voice. Not the way he was accustomed to hearing it.

When he reached the door, he waited beside it until she had gone through, slipping past him and leaving a gentle waft of rosewater in her wake. When she was inside, he stepped into the room and closed the door behind him. His hand on the knob, he stood before it a moment. He needed to apologize for his earlier slip of the tongue and was not quite sure how to go about it.

"I am so sorry," Bella said. "I know that the vase must have had great sentimental value to you and that it was terribly expensive as well. I don't suppose..." She hesitated.

"What don't you suppose?" he asked finally.

"That you would allow me to pay for it. It might take me a long time, but I assure you—" The halting words stopped in response to his shout of laughter.

"Good God, Bella, you're my wife. I don't expect to become your creditor. Besides, you have leave to smash anything in this house. Leave to get rid of the lot and redecorate the whole if you like. This is not a museum. It's your home. As it is Kit's home,'' he added, remembering the pleasantly solid weight of the child in his arms as he had carried him upstairs last night.

The darkness had been no deterrent to him on that journey. And when he had laid the boy in the very bed he had once occupied, he had stood in the room for a long time, breathing in the scents— and the memories—of his own childhood.

"Even so, he must be punished,'' Bella said, bringing him back to the issue at hand.

"He's a child. Accidents happen.''

"Not accidents of this magnitude. And not if Kit does as he's told,'' she said. "I can't imagine why he would have disobeyed.''

He could hear the anxiety and the disappointment in her voice. The fact that Kit had felt free to come downstairs was as much Hunt's fault as it was any failure of discipline on the boy's part. Perhaps if Bella understood Kit's reasons, she might be more willing to forget and to forgive.

Besides, if Hunt remembered correctly, and he knew that he did, the vase in question had stood on a tall pedestal at the foot of the stairs. He might just as easily have broken it himself.

It wouldn't be the first household object he had disposed of in that fashion. Of course, that sort of accident hadn't happened in years, but had he been the one who demolished the heirloom, no one

would have said a word about *his* carelessness.
They would all have pretended it had never happened. He wished he had been around when Kit
had knocked the vase off its stand. He would have
taken credit for the destruction, and the scene in
the hallway would have then had a very different
tone.

"I think perhaps Kit was coming here," he said.

"Here?" Bella repeated.

"I found him at the height of the storm last night
hiding under my desk."

"Under your desk?" Again, she echoed his
words. "But…"

"He was afraid. And I promised him I wouldn't
tell you that, so please don't betray to him that I
have. The desk seemed safe, I suppose. In truth,
it's as solid as an oak."

"And were *you* afraid, too?" Bella asked. "Is
that why *you* were down here at the height of the
storm?"

Trust Bella to ask the one question he didn't
want to answer, Hunt thought. He found he was
far less willing to explain his reasons for being
here last night than he was to explain Kit's.

"I couldn't sleep," he said. "The noise of the
storm perhaps. I came down for a glass of brandy,
and found Kit. At first…"

He stopped, knowing that what he had thought
at first was not something he was willing to share.
Not yet, anyway.

"At first..." she prompted.

"Dear Echo," he said, smiling at her, "are you to repeat everything I say?"

"No, my lord. Only the things you *don't* say."

"And that is something else that must change," he said. "We can't go on in this fashion."

"In what fashion?"

"You are not Mrs. Simmons. And I am not your lord."

"And *master,*" she said sotto voce, but the amusement was clear, even in the whisper, and he was relieved to hear it.

"I shall call you Bella, and you shall call me...Hunt? My friends do. Or Huntingdon if you prefer. Anything besides my lord."

"And when we're alone?" she asked.

He could have sworn there was something else in the husky timbre of that question. Something carefully hidden under the laughter. Perhaps it was simply the intimacy of the phrase. *And when we're alone.* They were alone now, of course, but her tone seemed to imply a future situation entirely unlike this one.

"My name is Alexander," he said.

"I know."

The silence grew, and then he heard the rustle of the newspaper she had been reading from when they had been interrupted. It seemed she had crossed the room to take it up again from his desk where she had laid it when she heard the commotion. Apparently, she was ready to return to work.

Fighting disappointment, he walked across the room. As he reached out to touch the edge of the desk, which he had done every morning for years, his fingers encountered something quite different from its hard wooden surface.

"I beg your pardon," he said, mortified that he hadn't known she was there.

And she was still there, he realized. Close enough that the subtle scent of rosewater washed over him in a great roiling wave of heat and desire. There. Near enough that he could grasp her shoulders and pull her to him. Bend her pliant body to his and hold her in his arms. Put his mouth over the soft trembling sweetness of hers.

He did none of those things, of course. He took one step back, away from his desk. Away from his wife. And then he waited.

"My mistake, my lord," she said after several long tense seconds. "Please forgive me."

He heard her move to the chair she usually occupied. Clearing his passage to his own, he realized.

All afternoon, as he listened to her beautiful voice, moving smoothly from one topic to the next, it moved also within his heart. And the Earl of Huntingdon knew he was truly lost. He was no longer in love with a woman's voice. He was in love with the woman.

* * *

"I have come to apologize, my lord," Kit said, stumbling only slightly over the word.

"I thought perhaps you had come to visit me," Hunt said, smiling at the child.

He had been surprised when Ingalls had ushered the boy into his bedchamber, but perhaps, given the scene downstairs today, his valet had decided that coming here would be less traumatic for Kit.

"I am forbidden to visit you," his stepson said softly. "I have been very disobedient."

"Would you like to visit me, Kit?" Hunt asked, hearing the wistfulness of the reply. "If we can obtain your mother's permission, of course."

"She's very angry."

"Only angry that you disobeyed her, lad," Ingalls said. "She's not angry that you wished to visit the earl. Perhaps if his lordship spoke to her...?"

Huntingdon was surprised that John had taken a hand in the conversation, but since he was probably better informed about what went on in this household than his master, the earl could only defer to his valet's assessment of the situation.

"Would you do that, sir?" Kit asked anxiously. "I should like to visit you above all things."

"And perhaps the earl might return the favor. He knows more about those soldiers you've found in the nursery upstairs than anyone. I believe they were his. Weren't they, my lord?'' Ingalls asked innocently.

Knowing quite well when he was being manipulated, Hunt raised a questioning brow at his valet, but he didn't deny the truth of the assertion, of course.

"They once were mine. Now, however, they belong to Kit.''

"You could come play with them if you wish,'' the child said magnanimously.

"Would you like that?'' Hunt asked, flattered despite John's rather blatant attempt to solicit this invitation.

"Very much. If my mama doesn't mind you coming to visit me. Aunt Fanny doesn't mind anything I wish to do.''

Both men laughed at the honest admission.

"Then I shall ask your mama for permission for us to exchange visits,'' Hunt said.

"Now say good-night,'' Ingalls advised, "like a good boy, and I'll tuck you in upstairs.''

"You come, too,'' Kit invited.

Again the small hand slipped into the earl's. Hunt tightened his fingers around it, savoring the feeling the trusting warmth of that hand resting in his gave him.

"His lordship needs to speak to your mama, remember,'' John reminded. "And then maybe tomorrow...'' he said enticingly.

Huntingdon could only imagine the exchange of

looks that passed between the two, but Kit's fingers
freed themselves, reluctantly it seemed.

"Good night," the boy said politely. "Come
and play with us if you can. If Mama will let you,"
he added.

Stifling the grin that remark produced, the earl
put out his hand, accurately finding the child's
head. He ruffled the soft hair, as fine as silk under
his fingers. "Sleep tight," he said softly.

"Don't forget to ask," Kit begged.

"I won't."

"Tonight," John suggested.

There was a brief silence.

"Come on, lad," Ingalls urged, perhaps realizing he'd gone far enough. "We don't want to make
your mama angry again by missing bedtime."

Hunt listened to them cross the room. When the
door opened, Kit rushed out into the hall, but Ingalls turned back to say, "Her ladyship hasn't gone
to bed yet, my lord. Just in case you were wondering."

"I wasn't," the earl said succinctly. "And I
must thank you for your concern for my entertainment. Are you up to something, Ingalls?"

"Me, my lord? Now what would I be up to?"

"I can only imagine," Huntingdon said.

"Well, it doesn't take much imagination to
know that the two of you had better work out some
accommodation for the boy. He likes you, my lord.
And that's quite a compliment. Don't you go dis-

appointing him. It won't do, you know. He thinks
you're brave enough to face any challenge. Even
this one.''

The door closed before the earl had a chance to
ask the questions that sprang to mind. Why would
his stepson think him brave, when he knew nothing
about him? Unless, of course...

Ingalls had obviously been telling war stories.
And he would put a swift end to that. Bella would
not appreciate John filling the boy's head with tales
of derring-do. Hunt definitely didn't appreciate
them if they dealt with any of his own military
exploits.

War was not a fit subject for a child, he thought,
walking across to the window and opening it as he
had last night. There was no storm tonight to elec-
trify the air. Only the crisp bite of the cold. He
lifted his face, thinking about the other thing Ingalls had said before he ran off without giving him
a chance to respond. *He thinks you're brave
enough to face any challenge. Even this one.*

Perhaps because he knew John so well, Hunt
understood, despite the rather cryptic reference, the
challenge his valet had reference to. It seemed that
his feelings for Bella were no more a secret from
Ingalls than anything else about his life had been.
And he was forced to wonder, since he had obviously betrayed himself to his valet, if Bella could
possibly be aware that his motives for this marriage

were much different than he had portrayed them to be. And if she did, he also wondered what she felt.

What she felt about him. That was the real question, of course. And finding the answer to it was the challenge John thought he was up to. He only wished he himself were half that confident.

Chapter Four

It had been a very long day, the Countess of Huntingdon decided as she sat before her dressing table that night. And a most distressing one. Of course, that confession was made only to her mirror, so she was betraying to no one the doubts that plagued her.

First had been Kit's "accident," as the earl had referred to what had happened this morning. Despite his kindness in minimizing the loss, she deeply regretted that her son had destroyed an item of such monetary and emotional value.

Kit had always been a well-behaved child, but given the confines of his previous existence, perhaps that had simply been a lack of occasion for mischief. In this house, however, which he must naturally be eager to explore, the opportunities for getting into trouble seemed endless.

Poor Fanny was no longer up to watching over such a lively and inquisitive little boy, Bella admitted. She herself couldn't watch Kit, not and do the job for which she had been hired. *And wed,* she added, with an unaccustomed tinge of bitterness.

Despite the seriousness of the rest, this was, she admitted, the crux of her despair. She was married to a man who had no interest in her as a woman. The trouble was that she was most definitely a woman. A woman with needs and desires she had discovered during her first marriage and for which she had hoped to find fulfillment in this one as well.

Instead, she had found a husband who seemed to have no appetite for a physical relationship. He didn't even want to touch her. When his hand had accidentally brushed against her body this morning, he had moved away as if he had been scalded. Or contaminated.

The lips of the woman reflected in the mirror tightened. She had known there was a gulf between them when she had agreed to this marriage. A looming gap composed of differences in position, family, wealth, education and experience. Too wide a distance, apparently, for the Earl of Huntingdon to wish to span.

And worst of all, she had no right to complain. He had been quite explicit about the parameters of this marriage. He wanted the convenience of having her live in his home. Marrying her was the only way society would accept that arrangement, since her family and her birth, if not noble, were certainly respectable.

Convenience, she thought, her bitterness growing. That's all she was to him. Despite his calling her Dear Echo, a phrase she had examined in her memory again and again throughout the day, trying to believe it might have some significance. Despite his kindness about Kit. Despite—

The knock on her door interrupted the mental tirade. Her immediate thought was that Kit had gotten into trouble again, but surely he was safely tucked into bed by now. She had had Ingalls's promise about that when she had left them playing with the battalions of metal soldiers before the nursery fire, so she wondered what this could be.

"Come in," she called, half turning on the satin-covered bench of her dressing table so that she was facing the door...which opened to reveal her husband. Her heart stopped and then resumed its familiar rhythm, beating as fast as it had this morning when she had seen the shards of that priceless French porcelain vase scattered all over the gleaming hardwood floor of the hall.

"My lord?" she said. Her voice sounded slightly breathless, but considering that Huntingdon's visit was unprecedented, perhaps he would put its thready quality down to surprise.

"May I come in?" he asked politely.

"Of course," she said.

She rose, hurrying to the door, and realized belatedly that she was wearing nothing but her night rail and dressing gown. Luckily, the latter was of velvet and thick enough to be unrevealing. Even as the thought formed, she remembered that it could not matter to her husband if she were wearing sackcloth and ashes. Or nothing at all.

"Is something wrong?" she asked anxiously, denying that quick surge of regret. *Not allowed,* she reminded herself, her eyes anxiously searching the dark, handsome face.

"Not that I'm aware of," he said, sounding puzzled by her question.

And then neither one of them said anything for what seemed a very long time. She fought the hope that was slowly filling her heart as those silent seconds ticked by. After all, he had come to her room. Surely…

"Forgive my intrusion, but…I have a favor to ask," he said finally, his mouth tilting.

"A favor?"

"A favor, Echo," he said, the slight smile widening. "Only a small one, so I'm very hopeful you'll agree."

"Of course," she said, struggling to control the disappointment that had replaced the tender green shoot of hope. A "small favor" did not seem to imply he was seeking what she had been hoping for when she saw him in her doorway.

"Is something wrong, Bella?"

She fought the urge to say "Wrong, my lord?"
Echo, indeed.

"Of course, nothing's wrong," she said instead.

"You sounded…" He hesitated, and then he
shook his head. "Forgive me. When one is forced
to rely on the nuances of voice, one sometimes
reads too much into them."

"Is that what you do?" she asked. "Read our
voices?"

"Tone. Inflection. It helps me know what people
are thinking, I suppose. So much of communication is unspoken, and when one is deprived of
those telling clues of posture, gesture, and expression, one attempts to compensate. Sometimes I
overcompensate."

It was the first time in the two years she had
known him that he had spoken to her of his blindness. She drew an unsteady breath, knowing that
how she responded to this confidence might affect
their relationship for a very long time. Perhaps forever.

"I should think it would be difficult not to."

Noncommittal enough, she decided. Not fawn-
ingly admiring, which he would hate. And, she
hoped, not cutting off this unexpected discourse.
Which *she* would hate.

"Perhaps," he said. "However, I didn't come
to talk about my failings."

"I didn't know you had any," she said, her

voice tinged by the bitterness she'd admitted before his arrival.

"I beg your pardon."

"You never seem to fail at anything," she explained, realizing anew how true that was.

Despite the long hours of preparation it took him to become acquainted with every aspect of the topic under debate in the House of Lords, he was frequently the one whose well-reasoned opinion the papers quoted. When she read those articles, sometimes reading them aloud to him, more often perusing them in secret, she felt a sense of pride that she had helped him accomplish his goals. And undeniably a sense of pride in him.

"No obvious failing, anyway," she said. "Not since I've known you."

"I'm flattered, of course, but...perhaps you haven't known me long enough," he said, smiling at her again.

"Two years," she said.

"That hardly seems possible," he said softly.

It seemed he had been a part of her life for far longer than that. And of course, this was another indication that she was the one whose expectations of this marriage were out of line.

"Bella?"

"I'm sorry," she said, gathering her wits. "We seem to have strayed from the purpose of your visit."

"Of course. The purpose of my visit," he repeated, as if he had only now remembered there was one.

With a great deal of self-discipline, she denied herself the pleasure of calling *him* Echo.

"Do you suppose we could sit down?" he asked unexpectedly. "If I remember correctly, there are two chairs before the fire. Or have you rearranged the furniture?"

"This was your mother's room," she realized. The housekeeper had told her that, along with the cherished information that his lordship had expressly chosen his mother's suite for her.

"She would sometimes let me come in and watch her dress for the evening," he said. "Only the finishing touches, of course. The placement of a patch, perhaps. The selection of an ornament to go in her hair. Her jewelry."

"Did she let you choose them?" Bella asked, fascinated by the revelations, far more personal than he had ever made before.

"Occasionally. Occasionally, she even wore whatever I had selected. More often she explained why it wouldn't do."

Although his voice was full of amused nostalgia, Bella was horrified. She couldn't imagine doing that to Kit. If she had given her son freedom to choose something for her toilette, then she would certainly wear whatever he had chosen.

"Perhaps her early lessons account for your excellent taste," she said, trying to find something positive to comment on in the sad little vignette he had shared.

"I'm forced to rely now on Ingalls's taste, I'm afraid. Which I can only *hope* is excellent."

She could feel the blush rise into her throat. For the first time since she had known him, some of his reserve seemed to be melting, and she had had to spoil it by a thoughtless remark.

"You may rest assured that it is," she said stiffly.

"Thank you," he said. "And *now*, Bella, we really need to talk about Kit."

"Kit?" she echoed, taken by surprise.

She waited for him to tease her, and when she realized he didn't intend to, there was a frisson of disappointment to go along with her sense of dread. What could he want to say to her about her son? Obviously, something important enough that it had brought him to her bedchamber for the first time.

"By the fire?" he reminded softly.

A new anxiety stirred in her chest. Should she offer him her arm? If he had not been in this room since his mother's death, then it might be difficult for him to negotiate, perhaps even dangerous.

"Forgive me, Bella, if I'm being obtuse," he said in response to her silence. "Had you rather we talk tomorrow? Downstairs?"

"I would rather you tell me how to go about guiding you to those chairs," she said truthfully.

His laughter sounded almost as relieved as it made her feel. "Is the room a total maze?"

She looked across at the inviting fire and realized it really wasn't. There were almost no obstacles between it and them. "Not really."

"Then this should do," he said, holding out his hand.

She hesitated only a second before she took his fingers, which were warm and hard, especially when compared to the trembling uncertainty of hers.

"Are you sure you trust me to do this?" she asked, slanting a glance at his face, which seemed perfectly composed.

"Implicitly," he said, the thread of laughter still lurking in his voice.

She said a quick prayer that nothing disastrous would happen, and then she began to lead him to the wing chair that sat on the right hand side of the fireplace. When they reached it, she hesitated again, and he simply waited.

Finally, she placed his hand on the back of the chair. She watched as his fingers brushed along the top and down the arm. Then he stepped past her, keeping his hand always in contact with the chair, and sat down.

A sense of accomplishment—and gratitude— overwhelmed her. When she moved to take the other chair, she realized that her knees were trembling. Delayed reaction? Or fear of what he was about to say?

Oh, please, she prayed, *not that Kit and Fanny must leave.* The earl hadn't sounded upset this morning. Perhaps this was to be a simple admonition that she must make Kit keep to the nursery wing. Since she was in complete agreement with that restriction, she would readily accept it. That was what she had intended all along.

"I think that we must make some other accommodation for Kit," he said.

And her heart sank. "Indeed?" The word was only a breath.

"I confess I enjoyed his visit last night. And Kit seemed to enjoy visiting me. I hope you will not forbid him to come to my study again."

"*Not* forbid him?" she asked, unsure that she had heard him right. Even by firelight, she could see the quick tilt of his lips, but he didn't point out that she had done it again. "You want him to come?" she asked carefully.

"He seemed to enjoy his visit as much as I enjoyed having him. I thought at the time—"

He stopped, and she waited until it was obvious he didn't intend to complete the sentence.

"Yes?" she prompted.

"He doesn't mind these," he said, raising his right hand to touch those long, dark fingers to the scarred skin.

Her own eyes filled with quick tears, but she

blinked them away, determined he would not hear them in her voice. "Why should he mind them? They are very faint, I assure you."

His lips tightened quickly before he said, "I thought it was simply that he hadn't seen them clearly in the darkness, but this morning and even tonight—"

Again the sentence was cut off, and she knew then that this was something he had not intended to tell her.

"Kit came to your study tonight?" she asked. She couldn't believe that her son would disobey her again, not after this morning's fiasco.

"No," Huntingdon said quickly. "Forgive me, Bella. Ingalls brought him to my room to apologize for breaking the vase. In the course of that visit, Kit invited me to come to the nursery and play with the soldiers."

"And you want to," she said.

It wasn't hard to see that he did. He was fighting a grin, looking almost as young as Kit. And something very peculiar happened within her chest.

"They *are* my soldiers," he said, smiling openly now.

And with that smile, the fear that she hadn't even realized she had been living with these weeks disappeared.

"You like him," she said.

"Of course. More importantly, I believe Kit likes me. At least he doesn't seem to be afraid of me." His hand lifted, making what was almost a gesture toward his eyes. "Nor does he seem to be unduly uncomfortable about…this. So, with your permission, of course, we should like very much to continue to exchange visits." The earl stood, his left hand maintaining contact with the chair. "Do we *have* your permission, Bella?"

"And my blessing," she said softly, denying again the sting of tears.

"Thank you," Huntingdon said, his voice as low as hers.

"Thank *you*, my lord."

"Hunt," he corrected. "Or Alex, if you prefer."

When we are alone, she had said this morning. They were alone now. Alone in her bedchamber.

"Hunt," she agreed.

"That wasn't so bad, was it?"

"Not nearly so difficult as I had imagined."

"Good," he said. "Then I shall bid you good night."

"Do you need me to—"

"Not now. I know the way," he said, but he didn't move.

"Was there something else?" she asked finally, watching the play of the firelight over the strong features of the man she had married.

"Any regrets, Bella?"

She knew what he meant, and she searched her heart for a truthful answer. She had no regrets about marrying him, of course, but many about the nature of their relationship. Despite tonight's disclosures, however, those were something she still couldn't share with him. Not yet.

"No," she whispered, forcing the words through the tightness in her throat. "No regrets."

"Good," he said again. He turned, and stepped away from the chair, moving without hesitation toward the door.

As he put his hand on the knob, her question stopped him. "And you. Do *you* have regrets?"

She couldn't see his face, and she realized this was what he had meant about missing those subtle clues of gesture and expression. She wanted to see what was in his eyes when he answered her. And it was a very long time before he did.

"Only that I waited so long," he said softly. Then he opened the door and disappeared into the darkness of the hall.

Had he made a fool of himself? Hunt wondered as he sat at his desk the next morning, waiting for Bella to come down. When she greeted him, he thought he would be able to tell if he had from her voice, which was so richly textured that it expressed far more than her words. And there had been something in it last night—

"Planning to get an early start on the work, are we, my lord?" Ingalls said as he came into the room.

John Ingalls had obviously expected his em-

ployer to wait until his normal hour to come downstairs, although he was certainly aware of how
early Hunt had sent for him to help him dress.
What he probably hadn't been aware of was how
little his master had slept last night.

"Why not?" Hunt said.

Ingalls set the tray on the desk, but there was
no clink of china to indicate that he was removing
the earl's cup and saucer.

"Something troubling you, my lord?"

Hunt briefly debated asking for John's opinion.
After all, very little that went on in this household
escaped Ingalls's notice. This seemed too private,
somehow, despite all they had shared through the
years. And he couldn't be sure, in spite of its importance, that John would tell him the truth.

"Only the lack of my coffee," he said.

"Of course. And I took the liberty of bringing
in the most recent invitations. Now that the Season
is upon us, they are beginning to pour in. I thought
you and her ladyship might wish to confer together
on which to accept."

Ingalls certainly knew that he declined almost
all of the invitations he received. Most were sent
as a matter of course by those with whom he as-
sociated in Parliament or strictly on the basis of
his title. The few he did accept were for very private entertainments at the homes of close friends.

"You know—" he began, when John's voice
continued, just as if he hadn't spoken.

"Her ladyship must be excited. It's been a long time, I should imagine, since she's been out and about in society. And that's a shame, as young and as lovely as she is. If you'll forgive me for saying so, my lord, she'll be even lovelier when she's a bit more fashionably dressed. I've been expecting her modiste to call any day now."

"Have you, John?" the earl said softly.

There was no doubt of Ingalls's intent. And no doubt he was correct about everything he'd said. Unforgivably correct. It had been too long since Bella had been in society. And too long, apparently, since she'd had a new dress.

"Indeed I have, my lord."

"Are you implying that Lady Huntingdon is dowdy?"

"I'm saying it's a crime that a woman who looks like that isn't the most fashionably dressed in the capital. And if you could see her, my lord, you'd be agreeing with me."

If you could see her.... It was the perfect opportunity, of course, to do something he had wanted to do for a very long time. Long before he had considered asking Bella to marry him. Despite their friendship, however, he had never asked Ingalls to describe his wife to him. He didn't now.

"I have received Lady Huntingdon's permission for the boy to call on me," he said instead. "I would appreciate it if you could bring Kit here this afternoon. If he wishes to come."

"Oh, he'll want to come. Don't you be worrying about that. He has a thousand questions to ask you, my lord. He's very excited about the possibility."

"Questions about what?"

"About you, primarily. About your experiences on the Peninsula. And don't be angry at the lad about that. It's my fault, I'm afraid. I told him a little about what we did there."

"A rather bloodthirsty topic of conversation for so young a child. I'm not sure his mother would approve."

"Maybe not," John allowed. "But he's got a good mind and a lively intelligence that won't be put off with short shrift. He'll pester you until he's satisfied about a subject."

"I'm afraid I haven't been around many children," Hunt said.

He was beginning to wonder if attempting to further his relationship with his stepson was a good idea. And at the same time beginning to recognize the fine hand of his valet in far too many of the changes that were suddenly taking place in his life.

"It's time you were," John said. "Time you had some of your own, if you ask me."

"I don't believe I did, thank you, Ingalls," Hunt said, allowing the coldness in his voice to convey his displeasure with the direction of this conversation.

"That's half your trouble, my lord," Ingalls

said, setting his coffee down with a clink. "You never do ask me."

"Good morning," Bella said from across the room.

Hunt wondered if she had heard any of that, especially John's suggestion that he needed children of his own. Despite his belief that he could read her voice, he couldn't tell a thing from the two words she had spoken. She sounded exactly as she had every other morning she had come to work.

"Your ladyship," John said. "And will you be having tea this morning?"

"Thank you, but no, Ingalls. I've had my tea."

"We may manage to stretch the household budget to allow you another cup," Hunt said. Thankfully, his voice seemed to betray none of the nervousness he felt.

"Thank you, Hunt. It's very good to know we aren't in dun territory," she said.

He could almost sense John's listening stillness. It must be obvious that there had been a subtle change in their relationship. He wasn't certain what aspect of his visit to her boudoir last night had effected that change, but he was encouraged by it.

"Of course, the Season hasn't properly begun," he said, remembering Ingalls's admonition. "Your dressmaker's bills may change all that."

"My...dressmaker's bills?"

"That will be all, I think," he said in an aside

to John, amused by the knowledge that his valet would be very reluctant to leave now that the subject he'd brought to his master's attention had been broached. There was no doubt in Hunt's mind that John would give his right arm to hear the rest of this.

"And her ladyship's tea?" John asked.

"Perhaps later," Hunt instructed, struggling not to smile.

"Very good, my lord," Ingalls said, his voice stiff with indignation.

John played with the dishes on the tray a moment, prolonging his departure as long as possible, but as the silence stretched, it must be obvious that Huntingdon didn't intend to go on until he and Bella were alone.

Two can play at manipulation, my friend, Hunt thought in satisfaction. A petty victory perhaps, but after what Ingalls had been doing, he deserved this defeat.

When the door closed finally behind the valet, he said, "You haven't been fitted as yet for the gowns you'll need for the Season?"

"I didn't realize we should accept enough invitations to require new gowns," she said.

We. Hoist on his own petard, Hunt admitted wryly, but he realized with surprise that this was a sacrifice he was willing to make. Because John was right, of course. It had certainly been too long since Bella had been to a party.

He, of all people, understood how hard her life had been since Bertrand's death, especially in the years before she had come to work for him. Both Bella and her husband had been orphaned, and neither had family in a position to offer financial assistance when Bertrand died. Or to offer Bella a home. She had told him quite openly during the initial interview how she had hoarded the small sum her husband left her, spending it only on necessities, until it had been used up and she had been forced to seek employment.

Necessities. And knowing Bella that would mean nothing for herself. He wondered how long it had been since she had had a new gown. He realized in self-disgust that Bella had been his wife for over a month, and he had never even thought about enlarging her wardrobe. Despite the change in her circumstances, he knew she would never have undertaken to do that herself.

Nor could she have, he realized. Dawkins, his man of business, would quite naturally have assumed that he would no longer pay the Countess of Huntingdon a salary. Which meant...

"You have no money," he said aloud.

She laughed. "If you were expecting to receive marriage settlements, then you will be disappointed. I thought you understood that *before* we wed."

"Forgive me, Bella. I meant that I have made you no allowance since we've been married."

"Pin money, do you mean?"

"Of course. You are my wife."

"The Countess of Huntingdon," she said, her voice still amused.

"And you must dress the part," he advised, deciding he could manipulate as well as John.

"So I won't embarrass you at all these entertainments we shall be attending." Her voice was mocking.

"Of course. What I have got away with as a bachelor will not be tolerated in a man who is newly married."

"Do you seriously intend..." she began before her voice faltered.

"To take you dancing?" he suggested softly, realizing even as he said it that it was exactly what he wanted to do. He wanted to take Bella in his arms, even if only briefly, and lead her slowly around the floor.

He had once been accounted a very good dancer, a skill that was as necessary for a member of Wellington's staff as being a good shot or a good rider. There was no reason why he couldn't manage one waltz. Was that so much to ask?

Into her shocked silence he asked, "Do you have a favorite modiste, Bella?"

"If I had," she said brusquely, "she is probably dead or out of business by now. Or she would refuse my custom after such a long, dry spell of inactivity."

"Then it's settled," he said.

"What's settled?" she asked in bewilderment.

"You shall have a new wardrobe, one suitable for the Countess of Huntingdon. And it shall come from the most fashionable dressmaker in London. With your permission, of course."

It seemed a very long time before she answered, and in her voice was a tone he had never heard before. Of course, in this case, it was only the words that mattered.

"Of course," she said softly. "Whatever you wish. I shall be very honored to go out into society on your arm."

Royally hoist on his own petard, Hunt thought in amusement, and found he had no regrets.

Chapter Five

"That fabric is perfect with your coloring, my dear. And the style could not be more becoming. You are truly a picture, Bella. A picture!" Fanny said proudly. "Don't you agree, my lord?"

The silence that fell after that unthinking remark was suddenly full of tension, almost as tense as Hunt himself felt, as he stood at the foot of the staircase waiting for his wife to descend. Not over what poor Fanny had said, of course, but because he really wanted to see. To see Bella. And for the first time in almost ten years, the anger he had vowed never to reveal threatened his control.

"Please forgive me, Lord Huntingdon," Fanny said, her voice trembling. It was obvious the old woman was deeply embarrassed.

"There's nothing to forgive, Mrs. Hargreaves. I'm sure Lady Huntingdon is indeed 'a picture,'" Hunt said, holding the years-old facade in place.

Inwardly, he wondered how he would manage

to get through this night. Despite what Ingalls had said, despite what he'd felt when he'd suggested taking Bella into society, this was a mistake. He had known that long before it was time to don his evening clothes. No matter how much he wanted Bella to enjoy herself, no matter how much he had fantasized about holding her in his arms as they slowly circled the floor, he knew neither of those things was likely to come to pass.

Instead, other uncomfortable remarks would be made during the course of the evening. There would be whispers as Bella led him into the ballroom. Although he was certainly accustomed to the curiosity his appearance aroused, she would not be, and he wondered what she would feel. And he knew he would never find the courage to propose the waltz he had dreamed about in the fortnight since he had foolishly accepted an invitation to tonight's ball.

Hunt realized suddenly that Bella was standing beside him, the subtle scent of roses surrounding him. It was indicative of his state of mind that she could be this close and he hadn't even been aware of it. He knew his distraction didn't bode well for the remainder of this evening.

It would take every ounce of his concentration tonight to keep from making a fool of himself. A fool or an object of pity. Except, if some embarrassing disaster did occur, the pity of the ton would be reserved for Bella, of course.

"Here," she said. She took his hand, carrying his fingers to touch the silk of the gown she was wearing. "It truly is a remarkable fabric. The color of moonbeams and as fine as a cobweb. I can't imagine how they fashioned the cloth, but they tell me it was made in Cathay."

At the lack of tension in her voice, Hunt began to relax. Or perhaps that was because she had not released his hand and seemed in no hurry to do so. He brought her gloved fingers to his lips, pressing his mouth against the soft kid.

"You'll be the most beautiful woman at the ball," he said softly. By design, his tone was so low over the next words that only she might hear. "And I wish more than you can imagine that I could see you."

Her fingers trembled in his, and he released them, immediately regretting his confession. She would undoubtedly hear enough references to his blindness tonight, most of them unintentional and as harmless as the one Fanny had just made. He could only hope none would be truly malicious. He wanted nothing to spoil her evening.

"It's far better that you can't," she said, her voice equally low, the words laced with self-mockery. "I should so hate to disabuse you of the notion that I could be the belle of this or any other ball."

More of his tension dissipated at the wry amusement in her tone, and he presented his wrist. She placed her fingers, no longer trembling, on his arm, and he led her to the wide doors of the town house. This was the easy part, Hunt acknowledged, as the footman helped them into the waiting carriage. Everything would be much harder once he was away from the safe familiarity of home.

It was always so damn hard. Meeting new people. Trying to keep track of the changing speakers in a conversation, despite the music and the flow of noise around him. Negotiating his way through a totally unfamiliar place, which would be crowded with people. Having to depend on the guidance of others, something he hated.

For Bella's sake he could survive one night, he told himself sternly, calling on the courage that had sustained him through the years with Wellington. And more importantly, on that quite different kind of courage which had carried him through the long, dark years since his last battle. This was simply another, and the greatest enemy he would face tonight would be, as always, his own stubborn pride.

The evening had been nothing like what she had anticipated, Bella thought, as she was whirled competently around the floor by another of Huntingdon's friends. This one had served with him in Iberia, as had several of the gentlemen who had asked her to dance. Of course, ex-soldiers weren't the only ones paying quite flattering attention to the new Countess of Huntingdon. Bella had danced with some of the most prominent men in the current government as well.

As the evening wore on, their names and faces had begun to run together. All she knew for certain was that she had not been without a partner for any set.

Had she been vain, she might well have attributed her popularity to her own person. Or perhaps to the gown she was wearing. Hunt's promise about choosing the most fashionable modiste in London had certainly been fulfilled. This was the most beautiful dress in the room, and her mirror had confirmed that its elegance was vastly becoming to her.

Not being vain, however, Bella had quickly begun to suspect there was a conspiracy afoot among her husband's friends. And even to suspect that Hunt himself had taken a hand in it.

Her gaze went straight to her husband, despite the throng. He was standing across the ballroom, his dark head bent slightly because of his height, the better to hear what the prime minister, who was on his other side, was saying to him. As she went mindlessly through the motions of the waltz, Bella continued to watch the small group gathered around her husband.

It seemed she had been aware of exactly where Hunt was throughout the evening, although she had spent most of its long hours away from him, in the arms of some handsome man or another. *Never in his arms,* she thought with regret. And of course, she had no right to have expected that she would.

She only wished that he might display a little more reluctance in sending her onto the floor on the arm of each gentleman who applied to him for permission to dance with her. He hadn't, seeming instead to be pleased at the attention she had garnered.

Knowing him now as well as she did, however, she knew Hunt would be finding this evening a dead bore. The ball was, by its nature, devoted to dancing, an activity in which he obviously did not participate. To her certain knowledge his social calendar during the last two years had never included this kind of entertainment. Not until tonight.

As soon as she had realized she was to be partnered in every dance, almost certainly by prior design, she had known Hunt was here only because he believed this would give her pleasure. And it had, of course. The greatest pleasure had been the knowledge that her husband had carefully planned this evening with her enjoyment in mind. Now if only—

"Am I boring you, Lady Huntingdon?" her partner asked. "That's the second comment I've made to which you've failed to respond. At this rate, even I, acknowledged wit that I am, shall run out of commonplaces with which to entertain you before the music ends."

Startled, she pulled her gaze away from her contemplation of her husband and looked into a pair of very fine brown eyes, sparkling with amusement.

"One is supposed to converse with one's partner, you know," the man holding her in his arms said in a confiding whisper. "I don't know who began the custom, but by now it's rather widely accepted."

"I am *so* sorry," Bella said, feeling the blood rush into her cheeks. "Forgive me, please, Lord..." For the life of her, she could not remember his name. And her blush deepened when he laughed.

"Ardley. Actually, it's quite refreshing to see a lady in love with her husband. Very rare in our set, even for newlyweds, I'm afraid. Hunt's a lucky man," he added. "Swept him off his feet, did you?"

His eyes were still smiling at her, so she didn't take offense. "I think that's supposed to be phrased the other way round," she countered, and then lowered her own voice. "I don't know who began the custom..."

He laughed, just as she'd intended.

"But you *are* in love with him," he said. "It's quite useless to deny it, as unfashionable as that may be. You're in love with your own husband, as much, perhaps, as he is with you."

"In love with *me?*" she repeated, remembering

with a jolt in the region of her heart how Hunt teased her about that unfortunate habit. *Dear Echo.*

"Of course," Ardley said. "We all wondered when we heard the news of your marriage, since Hunt had sworn he'd never burden a woman with…what he has become. And then, when we saw you, we understood why he would—"

Their eyes met and held, the laughter disappearing suddenly from his. "But Huntingdon has never seen me," she said softly.

And he never will. That was somehow harder to bear now than it had ever been before, perhaps because of the words her husband had whispered as he kissed her hand at the foot of the stairs.

"Did he tell you how he lost his sight?" Ardley asked.

"No," she said, wondering if this was a story she wanted to hear. Wondering if her husband would want her to hear it. She knew that Hunt would never tell her, however, and she would never have dared to ask him. And so, although she felt that she should, she didn't stop Lord Ardley when he began.

"He was a staff officer. One of the Beau's pets. Everyone knew it, but no one resented the favoritism. Hunt had earned our respect in more ways than I could possibly recount to you. Earned it again and again. The more difficult the mission, the more certain one could be that it would fall on Hunt's shoulders to carry it out."

He took a breath, deep enough that his shoulders lifted, moving against her hand as it rested lightly on top of the left one. "There was a rather reckless young lieutenant, newly out from London, who believed that war was all glory and honor and tilting at windmills. He was the kind of nincompoop that battle-hardened veterans like Hunt were sure to avoid as bad, mad and *very* dangerous to know."

She laughed. "And was he?"

"Oh, far more than you can imagine. It took him less than a month to get into trouble. No one was surprised by that speed, of course, and most of them would have said, 'Devil take him.' The only trouble was he had gotten the men under his command into trouble, too. And a lot of them stood to die because of his foolishness."

He paused again, his eyes finding Huntingdon in the throng as surely as Bella's had earlier. The earl was laughing at something someone had said to him, his head thrown back a little in what appeared to be genuine enjoyment. Bella hoped it was.

When Lord Ardley's brown eyes came back to hers, however, they were sober. "Huntingdon was sent to the rescue, of course. And he even found a way to get most of the troop out of the ridiculous mess our stalwart young hero had gotten them into. Most of them," he said. His lips tightened, and his eyes briefly sought Hunt again.

"And the lieutenant?" Bella asked.

"Took a French ball in his arm and fell off his horse. Grandly heroic, ain't it?" he said mockingly.

"And he died?"

"Oh, no, Hunt rescued him, too. Fought off a French dragoon who was about to use him for saber practice. Put the lad up on his own mount and sent horse and rider off in the direction of our lines with a good hard slap on the rump. The horse's, not the lieutenant's. The boy got back behind his own lines to discover that the ball he'd taken had gone through the flesh of his arm without touching bone. A miracle, the sawbones said." Again, he paused, his face set and his mouth grim.

"And Hunt," Bella whispered, knowing the answer from the question that had begun this story. She had been right from the first, she realized in regret. She did *not* want to hear this.

"A French shell exploded almost at his feet. And since he had given his horse away..." Again, the handsome mouth flattened before Ardley went on. "No one who saw what happened expected Hunt to live through that explosion, but when the patrol was sent out that evening to bring back the bodies, they found him still alive. The shell had set the grass where he had fallen on fire. Hunt had managed to crawl away, but the heat—"

"Don't," she commanded.

The horror of the story made her steps falter

until they were standing unmoving in the midst of the swirl of dancers.

"Forgive me," Ardley said softly. "I should never have told you all that, but I wanted you to know the caliber of the man you married."

"I knew already," Bella said, fighting the power of the terrible images his words had produced.

"You're quite pale, Lady Huntingdon. If I take you back to Hunt in this condition, he'll have my hide. And rightly so. Some fresh air?" he suggested.

Bella realized they were beside French doors that led into the garden. Perhaps she *would* feel better for a breath of the cooler night air. It had grown very close in the room. And much too warm. Besides, Ardley was right. Hunt would know from her voice that something was wrong. He knew her far too well.

Lord Ardley was already leading her toward the doors, and as soon as she stepped through them, she knew she had done the right thing. Hunt wouldn't miss her, and she would only stay outside a moment or two. Only long enough to put the story from her mind and regain her composure.

"May I bring you some refreshment?" Ardley asked.

"Oh, yes, please," Bella said. "You are so very kind."

"No, Lady Huntingdon. What I have done is unforgivable. And I have no excuse, except that it seems I am still the same reckless, unthinking fool I was that day in Spain.''

He bowed to her, his eyes meeting hers briefly before he turned and disappeared into the crowded ballroom.

The same reckless, unthinking fool I was that day in Spain. He was the lieutenant whose life Hunt had saved, Bella realized. Ardley was the man whose foolhardy exploit had cost her husband a price greater than any man should have to pay to the gods of war. And if Hunt had had his choice that day, she suspected that he would rather have died.

She took another deep, fortifying breath, trying to put the story and its implications from her mind. It had all happened more than ten years ago, and surely Hunt no longer felt that way. He had certainly by now come to terms with the consequences of his heroism.

She had truly understood only tonight how well he coped with his blindness, whether he was dealing gracefully with the unspoken discomfort of others, quickly putting them at ease, or enduring the confusing bombardment of sound that came at him from every direction, or putting up with her own inept and hesitant guidance through those close-packed bodies.

None of those were skills any man would have wished to acquire. Certainly not the man Ardley had just described. Not that gallant and respected soldier.

"Bella?" he said from behind her.

She turned in time to see Ardley slip away, leaving Hunt alone in the wide frame of the French doors. He tilted his head slightly, listening for her answer, despite the noise from the ballroom behind him.

"I'm here," she said.

She did not move toward him, her emotions too raw and exposed. Too vulnerable. A careless word or the hint of pity in her voice would be fatal to her cause. She knew that, although her instinct was to rush to him as she would have to Kit, taking him in her arms and kissing the hurt away.

This, however, was a ten-year-old hurt that no one, not even she, could ever make well. Nor was it her place to try. She was his wife, not his mother. Perhaps it was time she undertook to fulfill her proper role.

"Ardley said you were ill," Hunt said.

He sounded both concerned and puzzled. And why shouldn't he be? she thought in quick amusement. She had not been ill a day since he had hired her. Why would she believe that on a night he had planned as carefully as he might have planned a military campaign she, of all people, would succumb to a fit of vapors? She could hardly believe it herself.

"Not ill," she said. "Only stifled by the heat

and the noise. And quite tired of having my toes trod upon.''

"Shall I call him out?''

"Who?'' she asked, feeling a flutter of anxiety that Lord Ardley might have confessed that he had told her.

"The cad who trod on your toes, of course.''

She laughed, the tension of the last few minutes melting away in the face of his calm serenity. In the security she always felt in his presence. Hunt did make her feel secure, she realized, because she knew that he would always take care of her, just as he had tonight.

"I shall forgive him if you'll take me home,'' she said softly.

"Tired, Bella?''

"Only of this,'' she said truthfully. "Only of the ball and the noise and the heat.''

"I thought you would enjoy it. You were quite the belle, despite your doubts.''

Her lips lifted, knowing full well why that had come about. "The dress, perhaps,'' she suggested.

"The woman wearing it,'' Hunt corrected. "Two score people went out of their way to tell me what a lucky man I am. Most of them shortly after they had danced with you.''

"Well, *I* didn't tread on *their* toes,'' she said.

She was rewarded by his laughter. This time, the impact of that ghastly story fading, she was able to laugh with him.

"I'm sure they should not have minded if you had," he said.

"Would *you?*"

Her voice was teasing, the suggestion lightly made, though it had been carefully worded. Despite her tone, she watched his face change, the laughter disappearing to leave the spare planes and angles arranged in the same austere lines they assumed whenever he was concentrating on something very difficult to comprehend.

As she waited for his answer, the silence grew and then expanded. Through it the sounds of music floated to her, spilling from the dance floor out into the cool darkness. And when he spoke again, it was not in response to her question.

"As soon as we've made our farewells and apologies, I can take you home. I'm sure you'll feel better when you're away from this mob."

She had accomplished nothing, other than to embarrass them both. And to put a damper on an evening that had been planned strictly for her pleasure. It was a mistake she would not make twice.

"I'm sure you're right," she said.

She raised her chin, holding her head high, and walked across the terrace to take his arm. Then she turned, prepared to lead him into the ballroom, but he didn't move.

"Did you enjoy yourself, Bella?" he asked.

"Thank you, yes," she said, the words sounding more formal than she had intended.

"Then...perhaps another night?" he said softly, the inflection almost a question.

He took a step forward, forcing her to move with him or send him into the throng without guidance. And he never spoke to her again on the way home.

Chapter Six

"*I'm sure they should not have minded if you had.*"

"*Would you?*"

There was no other logical interpretation that might be put on that question, the Earl of Huntingdon decided, as he paced back to the window of his bedchamber, mentally reviewing the conversation, something he had done a hundred times since they had returned from the ball.

Bella had wanted to dance with him. And, fool that he was, he had ignored her suggestion. As he had feared at the beginning of the evening, his pride had defeated all his expectations.

Not all, he amended. Bella had said she had enjoyed herself. Since that had been his primary purpose in accepting the invitation, he could not regret that they had gone, despite the strain the evening had proven to be.

It was over now, thank God, and alone in his

room he could finally relax. He had allowed Ingalls to help him off with his coat, and then he had sent the valet away.

He didn't want to answer the questions he knew John would be eager to pose. After all, his valet's anticipation of tonight's success had perhaps been as great as his own. And from the beginning they had both been destined for disappointment, he acknowledged, still pacing restlessly.

Bella had, however, been introduced to a number of his friends, who could now be called upon to provide an escort for any of the Season's events she might wish to attend. From that aspect the evening had been a success. An unmitigated success, he thought bitterly, remembering the many comments about his wife's beauty. Which had only reinforced—

The soft tap on his door was unexpected. Ingalls, he thought, come to question why he was still up. More and more frequently of late John had been poking his nose into things that were really no concern of his. The earl felt an unaccustomed spark of anger, which, had he been honest, he would have admitted had nothing to do with his valet's actions, but rather with his own. Or the lack of his own.

He walked over to the door and threw it open, ready to chastise Ingalls for hovering over him like some damned mother hen. As he drew breath to begin that angry lecture, the subtle scent of roses surrounded him. He fought the urge to close his eyes and savor the fragrance, as he had during the carriage ride home.

"Bella?" he questioned instead. "Is something wrong?"

"Most wives would take offense if their husbands greeted their appearance at the bedroom door with that question."

But Bella was *not* most wives. Nor was he, of course, most husbands. He was a blind man, who had felt more blind tonight than he had at almost any other time in the last ten years. A blind man in a marriage of convenience. A blind man in love with a woman he had never seen.

A woman who was, according to his friends, incredibly beautiful. A woman to whom he had offered a home and financial stability. There had been nothing else, stated or implied, in that arrangement. And no matter how he felt, he didn't see how he could legitimately expect to change the terms of their agreement now.

"May I come in?" Bella asked.

"Of course," he said, more from a lifelong habit of politeness than because he was eager to add to the chaos of emotion that had tormented him since their return.

"Thank you." Her voice seemed almost amused.

She came into the room, and when he heard the door close behind her, his heart rate accelerated. Unaccountably accelerated. After all, he was alone with her every day. Not in these circumstances, he admitted, which somehow seemed even more intimate than the night he had gone to her bedchamber to speak to her on Kit's behalf.

Kit. Perhaps Bella had come here for that same purpose. To talk about her son. He took another deep breath, controlling his wayward imagination, which had stupidly been suggesting that Bella might have sought him out for a very different reason.

"I wanted to thank you for tonight," she said. "The evening was almost perfect."

There was something in her voice—some subtle undertone—that he was aware of, but couldn't identify.

"*Almost* perfect?" he asked, smiling at her. "Did you wish to lodge a complaint, Bella?"

"Your friends are delightful. And I very much enjoyed being treated like a diamond of the first water. That's flattering, of course, for any woman, especially for one of my...advancing years," she said, the amusement back in her voice. "However, I must confess..."

And then she didn't. He waited through the long silence, still uncertain where this conversation was headed.

"What I wanted most of all was to dance with *you*," she said finally, and his heart rate, which had almost returned to normal, began to race again.

"Forgive me, Bella. I no longer dance. I thought you understood."

"Why?" she asked.

There were, of course, a number of quite legitimate reasons he could give her. He chose the truth instead.

"Because I'm very much afraid I should make a fool of myself if I tried," he said, and then to soften the harshness of the words, he smiled at her again.

It was not a plea for pity, and he believed that by now he could trust her to understand that. This was simply the ultimate truth of his situation. Making a fool of himself, especially before her, although he did not confess to that, was the one thing he feared above all others.

And it was why, of course, he had never told her what was in his heart. He still didn't, although the silence stretched beyond comfort as he waited for her response.

"Isn't it strange that we've been afraid of the same thing and didn't know it," she said.

He shook his head. "The same thing?"

"Yes, my darling Echo. We've both been too afraid of making fools of ourselves to admit how we feel."

My darling Echo. He had revealed too much of what he felt for her that day. And yet, hearing what was in her voice, he could not regret that he had.

We've both been too afraid of making fools of

ourselves to admit how we feel. How we feel. Which could only mean...

And then, the old doubts flooded his heart, forcing out that sudden glorious certainty. This was the same battle which had kept him from taking her in his arms tonight and swirling her around and around to the music drifting through the terrace doors.

Fear was his enemy. Fear and his own stubborn pride, which had told him for years that he could never reveal to anyone how vulnerable he felt.

He knew, however, that he must somehow find the courage for this. The same courage he had called on when the surgeons told him he would be permanently blind. The courage that had been required then simply to face each day. To decide to make something meaningful of his life. To accept every challenge this eternal darkness had presented. A darkness which he still hated, even after all these years.

We've both been too afraid of making fools of ourselves to admit how we feel.

"And if I tell you how I feel, Bella? Will I be making a fool of myself?" he asked.

"Love makes fools of us all. I'm surprised you didn't know."

"Then...I love you, Bella," he said, forcing the words through the constriction of his throat.

"And I love you, my darling," she whispered.

She moved into his arms as if they were not only

dear to her, but familiar. He lowered his head, finding her mouth unerringly, as though he had kissed her a thousand times.

Her lips trembled under his. He caressed them with his own, trying to control the flood of desire and longing that swept through him so fiercely he was terrified he might frighten her. He need not have worried. Her mouth opened, her tongue seeking his to engage in a dance more primitive than any a London ballroom would ever witness. That slow, tender waltz of mutual passion.

The kiss seemed unending. Their mouths met, melded, and then released, only to seek the same sweet pattern again. And then again. To cling. To break apart. To reunite.

Learning. Learning one another. After a very long time, he put his hands on her upper arms and set her away from him, positioning her body almost at arm's length from his. As he did, her lips still clung, as if they could not bear to be separated from his.

"Bella," he said, almost in wonder. "My darling..."

He wasn't sure she would understand, but this was something he needed to do. Something he had wanted to do far longer than she could know.

"What is it?" she asked. When he didn't answer, she put her hand on his cheek, her thumb pulling slowly and sensuously across the fullness of his bottom lip. "What's wrong?"

Because there were no words to tell her what was in his heart, he said nothing. Instead he raised his hands, putting his fingertips lightly on either side of her face. His thumbs brushed over her forehead and then more boldly down the narrow bridge of her nose. And when they had finished there, his fingers examined her brows, following the arch of bone they outlined. As they trailed across her eyelids, her eyes closed, the long lashes lying like fans below them, allowing his examination.

The movement of his fingers didn't stop until he had traced over all the delicate structures of her face: brow, nose, cheekbone and jaw. They had molded each feature, following not only the outline of her eyes and brow, but tracing the bow of her top lip and the sensual fullness of the bottom. He even followed the shape of her ears and touched the softly curling tendrils that floated against her cheek.

When his hands finally rested unmoving around the slender column of her throat, their journey of exploration complete, with the smallest of pressures, he urged her to him again. He bent his head, putting his lips against the soft skin below her ear, his tongue trailing provocatively along the underside of her jaw.

The progress of his mouth was as unhurried as that of his hands had been. He stopped to examine the pulsing hollow at the base of her throat. To follow the fragile line of her collarbone, returning to glide over the beginning swell of her breasts. Her sudden intake of breath as his tongue delved into the shadowed darkness between made him pause. He lifted his head, listening to the subtle change in her breathing.

"Don't stop," she whispered.

"Are you sure, Bella? Because once I touch you, my darling, there can be no turning back. If you can't endure the fumbling caress of a blind man…"

She stopped the words by the simple and effective expedient of stretching on tiptoe to put her mouth over his. Briefly then, hers was the guidance, but only until she had convinced him that whatever doubts he had, she did not share them.

As his hands dealt efficiently with the intricacies of feminine apparel, a task at which he had excelled in his younger and admittedly wilder days, the Earl of Huntingdon found there are some skills one never forgets. And he was inordinately delighted only a short time later to realize that darkness had never, in the history of the world, been any impediment to making love.

"Yes," She breathed, the word softly sibilant, almost a whisper.

"And here," he said.

His breath was moist against her skin. His tongue circled her nipple, laving it lazily, applying no pressure. Teasing. And tantalizing.

Everything he had done during the long dark hours of the night had tantalized her, arousing feelings she had not known she was capable of experiencing. She had never dreamed there were so many ways to give pleasure. Or to receive it. It seemed she had learned new ones with each touch of his lips and every movement of his tongue.

"And here," he said, his mouth leaving her breasts to glide downward over the sweat-dampened skin of her stomach. She didn't have the strength to speak again. Or the will to deny him. Not anything.

And he wasn't really seeking her permission. Any barrier she might have thought to erect between them for modesty's sake had long ago been destroyed. Every portal had been thrown open. Lovingly invaded. The citadel of her body joyfully surrendered.

This was only the shivering aftermath. The heated shimmer of nerve endings tested beyond their endurance, so that they, too, quickly surrendered again before the knowing touch of his lips and his tongue and his hands.

Those long, dark skillful fingers had caressed her body as if it were infinitely precious. As if every part were beautiful, something to be cherished. And they had moved with a sure mastery which proclaimed she belonged to him. After tonight, of course, there was no longer any doubt that she did.

Love makes fools of us all, she had told him. Until now, lying in his arms, boneless and spent, she had not realized how true that was. Her fingers tangled idly in the dark silk of his hair, allowing the strands to curl around them. Savoring the texture against her palm as she drew her hand through its thickness.

She had willingly entered his world of sound and touch and taste. There was no light in the room, nor had there been any throughout the night. In the darkness, they had discovered one another tactilely, and for her that had meant a freedom from inhibition she had never before experienced.

He had delighted in her body, but she had been given an equal liberty to explore his. To daringly run her fingers over its hardened contours. To draw her bare insole along the muscled ridge of his calf. To caress the broad, hair-roughened chest. To lay her cheek against it, exhausted by his lovemaking and content to listen to the rhythm of his racing heart slow and finally steady.

She had believed they were both sated, beyond need or desire, long past satisfaction. She *had* believed that until suddenly his tongue flicked against the very core of her sexuality. Heat spiraled upward, running along those same over-stimulated nerve pathways, liquid fire leaping through veins and arteries and rushing like a reviving drug through still-trembling muscles.

She gasped, fingers reflexively tightening in his

hair. There was no response. His tongue didn't cease to caress, and slowly, despite her shock, she began to relax into the waves of sensation that poured like torrents from a seemingly endless spring throughout her body. No one had ever touched her like this, and in her wildest fantasies, she would never have been able to imagine that he would.

She felt as if she should protest, in spite of the fact that he was her husband. Despite all they had already shared. This was too intimate, the feelings it created too powerful, almost frightening in their intensity.

Before that thought was fully formed, however, she knew she didn't want him to stop. Despite her satiation, that slow, spiraling journey had already begun. Fulfillment awaited, hovering just beyond her reach, and her body strained wildly against the movement of his mouth.

This was something she had wanted almost as much as she had wanted the acknowledgment of his love. This had been a part of that longing. To know that he wanted her physically. And now, after tonight, after this, there could be no doubt that he did.

Racked with need and desire, her body writhed, trying to hurry him. As through every moment of the long dark hours they had spent together, however, he would not be rushed. The control was his, and ultimately she surrendered her will to his as completely as she had given him her body.

Again and again, he brought her to the very edge and then retreated, deliberately allowing the sensations to ease, to withdraw their dominion until she could again think. And she didn't want to. Tonight was not about thinking, and she had welcomed the permission his lovemaking had given her to allow her mind to simply drift, all the intellectual decisions already made.

She had again reached the cusp, and she knew this time there would be no turning back. Apparently, he knew it too. His body shifted, moving over hers in the darkness. Suddenly his mouth again sought hers, which was open and waiting, as her body waited breathlessly for his entrance. And it was as powerful as the first time he had taken her.

With his thrust, she cried out, her nails scoring his back as she rode the crest of sensation that caught them both. His body arched and then convulsed, and she could feel the hot, jetting release. In response she wrapped her legs around his waist, pulling him closer, trying to become one with him forever. Holding him to her as the darkness spiraled around them.

His darkness. And he had taught her tonight there was nothing in it to fear.

Slowly his body stilled, and then he pushed himself up a little, propping on his elbows, just as if he were looking down on her. And she could see him, she realized, his face pale against the blackness that was beginning to fade with the faint light of dawn. She put her hand against his cheek, the gesture almost consoling.

He turned his head and pressed his lips into her palm. And when he turned back again, once more seeming to look down into her eyes, he said, "I wish I could see you when that happens."

She tried to read the tone. There was regret, she thought, but no sadness. A simple statement of fact.

"I know," she whispered.

She thought about telling him that only now, with the breaking day, could she see him. And then, looking at his face, she decided there was no reason to tell him that for her the darkness they had shared all night had broken. As it would each morning for the rest of their lives. Instead, she raised her head and put her lips very gently against his.

There was no passion in their touch. The driving need that had guided their actions had been exorcised—at least for now. It was time for other things. The simple but important tasks of living, as well as they could, new each day. Beginning with this.

"What was that for?" Hunt asked, smiling at her when she lay back on the pillow, her eyes still feasting on the sight of his face, emerging from the shadows.

"Just in case you've forgotten."

"Forgotten?" he asked, tilting his head a little, the familiar gesture more endearing than it had ever been before.

"My darling Echo," she said softly, touching the tips of her fingers against his lips. "Just in case you've forgotten how very much I love you. Even when you are *not* making love to me."

"And when I am?" he asked, his tone wickedly suggestive. The smile had become a grin, and it destroyed the slight melancholy she had felt with the arrival of dawn.

"Then you shouldn't have to be told," she said. "It should be obvious."

"Even to me," he said softly. The smile slowly faded. "And will you eventually tire of telling a blind man all the things that should be obvious?"

She thought about what he had asked, wondering if she might. "Did you tire of explaining all those parliamentary bills to me?" she asked.

And was relieved to see the grin return. "Occasionally," he admitted, "but not often. Those are things I feel very passionate about."

"Exactly," she said, and pulled him down to her again.

When Bella awoke, she could tell by the sun it was very late. She turned her head and found the pillow beside her empty. As was the room, she discovered. She was alone in her husband's bed-chamber, and he was probably downstairs, forced to make do with Ingalls's less than fluid reading of the day's headlines.

It was not until she had found her dressing gown, thoughtfully laid out for her on the foot of the bed that she remembered it was Sunday. Her day off, she realized with a smile. And in all honesty, after last night she needed one.

There was a discreet knock, so well-timed she wondered in amusement if the servants had been spying, ears against the door. In response to the permission she called, however, Ingalls entered with a tray bearing a pot of tea. His face was perfectly controlled, his eyes averted from her state of undress.

Bella was just as glad that she didn't have to meet them. She knew she'd blush, which was probably not the response a *proper* countess should make to being found *en dishabille* in her husband's bedchamber.

"Will that be all, my lady?" Ingalls said after he'd put the tray down on the table before the windows.

"Thank you, Ingalls. Is the earl already at breakfast?"

"I believe Lord Huntingdon is in the nursery, my lady."

"The nursery?" she repeated, and then realized

that was where she wished to be as well. With the two people she loved more than anything else in the world. Especially today.

"Shall I ask him to join you?"

"Thank you, no, Ingalls. I think I shall join them instead."

"Very good, my lady," the valet said, bowing in preparation for leaving.

"And John?" He turned back, his eyes meeting hers for the first time. They were alight in a way she had never seen them before. "Thank you," she said softly. "Thank you for everything."

"Sometimes Quality don't know what's good for them, my lady. Those of us in service occasionally have to give them a push in the right direction, if you take my meaning. After that, things are generally better for everyone concerned. As I'm sure your ladyship will agree," he added. And then he winked at her.

The blood she had denied before rushed into her cheeks. Seeing it, Ingalls grinned, and then, without another word, he crossed the room and went out, leaving her alone.

Bella could hear Kit's piping voice, full of excitement, even before she opened the nursery door. She hadn't taken time to return to her own room to dress. Luckily, she hadn't encountered any of the servants in the halls or as she'd climbed the stairs to the third floor. Facing Ingalls's knowing grin had been quite enough embarrassment for one morning, she thought.

She opened the door in time to hear Kit offer magnanimously, "Now *you* may be the Iron Duke, if you wish. I'll help you set up your army exactly the way that he did at Vitoria."

"Thank you," the Earl of Huntingdon, who had had a hand in the strategic planning of that battle, said humbly.

By that time, however, Kit had seen his mother standing hesitantly in the doorway. "Mama!" he shouted, jumping up and running across the battlefield, which was really only the worn rug before the nursery fire. More than one of the gallant tin soldiers inadvertently broke ranks as the little boy flew across the room to throw himself into his mother's arms.

Bella bent just in time to stop his headlong rush by scooping him up. She hugged him tightly, as if they had been separated for days rather than hours. She swung him around once or twice before she set him on his feet again.

"Did you have a good time last night?" Kit asked.

Despite herself, Bella's eyes lifted to find her husband, still lying on his side on the rug. His dark head was propped on one hand while the other toyed with the soldiers scattered before him. Even from where she stood, she could see the amused quirk of his lips in response to Kit's question. And again she blushed.

"A very good time, thank you, Kit. The earrings you choose to go with my gown were the perfect touch. I was quite the belle, I assure you."

"Good," Kit pronounced in satisfaction, and then moved on to a subject of far more importance. "Did you come to play soldiers with us?"

"Only to watch, perhaps," she said, her eyes still on her husband.

"I suspect girls aren't very good at playing war," Kit said.

"Perhaps they have other interests," the Earl of Huntingdon suggested. "And other...talents."

The long fingers of his left hand were still arranging miniature men into formation before the cheerful blaze. As Bella watched, knowing quite well what he meant, the memories of what had happened between them last night produced a different kind of heat.

"Thank you," she said softly.

"Thank *you*," he answered, his lips tilting again.

"Hunt says I'm to have a brother," Kit announced, drawing her eyes back to him.

"A brother," she repeated.

"Darling Echo," Hunt said, still arranging his troops.

"Or perhaps a sister. He doesn't know yet for sure."

"The earl seems to be making quite a few...
assumptions this morning. I only hope you won't
be disappointed if you have to wait awhile, Kit."

"Only the requisite nine months," her husband
said confidently. "I've explained all that."

"Indeed?" Bella said faintly, putting her hand
on the back of Kit's head and directing him toward
the fire. The little boy sprawled happily across the
battleground from his stepfather, his eyes excitedly
taking in the formations of both armies. "You
seem to be *very* sure of yourself this morning, my
lord."

"Oh, I am. I have it on the best authority. Ingalls
assures me it's time I should have children."

He lifted his hand to her, an obvious invitation
to join them on the rug. Smiling, she complied.
And when she was seated on the floor beside him,
he didn't release her fingers until he had brought
them to his mouth and kissed each one individu-
ally, much to Kit's fascination.

"And I *never* argue with Ingalls," Hunt said,
smiling at her. "If there is one thing I've learned,
it's that he truly does always know best."

Bella thought of that cold winter day when she
had come to his study to refuse the Earl of Huntingdon's offer and had watched John Ingalls
mouth those fateful words. *Say yes,* he had told
her, and for some inexplicable reason, she had.
And now...

She breathed a silent prayer of thanks for her husband's valet. She had no idea, of course, what other role he might have played in this, but it was obvious by Hunt's remark there had been one. Perhaps he had influenced the earl's decision to propose as much as he had hers to accept. If so, she owed him a debt she would never be able to repay.

"If you tell him I said that, however," Hunt continued, still holding her fingers in his, "there will be no living with him, I'm afraid. Shall we pretend we were unaware of his manipulations?"

"Pretend we thought this marvelous arrangement up all on our own?" she asked mockingly, setting a fallen soldier upright and in his proper rank. "But my dear, no one would believe a member of the nobility would have the rare good sense to fall in love with his own wife."

"I must confess I am finding that rather convenient," Hunt said, smiling at her over the small curly head of their son. Their first son.

"Of course you are," Bella said contentedly. "That's exactly why a match such as ours is *called* a marriage of convenience. I'm surprised you didn't know."

Then the Countess of Huntingdon leaned forward to kiss her husband, dealing Wellington's army such a defeat as it had never before known.

And properly distracted, the commander of all the British forces in the field that day didn't even seem to notice.

* * * * *

Dear Reader,

My Darling Echo is truly a story straight from my heart. The two central characters, Arabella Simmons and the gallant ex-soldier, Alexander Coltrain, seventh Earl of Huntingdon, have lived in my head a long time, just waiting for their chance to come alive. I'm very grateful that Tracy Farrell and Harlequin Historicals have given me the opportunity to tell you about them.

Actually, they were inspired by two of my favorite stories, both written in the early 1900s, a period when writers such as Ethel Dell were creating intensely romantic novels that are seldom read today. *Man and Maid* by Elinor Glyn and *Leave It to Love* by Pamela Wynn have been on my keeper shelf for years. Of course, I've always loved to read stories about strong, imperfect heroes, and now I love to write them.

Hunt, as the earl's friends call him, has long believed he would never marry because of his disability. As a result of a heroic military action during his service with Wellington ten years ago, the earl was blinded. Now a member of the House of Lords, Hunt's life is both productive and meaningful. It is also lonely, at least until he employs as his reader the widow of an old schoolmate and finds himself falling in love with a woman's voice.

Arabella has struggled since her husband's death to support her small family in a society in which gentlewomen do not work. The employment Huntingdon offers her is a salvation, and she is enormously grateful. And then, as she comes to know her employer, gratitude and admiration are not the only emotions she begins to feel for him.

It is only with the behind-the-scenes machinations of the earl's faithful valet, however, that two lonely people are tricked into a marriage of convenience, which will in the end, of course, become something very different. And something I hope is as romantically satisfying for you as those old stories on my keeper shelf have always been for me.

I sincerely hope you enjoy *My Darling Echo*, my small tribute to some of the pioneers in the field of romance who have been virtually forgotten by modern readers.

Gayle Wilson

**Don't miss
an exciting opportunity
to save on the purchase of
Harlequin and Silhouette books!**

Buy any two Harlequin or
Silhouette books and save
$10.00 off future Harlequin
and Silhouette purchases

OR

buy any three
Harlequin or Silhouette books
and save **$20.00 off** future
Harlequin and Silhouette purchases.

*Watch for details
coming in October 2000!*

PHQ400

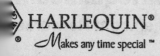

Romance is just one click away!

online book serials

➢ *Exclusive* to our web site, get caught up in both the daily and weekly online installments of new romance stories.

➢ Try the Writing Round Robin. Contribute a chapter to a story created by our members. Plus, winners will get prizes.

romantic travel

➢ Want to know where the best place to kiss in New York City is, or which restaurant in Los Angeles is the most romantic? Check out our Romantic Hot Spots for the scoop.

➢ Share your travel tips and stories with us on the romantic travel message boards.

romantic reading library

➢ Relax as you read our collection of Romantic Poetry.

➢ Take a peek at the Top 10 Most Romantic Lines!

Visit us online at

www.eHarlequin.com

on Women.com Networks

If you enjoyed what you just read,
then we've got an offer you can't resist!

Take 2
bestselling novels FREE!
Plus get a FREE surprise gift!